FRACTURED OAK

DANNIE BOYD

INDIGO
DOT
PRESS

Indigo Dot Press
indigodotpress@gmail.com

First edition, 2023

Library of Congress Control Number: 2023901925

FIC061000 FICTION / Magical Realism
FIC022000 FICTION / Mystery & Detective / General
FIC014000 FICTION / Historical / General
FIC035000 FICTION / Medical

ISBN 978-1-958160-04-6 (trade paperback)
ISBN 978-1-958160-05-3 (ebook)
ISBN 978-1-958160-06-0 (audiobook)

Cover design by Tea Jagodic

PRAISE FOR FRACTURED OAK

"Fractured Oak by Dannie Boyd is a fascinating murder mystery about two extraordinary women belonging to different generations ... Comprehensive, well-researched, and above all mesmerizing"

— MARIA VICTORIA BELTRAN FOR
READERS' FAVORITE

"Two remarkable heroes enliven this absorbing crime story."

— KIRKUS REVIEWS

"Catherine [is] a superbly written character ... Boyd's efforts, both evidenced by the detailed research and great writing, made this book a worthy addition to the crime fiction scene"

— NICHOLUS SCHROEDER FOR READERS'
FAVORITE

FRACTURED OAK

For Dan
Gone too soon but never forgotten

PROLOGUE

1853

CATHERINE

As a woman...

Unaware she was about to die, Catherine Miller, a young woman delicate in build but determined in mind, hurried down the sidewalk of Cleveland's Superior Street, her velvet cloak flapping against her gown in the March wind. Having just become the third woman in the United States to graduate from a medical college of repute, she was in need of an escape to steady her nerves.

Neither her pounding heart, which galloped as robustly as the clopping horses and peopled carriages crossing the stone road, nor her dizzying thoughts had received a moment's respite from the day's excitement. She would return to the commencement celebration once she calmed down.

Perhaps if she had been less heady with emotion, she might have noticed the pursuer behind her. At the very least, her common sense would have kept her from venturing too far beyond Public Square and leaving the crowded protection its taverns and hotels provided. But on that brisk but pleasant afternoon her thoughts were elsewhere.

Doctor Catherine Miller. That is who I am now.

Soon she, a humble girl from a dusty but growing settlement in Pennsylvania, would be working alongside her new partner, Dr. Isaac Fitzgerald, performing physical examinations and dispensing treatments as a full-fledged physician of Cleveland. It was a dream come true, albeit one fraught with resistance at every turn.

I showed those naysayers, I surely did.

A sudden gust of wind whipped her honey-hued locks against her bonnet and threatened to whisk away her diploma. She clutched the rolled paper, along with her engraved class tickets, firmly against her bodice. A German bakery across the street floated the cinnamon scent of cakes and pastries her way, but the establishment, like the many other immigrant-owned businesses lining the commercial avenue, passed by with little notice from her. So, too, did the steepled churches and boxy colonial houses that followed, and soon the distance between even them grew far. When she reached the weedy edges of Cleveland and the forests beyond, nothing but towering trees and cawing seagulls in the distance near Lake Erie watched over her.

Finally, Catherine slowed her pace and escaped into a thick copse of trees, unaware of the lone figure still trailing behind her. Within the shadowy refuge of pines and spruces she could at last breathe and gather her spiraling thoughts.

What a whirlwind of a day this has been.

She leaned against the cool bark of a thick trunk and closed her eyes.

How proud she had felt upon the amphitheater stage, collecting her diploma as the only woman in a class full of men. Her mother and father had beamed in the audience, and even her older brother, Charles, a pastor and one of her strongest critics, had grudgingly applauded her accomplishment. From the moment she had been accepted into Cleveland Medical College, she suffered a litany of reasons why a woman was unfit to be a doctor. Frightening threats too, from fellow students and teachers alike. Even community members (of both genders) had passed judgment, and newspaper editorials never held an opinion back:

"This folly of turning our country's future wives and mothers into doctors must come to an end," a columnist had written. "Their presence in the field has been an amusement, one can fairly concede, but this social experiment has now run its course. By allowing yet another woman to graduate from the Medical Department of Western Reserve College, we have set an undesirable precedent, not to mention a dangerous one. How soon before our good citizens die from an error at the hands of a lady doctor, no matter how well-intentioned her treatment? In this fine year of 1853, as Cleveland burgeons to a population of nearly thirty thousand people, and our railroads, waterways, and manufacturing bring tremendous progress our way, we must not risk unraveling our social fabric because a few scandalous women deem themselves on equal footing to men."

Although Catherine had tried to disregard the overt contempt from men of that journalist's ilk and draw instead from the supportive ones in her circle, his type of rhetoric was far more common than the opposite. In fact, the public outcry over her education had been so intense that a young constable was tasked with overseeing that afternoon's commencement. As friends and family members took their seats on the amphitheater benches in the stately Medical College on St. Clair Street, the rather studious-looking officer with unruly hair and a cleft in his chin had pulled Catherine aside and reassured her his presence was merely a precaution.

After introducing himself as Constable Henry Whitaker, he had surprised her with a hearty congratulations and handshake. "What you've achieved is truly remarkable, miss…I mean, *doctor.* If you should need anything, anything at all, you can call on me." Despite her distraction she noticed his lingering grasp and infatuated expression, both of which seemed to extend beyond the professional.

She had thanked him but assured him the animosity of others was on the road behind her. Her newly acquired skills were about to shine, and not only would they earn her a healthy respect from her fellow citizens, they would bring her a sound income.

At last, Catherine's breaths, heartbeat, and emotions all reached the same plane of calm. She pushed away from the protective oak. It was well past time she return to the celebration. Her mother and father—and yes, even her brother Charles—might worry. They had traveled by carriage from Pennsylvania to celebrate her big day, and she shouldn't delay them any longer.

When she stepped away from the tree, a twig snapped behind her.

Startled, she turned to find the source, but before she could see what it was, something hard smashed into her skull.

Like an explosion of firecrackers, pain erupted inside her head. She fell to her knees, her gown billowing in all directions. Tree bark and muddy ground blurred before her. She began to cry out, but a second blow silenced her scream.

Blackness enveloped her.

Her thoughts were no more.

CHAPTER ONE
PRESENT DAY

CATHERINE

As a tree…

On a *Guardians of the Galaxy* calendar displaying five other-worldly misfits, the man inside the house draws an X over March 24, 2023, and this is how I know it's been one hundred and seventy years since I died.

From above the thawing winter terrain, my fractured bark and arthritic branches study Mr. Mark Carver through the window, his preference for curtains nonexistent. Of all the home dwellers to inhabit this remote bundle of land, he is my least favorite. I can't define why, no more than I can define why my soul became trapped in a tree, but I feel it none-theless. He radiates a subtle malevolence. A bad humor, perhaps. One I should like to purge with bloodletting were I still a living, breathing doctor named Catherine Miller instead of a hunk of twenty-first-century timber.

There was a time every branchlet and leaf of my oak form shook with sorrow over the murder of my human body. Although not the first attempt to banish me from medicine, it

6 | DANNIE BOYD

was definitively the last. If only I knew by whose hands. After all this time, that unsolved mystery is what torments me most, and I'm desperate to solve it. One moment I was reveling in my scholarly accomplishment, the next I was nothing but a sapling, surrounded by a babbling creek and fertile Ohio soil that over the many years has sprouted a microcosm of vegetation, from the tallest of firs and birches to the smallest of mushrooms and clovers. Throughout it all a litany of wildlife roams.

But as lovely as the singing birds and croaking bullfrogs are, stimulating companions they are not, for the rest of Mother Nature seems not to share my strange reincarnation. I feel their intimacy, to be sure, exchanging nutrients with the roots of my fellow trees and gases with my kin-like plants, but if not for the human inhabitants who have come and gone from this house over the years, a house that has been built and rebuilt, painted and repainted, shingled and reshingled, I'd be quite mad by now.

At least this ominous homeowner, who has resided here alone since his superhero calendar said June of last year, keeps me occupied.

No sooner have my thoughts returned to him than he slides open the glass door that separates the kitchen from the stone patio. As it often does when too much force is applied, the door slams with a bang. He steps outside in his puffy coat, made from a fabric I have no name for, and glances up at the morose sky, his dark hair lifting in the chilly breeze. His beard is nothing more than a few days' growth and thus not a beard at all. From a previously overheard conversation with his sister, I deduced he is thirty-seven years old.

In a blur of brown, white, and black fur, a beagle named Iggy bounds out after him. Mr. Carver strolls to the fire pit and mutters to the dog, "Stupid door. I swear to God, if I ever move again, it'll be to a new house and not some eighties nightmare."

Why he swears to God over such a trivial matter, I don't know, but his suggestion the russet-colored house is old amuses me. What would his thoughts be of the tiny cabin that originally marked these three acres one hundred years ago? Or perhaps it was one hundred and twenty years now. Time is elusive when one is a tree. If not for Mr. Carver's visible calendar, I would remain lost as to its passage.

I only know I spent many decades alone with nature before the foundation of a home was placed, along with a carriage house. The latter is now called a *garage* and is connected to the main residence by an arched trellis whose white paint come spring enjoys a burst of color from the lilac and rose bushes that nestle against it. Although Mr. Carver grumbles about having to walk outside from home to carriage house, he boasts about its history to visitors.

I suppose accuracy demands I refer to him as *Doctor* Carver, but as he is not the sort of doctor I'm familiar with, and perhaps, too, because of his dark essence, he remains simply *Mister* Carver to me. From his conversations with guests, it's clear he conducts research with medicines at Cardon University in Cleveland, not unlike my former Materia Medica teacher, an apathetic fool of a man if there ever was one.

Despite my reservations about Mr. Carver, I'm indebted to him, because he is a talkative and social man who holds numerous parties and prefers the outdoors, even in winter. Out of all the inhabitants who have graced this domicile, I've learned the most from him, even in this short time.

When the weather is warm, he enjoys his second-story deck off the bedroom or his elegant patio off the kitchen, both of which hold outdoor furniture as beautiful as anything one might expect to find inside. Come winter, he prefers the fire pit, enclosed in handsome cut stone and shiny maroon tiles and surrounded by four colorful Adirondack chairs. During all seasons, he soaks in what he calls his *hot tub* or *spa*. It sits on the far edge of the deck—which has been reinforced to support it —and bubbles and steams at the push of a button. Most intriguing of all these wonders, and most useful to me, is that wherever he sits, he speaks on a talking box he calls a *cell phone* or a *mobile* (who could ever have imagined such a thing?), and sometimes, have mercy on me, a face even speaks back to him.

Maybe the childless couple who lived here before him had similar devices, but if so, they never used them in my presence. They spent little time outside, always working late into the evening and returning to a darkened home, the curtains still drawn. It was a tedious few decades on my part, so yes, Mr. Carver's arrival was no less exciting to me than a traveling carnival come to town.

The dog, who has been sniffing around barren bushes and empty flower gardens ever since Mr. Carver released him from the house, finally raises a brown and white leg and relieves himself. When he finishes, he scampers over to the base of my tree, where his frequent repose has thinned the post-winter grass and hollowed out the soil between two of my exposed gnarly roots.

"Come on, Iggs," Mr. Carver says, having just started a fire in his pit, "what's that tree got that I don't?"

From his pocket, he withdraws a delicate lace undergarment and tosses it into the crackling flames. The act raises my curiosity tenfold, and I wonder who the intimate clothing belongs to.

After watching the fabric burn and shrivel for a few seconds, Mr. Carver sinks onto the green Adirondack chair, which is the one that gives me a view mostly of his back.

"Who would choose cold bark over a warm fire?" he asks the dog. "Besides, don't you think that old thing is kind of creepy?"

Iggy, like me, is voiceless. He simply lifts his droopy ears toward his master and then resettles at my base. We seem to have a connection, the canine and I, and he, along with the squirrels who forage my branches for my ever-dwindling acorns, is another reason I have not yet gone mad. Like the homeowner in front of me, Iggy is to whom I talk.

Mr. Carver chuckles at something on that peculiar object he calls a phone. Colorful lights flash from its rectangular glass, and playful music pours from its edges. He swipes his finger over the surface, watches a man fall comically down a flight of stairs, and laughs with even more jolliness. Despite my doubts about him, not to mention my confusion over the burned clothing, the sound of his mirth is always pleasant to hear.

How I'm able to hear or see anything, I'm not sure. Maybe it comes from the oxygen pores on my bark and limbs. But although my vision is keen, the higher my boughs go, the less clear the world becomes. The greater density of small branches at that height distorts my sight like a prism.

My beagle companion raises his head at his master's chortles, but when Mr. Carver calls him over again, Iggy simply wags his tail and resumes his restive pose near my trunk.

The researcher shrugs. "Suit yourself. Guess you might as well enjoy your tree now because you won't like me much when you see who's coming."

It's unclear what Mr. Carver means by this statement, but an unsettling sensation stirs in my roots. Whether from my own control over my limbs, which I've struggled to develop over the years, or the March wind, a gust rushes through my leafless branches, making them creak and moan like a haunted forest.

Before I have time to consider Mr. Carver's sinister implication, his phone rings. When he sees who the caller is, he curses and quiets the device without answering. To my canine friend, he says, "Don't look at me like that. I can't handle talking to Tony right now."

Although Iggy ignores him, my arboreal senses spark like

Mr. Carver's fire. Tony? My Tony? Who wouldn't want to speak to such a lovely man?

"Tony thinks he's found something in our research," Mr. Carver says to Iggy. "Something that could bring the whole thing down. Jeez, he's always overreacting." He grabs a long stick on the ground next to his chair and pokes at the fire like a jousting knight. My boughs bristle in annoyance to hear him speak about the gentle university student in such a rude manner.

A vehicle pulls onto the driveway and jerks to a stop. Although it's been decades since I saw my first car, driven home by a young couple who produced three children, the idea of one still fills me with awe, especially as I witness their evolution over the years. How convenient they would have been in my time. No horse and carriage to get stuck in the Ohio muck when the planks loosened and separated. No packed stagecoach to deliver me sweaty and cramped to my destination. Although the arrival of locomotives to Cleveland was a welcomed luxury, a modern vehicle offers far more freedom than I ever knew as a woman.

Through the gap between the carriage house and the home, I spot the back of a long black truck, and through the square windows of the carriage house, my lower branches make out the white letters emblazoned on the truck's side: Lockhorn Landscaping. Although I don't know what this means, my disquietude grows. Iggy jumps up and sets to barking.

A man dressed in a bulky coat and beige trousers exits the truck, disappears from view, and then reappears near the pretty white trellis. When he strides toward the front of the house, he vanishes again, and despite the dog's barking, I hear the familiar ding-dong noise of a bell from inside the home. Mr. Carver has already left his Adirondack chair and returns to the sliding door that leads to the kitchen.

"Sorry, Iggs," he says to the beagle, who lopes back and forth in front of my tree. "The bad guy's here."

Perhaps sensing my own unrest, the dog stops and stiffens. In that tense position, the black marking on his back resembles the saddles my father once sold at the back of his general store.

After a few moments, Mr. Carver reappears from the house, side by side with the man from the truck. Iggy zigzags around their feet, sniffing at the visitor's boots. Mr. Carver thanks the stranger for coming out on a Sunday.

"No problem. My schedule's packed, and you're not too far from where I live." The man's eyes widen, and his gaze lands on me. "Yikes, I can tell from back here. Shame too. She's a beauty. How old is she?"

Although he is an avid outdoorsman, Mr. Carver seems uninterested in such minute details as a tree's age. As the two men approach me, he says, "No clue, but its branches are starting to split. Don't want the thing toppling over and crushing my deck."

Despite my distance from his wooden oasis, I believe such a thing might be possible, but I'm not positive. I am, however, concerned about what exactly is going on.

The stranger in the bulky coat, which bears the same name as his truck, places a meaty hand on my bark. His weathered face scrunches up, and bristly hairs poke from his nostrils. "She's gotta be over a hundred years old. A hundred and fifty, maybe."

A hundred and seventy to be precise, I wish to say.

"It's a Quercus rubra, also known as a Northern Red Oak. They can live a mighty long time." The stranger rubs his chin and glances up at my highest point. "And this one's a tall gal. What, a good sixty, seventy feet? And with that bisecting trunk, a wide one too."

Mr. Carver shrugs. His phone beeps. He pulls it from his puffy coat and checks the screen. With a grimace, he returns it to his pocket, bends down, and pets Iggy under the chin. He is rarely affectionate with the beagle, so this is a welcome sight. The stranger plucks at my bark. A brittle piece breaks away. "See here? These cracks? Shows she's dyin'. No fresh bark growing in either."

I don't like the direction this conversation has taken. There are days I loathe my mute and immobile existence, to be sure, but whether human or tree, the prospect of another death is frightening. Was I truly meant to live a long second life in nature without any purpose or meaning attached to my soul?

"And see here?" The stranger reaches up and tugs at a small branch sprouting from one of my thicker ones. It easily snaps away. Although I feel no pain, sadness washes over me. "Even in March you should be able to find small leaf buds, but this beauty's hardly got any, and the ones she does got are dry and shriveled."

"Sounds like my department head," Mr. Carver says with a snort. "She's just a step away from the grave."

I'm not sure what a "department head" is, but nevertheless his joke seems cruel. The stranger must think so too because he says nothing, simply stares at my bark and plucks away another piece, as if pulling a licorice stick from my father's candy jar. The stranger then reaches into the pocket of his trousers and retrieves a small knife, which he flips open and uses to scratch away a spot on one of my twigs. He shakes his head. "Just as I suspected. Should be moist and green under here, not brown and brittle."

"Again, like my department head." Mr. Carver ruffles the dog's fur. "Right, Iggy?"

Iggy responds by leaving his master's side and plopping down once again at my base. It's as if he, too, suddenly understands what Lockhorn Landscaping means and what lies ahead for my future.

After scraping a few more of my smaller branches, all of

them above his head so that he must tug them down toward himself, the stranger pockets the knife and wipes his nose with the back of his hand. "Yeah, she's nearing the end of her life, all right. She's splitting apart too."

He points to the deep fractures that cleave my bark near the crooks of my branches. One stores trapped acorns, and another, about six feet above the ground, is fissured so deeply that anything hidden within its depths would likely never be found.

The stranger clicks his tongue. "You got a bit of time still, which is good because my schedule is jam-packed and there'll be a delay, but you won't get a better price than me, guaranteed."

"Sounds good," Mr. Carver says. "What kind of number are we talking?"

The stranger with the weathered face and nose full of bristly hairs gives the researcher a cost estimation. Once accepted, he extends his hand to shake Mr. Carver's, but Mr. Carver, who often rubs something that smells of moonshine over his palms as if to purify them, declines and bumps fists with the man instead.

With a devilish smile, Mr. Carver looks at his dog. "Sorry, Iggs, but your favorite tree is coming down." He draws a finger across his neck in a cutting fashion and adds, "Chop, chop."

His tone is so callous and his smile so cruel that I want to box his ears with two of my dead branches. Who is he to order me cut down at all? In May of last year, a month before Mr. Carver took up residence in the house, an efficient woman whose car advertised "Mercer Kline Realty" pointed to the creek to my immediate south and informed Mr. Carver that the home's property line fell four feet north of the slender brook and a good three acres east to west. Therefore, aside from a few meandering roots and arching branches, the bulk of my oak mass stands on city property. Has Mr. Carver forgotten Miss Mercer Kline Realty's descriptive details or was he too preoccupied with her half-exposed bosom to hear them?

I suppose it doesn't matter. Whether at Mr. Carver's expense or the city's, a swift "chop chop" will truncate any meager life I have left. The thought of yet another violent departure from this world squeezes my shriveled leaf buds in fear and stings my dried bark with powerlessness.

My absent eyes begin to weep.

CHAPTER TWO

CATHERINE

On this late-March afternoon, which is a good twenty to thirty degrees warmer than it was three days ago when my grim reaper from Lockhorn Landscaping came calling, Mr. Carver relaxes outside on his stone patio and sorts his mail. Loose-fitting pants and a buttonless shirt that reads *Just Do It* replace his professional attire. The cotton fabric fits snugly against his torso and showcases a fine physique, proof of his daily calisthenics.

Next to him, on a clear stand that matches a larger table a few feet away, rests a small parcel wrapped in brown paper, and next to that is a beverage in a copper mug, adorned with a slice of lime. In the past, he's referred to this spirited drink as a Moscow Mule. Usually it's his weekend libation, but since the calendar in his peach-colored kitchen tells me it's Wednesday, today's gift of a cloudless spring day must have enticed him to indulge a bit earlier.

All around him birds flit back and forth—from the pretty trellis, to the house's scalloped wood trim, to the many trees that dot the lawn. He takes little notice of them, and I can't help but wonder about a man who offers neither feeder nor birdbath to thank them for their songs.

Completing this backyard serenity is a soft breeze that sways my small branches and delivers an earthy scent from the creek to my south. As always, Iggy the beagle reposes at my base.

While Mr. Carver sips his Moscow Mule and opens his envelopes, alternately grunting at the contents or crumbling them up and tossing them into a trash bin near his shiny grill, I work on freeing the trapped acorns in the crook of my branch. Over the past three days, I've labored at this task because I don't know when my murderous arborist will return. It could be hours; it could be months. "Chop chop," as Mr. Carver said.

Perhaps one deeper crack is all that's needed to break the thin limb and let loose the acorns. Feeding the hungry squirrels that scurry over my boughs would at least give me a small purpose before I die, but today my branches refuse to comply. I keep trying, though, because as my mother often told me, "My tenacious little Cat, if something is impossible, you'll scratch your paws at it until it's not."

Mr. Carver's phone rings a musical jingle and startles us both. After he answers, he props the phone up on the side table, and from that angle I see the smiling face of his sister, Melissa, whose pert nose and broad forehead offer a pleasant balance to her wide-set eyes. As always in her presence, Mr. Carver's suspect nature shifts to adoration. Anyone can see how much he loves her.

"Hey, you," Mr. Carver says. "What's up?"

"Why am I staring at a tree?"

Mr. Carver laughs. "Sorry." He adjusts his phone so that only half of Melissa's face is now visible to me. "Is that better? The day is too nice to sit inside. Sixty-three degrees in March, can you believe it?"

"You'd sit outside even if it was twenty below. You're like a crackhead, only for fresh air."

"You try spending all your time in a lab or classroom." Mr. Carver bursts up from his chair and starts jumping up and down, his feet moving in and out and his arms waving in an arc. It's an exercise I've watched him do many times.

"You know your chubby days are behind you, right?" Melissa says. "You can put a kibosh on the jumping jacks."

"I ate a whole calzone for lunch. That was stupid."

"You're not getting obsessed on me again, are you? How goes the fatso drug, anyway? You and your nerdy minions any closer to clinical testing?"

Mr. Carver ceases his jumping jacks, stretches his sides, and retakes his seat, his cheeks flushed and his dark hair ruffled. "Leave it to the woman who called my fourth-grade bully a 'dildo-head butt-licker' to reduce my revolutionary drug discovery to an un-PC handle."

"You held your own by middle school."

In my suspended existence, there are many times in which I have no understanding of Mr. Carver's words or those of his friends and family. This is one of those times. It doesn't matter, though, because I enjoy the playful banter between brother and sister. To have had such a lighthearted relationship with my oldest brother instead of our constant rancor would have been wonderful.

While Melissa talks about her "tweens" no longer finding her "cool," Mr. Carver opens the parcel awaiting him and withdraws an elegant rectangular box. He lifts the lid and removes a sharp object with a silver blade and a mahogany handle.

Holding it up in front of his sister's face on his phone, he says, "Look what Harrison sent me. A fancy letter opener." Mr. Carver studies the handle. "It's even engraved. My name, and below that, Price Industries. What do I need a letter opener for?"

"I'll take it off your hands if you don't want it."

Mr. Carver waves it around and wields it like a weapon.

"No, no, I'll keep it."

"Careful. You'll stab yourself."

"Must've been expensive, it's heavy. Probably cost more than my flat screen."

"Guess that's an investor's way of saying get your butt moving."

My attention to their conversation is cut short when a man on a bicycle, which is another mode of transportation I learned about from the family with three children, glides onto Mr. Carver's driveway. He flashed by so quickly, I didn't make him out before the carriage house blocked him from view, but I imagine an arborist and his deadly saw would not come by bicycle. For this my boughs heave in relief, and I thank the Lord for another moment of life.

When I see who the caller is, I bristle with excitement. It's Mr. Tony Habib. My Tony. A slight man with dark eyes and a Cupid's bow for lips who's visited Mr. Carver several times, both in a social and professional capacity. If he no longer graced this soil my days would grow dark indeed. Despite his shyness, he reminds me of Mr. Mansour Younis, the exotic lawyer from Persia with whom I often strolled down Cleveland's beautiful Euclid Street, its dozens of baronial mansions rivaling even that of my preceptor's.

With a stiff gait, as if the bike ride bruised his thighs, Tony walks toward the trellis. His dark shirt, plastered to his lithe chest, is even tighter than Mr. Carver's, and his pantaloons seem glued to his body. So revealing is the outline of his masculine form that one might wonder why he chose to wear any clothes at all. Mr. Mansour Younis would never have worn something so explicit on our walks. But it doesn't matter. Tony is as handsome as Mr. Younis, and he makes my nonexistent heart flutter with the same palpitations.

When he passes beneath the white trellis, his palms delicately graze the still dormant lilac and rose bushes that flank it, and my affection for him grows even deeper. His athletic shoes are so quiet on the stone pathway I doubt Mr. Carver hears him approach. Even Iggy still snores at my base, proof he must be in the deepest of dreams because he usually rouses at the slightest noise.

I return my attention to Mr. Carver's phone conversation, which his sister is now ending. "Sorry, I gotta go."

"Hot date?" Mr. Carver asks. When Melissa offers a look of surprise and then hesitates, he laughs. "I'm kidding. You married people are so boring."

"Says the man with no girlfriend."

They disconnect, and it is only now that Mr. Carver spots Tony creeping over the spring grass as if trying not to startle the homeowner.

"Hey, Tone, what are you doing here?" Mr. Carver rises. He seems neither pleased nor displeased at his caller's unexpected arrival. He scrunches his nose. "Nice bike shorts. Get a free dose of humility with those?"

Tony glances down at his clothes, and his olive coloring pinks to a faint blush. "Sorry. Just got my bike out for the season."

Mr. Carver approaches Tony and bumps fists with him. As always when the two men are together, I feel protective of the younger researcher. Whether it's because I don't yet trust Mr. Carver or because of something deeper, I'm not sure.

"I'm just messing with you," Mr. Carver says. "The shorts look fine, and all that biking clearly keeps you trim. You and I should ride together sometime. Take the towpath from Cleveland to Akron."

Tony's face brightens. "I'd like that."

"Then it's a date." Mr. Carver bumps fists with his student once again and indicates he sit by the fire pit so they can talk.

As Tony glides toward the Adirondack chairs, I long for human fingertips so that I might reach out and stroke the soft skin of his face or smooth the tousled hair on his forehead. Foolishly, I want him to notice me, to recognize the soul embedded within my cracked and fissured exterior. *I am here,* I wish to cry. *See me.* Of course he doesn't. He simply mentions how beautiful Mr. Carver's yard is and makes his way to the fire pit, which is unlit on such a fine day. I'm relieved when he chooses the orange Adirondack chair because it means he'll remain in full view.

"Can I get you a drink?" Mr. Carver offers. "Sparkling water?"

"Yeah, that'd be great."

Mr. Carver strides through the sliding door that leads to his kitchen, and through the large pane of glass, I see him retrieve a bottle from his cooling box and dump ice into a glass from the same machine (how I would have loved such an appliance in my day). After filling the glass with the bottle's contents, he tops it with a wedge of lime. Meanwhile, Tony smooths his hair, adjusts his strange bike shorts, and fidgets in the chair. He seems a man full of nervousness, but when Mr. Carver reemerges from the two-story house, Tony's drink in one hand and a fresh Moscow Mule in the other, Tony straightens, and that same look of admiration blankets his face.

I struggle to understand this obvious adoration of his superior. Is it from mere respect as a student working alongside his teacher? Or is it something else, something that brings a blush to my boughs? Mr. Carver doesn't wear the same expression, and although he may not have a girlfriend now, in the months he has lived here, more than a few women have crossed his trellis. I've witnessed a few amorous trysts in his hot tub as well, which I would have preferred not to.

A fortnight ago, I was privy to a heated argument between Mr. Carver and a blond woman who, on a number of occasions, had made herself at home inside his kitchen and bedroom, at least the portion of it visible to me. So fierce was their outburst in the backyard that Mr. Carver seemed ready to shake the poor woman and throw her into the narrow creek. In my permanently frozen stance, I was unable to help her, and the lack of neighbors made any rescue unlikely.

The fight did indeed end with a smashing, but the one who got smashed was me. Mr. Carver shattered the glass he'd been drinking from against my bark, where it exploded into hundreds of shards that bloodied his palm. His fury was so venomous, my branches shrank away from him.

I have not seen the woman since, but I sense from Mr. Carver's mutterings that she's called his phone several times. He didn't answer those calls, but he did, oddly enough, take the striped umbrella she once used. The other evening he stood on his deck and twirled the confiscated parasol like a stage performer, humming in strange contentment.

Presently, he hands Tony the bubbling water and sits in the blue Adirondack chair next to his visitor, giving me ample view of his confident features as well. The late afternoon sun glints off the copper cup in his hand. "So, what's up, Tone? Problem at the lab?"

"No. Well, maybe. Probably."

Mr. Carver laughs, and the delicious nature of it seems to put Tony more at ease. "That doesn't exactly clear things up for me."

With the fingers of a pianist, Tony squeezes the lime wedge into his drink and takes a sip. "The results came back. It's conclusive."

"What is?"

"The mouse has it. Found it in his lab results last week, but I wanted to give it a few days to be sure. Today's necropsy confirmed it."

Mr. Carver's posture stiffens. "Confirmed what?"

"Come on, Mark. Don't pretend you don't know what I'm talking about. One of the mice got liver cancer. I think Skinny Z is responsible."

"Don't call it Skinny Z." Mr. Carver scratches at his neck in obvious irritation. "That's a stupid name for a drug that's going to change the way we manage obesity. Who came up with it, anyway?"

"Chloe."

"Leave it to the stats nerd."

Tony slides toward the end of his wide-based chair and places his glass of water on one of the maroon tiles adorning the fire pit's rim. Worry creases his face. "ZM6635, Skinny Z, call it whatever you like until Price or the pharma folks formally name it, but it might be giving the mice cancer."

Mr. Carver finishes his beverage in one long, slow drain. "Come on, one case of liver cancer out of tons of lab mice doesn't prove our drug is at fault. It's making the mice lose weight with none of the side effects of the drugs on the market."

"I know, but we at least need to take it seriously."

"I am taking it seriously, of course I am, but that doesn't mean we have to get our bike shorts in a wad." A brief hesitation and then Mr. Carver asks, "Have you recorded it yet?"

"No, only in my notebook. I promised you I'd discuss it with you first if the biopsy confirmed it, but now that it has, I think it needs to go on the official record." Tony picks at the tight fabric of his shirt. "I should have already done so. It's unethical not to."

Mr. Carver leans all the way forward and places a hand on Tony's forearm. The blush in the young researcher's complexion returns.

"Hey, nothing you did is unethical," Mr. Carver says. "There's no sense hindering our research for something incidental, at least not until we can better define it."

When I was a medical student at Cleveland Medical College, I helped with enough experiments to know Mr. Carver's words don't sound like accepted procedure. Of course, I was murdered before I had a chance to perform any independent research, so maybe I'm not the best judge.

"Yeah, but we need to record this." Tony's voice rises. "We need to do this methodically. We need to inform the rest of the research team. We need to—"

"Of course we do. You think I'd have brought you in on this project if I didn't love how methodical you are? You're the best PhD student I've ever had." Another squeeze to Tony's forearm, followed by a caress, and now Tony's cheeks are as red as the tulips that will color the tree beds come April.

"I…well…"

"One more case. One more case and we do it all by the book, I promise. But I need some time to make a plan B, come up with some drug modifications if need be, you know the drill. We've been here before."

"Not with cancer!" When Mr. Carver doesn't respond, Tony says, "This isn't like before. This isn't a side effect like gas or diarrhea. And we're so close now to human trials. You said yourself Price is putting a lot of pressure on you."

Mr. Carver glances over his shoulder toward the patio table where the letter opener from his investor, Harrison Price, lies. "That's putting it mildly, but don't worry. Price's impatience has nothing to do with my hesitance. I just want to make sure there's really a problem before we create one unnecessarily. If we go marking up our records with notes of how ZM is causing cancer in mice, even if it isn't in anyway related to the drug, we're finished. If Chloe, Montell, Alice, or any of the undergrads get a whiff of this, it'll leak like a septic wound. Everything we've worked for will implode. We still have time to let things play out over the next week or two. You keep your sharp eye on those mice like you have been, and let's see how things go."

"So if I find a second case you'll act?"

"Of course, Tony, of course. You think I want to put a

drug out there that causes cancer? My career—and yours—would be over."

"Still can't believe they might offer you full tenure already." Tony glances shyly at Mr. Carver. "Well, I *can* believe it because you're so good."

"Thanks, man. I appreciate that." Mr. Carver's smile is so luminous it could melt the ice in his Moscow Mule. "So I'm simply saying let's take this a day at time. Why risk all the progress we've made for something that might turn out to be nothing? After all, we've been testing ZM in mice for a while, and you haven't found any indication of this before, right?" After Tony shakes his head, Mr. Carver says, "Then it's most likely a fluke."

"Or maybe it just took time to develop, but if there's a second case, you'll—"

"Yes, yes, you know I will. Safety is my number one priority. Trust me." This last is said with a wink as charming as any Beau Brummell could deliver.

Tony blushes for a final time, and after another half hour of unrelated conversation, he says he needs to go. He plans on visiting his great aunt in the nursing home later that evening.

"How's she doing?" Mr. Carver asks.

"As well as anyone with bad Alzheimer's. Sometimes she recognizes me, most times she doesn't."

"God, that's awful. Raised you all those years and doesn't remember you? Dementia is a cruel beast." The homeowner displays a warm sympathy that mirrors my own.

"Yeah, it's pretty rough."

Mr. Carver embraces Tony in a hug that lasts far too long, and when he pulls away from his young researcher, he says, "Hang in there. She's lucky she has you."

Tony swallows and nods and then makes his way under the trellis back to his bike, at which time he cycles away and disappears from my view.

After his student's departure, Mr. Carver puffs out his

cheeks and sighs, and I'm touched by the empathy he showed Tony over his great aunt. Perhaps I've misjudged this research doctor. Perhaps his blood's humor is not so sinister, after all.

Without warning, a sparrow crashes into the large pane of glass that makes up the sliding door. Both Mr. Carver and I startle, him with a jerk of his body and me with a crack of a small twig that falls away from my upper half. Iggy, too, has jumped up to attention, and within seconds he trots over to the fallen bird.

Its wings flutter softly, uselessly, flight evidently impossible. As the poor creature lies there injured, tiny chirps squawk from its broken beak. Iggy sniffs at the bird, but rather than clench it within his jaws as I feared he might, he settles down next to it, stares at Mr. Carver, and whines.

"Ah, it's okay, Iggs." Mr. Carver bends down to stroke the dog's fur, and I again wonder if I have miscast him. "These things happen."

For a while, the two study the bird, as if unable to tolerate its suffering, but then Mr. Carver rises and grabs a stone from a dirt patch beyond the patio.

No, please. Please don't, I want to shout.

Mr. Carver returns to Iggy and the sparrow and crouches down once again. He raises the rock high above his head.

No! Please!

With lips curled into the same feral smile he displayed when telling Iggy I was to be removed—"chop chop"—he pounds the stone down and bashes the bird's head. Once, twice, three times in total, each smash echoing my soundless cries of sorrow.

Iggy, seemingly as horrified as me, scoots back and whimpers. Mr. Carver stares at him beyond the crushed bird. "Ah, lighten up, Iggs. You're as wimpy as the woman I got you from." When the dog blinks at him, Mr. Carver adds in a flat tone, "Some things are just better off dead."

CHAPTER THREE

LANI

The corpse sways from a sturdy ceiling fan in the middle of the living room, the rope around her neck taut, but fourth-generation homicide detective Lani Whitaker isn't convinced it's suicide.

"For one thing," she says to Brian Dupree, her young partner of seven months, "there are fingernail marks around the ligature as if she was fighting it." With her gloved hand, she points to the deceased woman's dangling heel where a pink Croc slipped off. "And what woman kills herself wearing plastic shoes?"

"Crocs aren't made of plastic. It's actually a foam resin called—"

"Yeah, yeah, Einstein. Save it for never."

"Glad to see you're as chipper as ever this morning. It's Friday. Cheer up."

"When they're kicking your butt out the retirement door you can be as grumpy as you like."

"You've always been grumpy."

Lani snorts. He isn't wrong. Her Grandpa Joe used to tell her she was just a few scowls away from becoming her great grandfather, Henry Whitaker, a man who brooded his whole life over the case of a pretty young doctor whose disappearance he could never solve.

She peers back up at the rope around the dusky woman's neck, the binding partially hidden by long blond hair. "What gal has that kind of rope just lying around a tiny house like this? Judging by the Pier 1 decor, she doesn't seem the type to keep a roll of it."

"Maybe planned it ahead of time."

"And what, decided she'd blow dry her hair to a glossy shine first?" Lani shakes her head, her own tresses a short dark bob, not counting the few grays her barber missed. The guy is older than a 1945 penny and probably sees about as well as one too, but she isn't about to pay a pink tax at some fancy salon when the local barbershop will do. Her parents went there for years.

"So you think someone else strung her up and kicked out the chair?" Brian asks.

"Maybe he killed her someplace else. Strangled her and then hoisted her up to make it look like a suicide."

"Wouldn't a neighbor have seen something?"

Lani shrugs. "People keep to themselves. No door camera outside either."

Brian's gloved hand points to the markings on the front of the woman's neck. "Maybe she had second thoughts, that's why the fingernail scratches. Plus, the rope pattern is an inverted V. You'd expect that from a hanging. If it was strangulation, the furrow markings should be different."

Lani raises a thin eyebrow and smirks. "Someone's proving he earned that top score on the detective exam. A few months as Columbo and you're already smarter than me."

"Nah." Brian winks.

Despite their thirty-three-year age difference, his boyish

charm stirs something long since dead inside her. Or maybe it's just gas.

"I'm learning from the best," he says. "Why do you think they paired me with you?"

"Because I'm almost sixty-five and about to be sent to pasture. I'll be a tube of glue in six weeks." She focuses again on the woman's neck. "You're right about the skin markings, but a smart killer would know that too, so he could've applied pressure in the same way a hanging would."

The door to the dead woman's home swings open, skimming an empty umbrella stand next to it. Two techs from the crime scene unit pour in with their cases and protective gear. Upon seeing Lani and Brian, the female tech relaxes. "Oh good," she says. "Glad you're the lead, Whitaker. Don't need to worry about you messing up our scene."

"Got my ruby slippers on and everything." Lani points to the white booties on her feet. "Might not be much of a scene though. Could be a simple suicide, but I have my doubts— some fingernail markings on the neck. Haven't touched anything yet."

Behind them is the medical examiner, Dr. Otis Fry, who's been on the job nearly as long as Lani and whose cynicism matches her own. He nods to her in greeting.

While the ME and the techs photograph and assess the body, Lani and Brian make their way to the lone bedroom in the Winston, Ohio home, the other bedroom having been converted to a walk-in closet. Though Lani lives up in Edgewater, a west-side neighborhood of Cleveland, she prefers not to work where she craps, so she slogs for the Winston PD instead.

As they sift through the woman's things, Lani taking the oak dresser and Brian a small desk, he says, "Made any plans for when you're a free woman? May tenth isn't far away."

"Probably just kill myself on my birthday three days later. Make you come figure out if it's suicide or murder."

Instead of giving her an appalled expression, Brian laughs, which is one of the reasons she likes him.

"I'll treat you with kid gloves," he says, "but I might steal a couple twenties from you while I do."

"I'd be disappointed if you didn't." Lani sorts through cotton underpants and 34-C bras and then moves on to the next drawer. "I don't know," she says, figuring she owes her young partner an answer. "What do you do when you suddenly become irrelevant? Just bum around, I guess. I need to clean out the attic—been putting it off forever—so I'll start there. It's been thirteen years since I moved into my parents' house, and I still haven't sorted through their stuff. It's not like they're going to rise from the dead anytime soon, and who knows what they've got hidden up there?" She pauses and glances at him, not sure she should admit the next part, worried he'll think she's crazy. "Been thinking about taking a long cruise, finally seeing more of this planet. Found an around-the-world one, and god knows I've got enough money saved. Plus, I've been poked more times than a voodoo doll with all those booster shots. I put a deposit down to hold the spot."

Thankfully, Brian doesn't mock her, just folds his brow in a pensive way as if weighing the idea around. "Not sure that's your kind of thing. You really want to eat dinner with strangers? And for a woman who treats her plants like babies, won't you miss them?" He makes a rocking motion with his arms and hips. "Nothing but a swaying sea all around you."

"They do stop for land trips, you know. Maybe you're not as smart as I thought." She exhales a heavy sigh, her breath ruffling a silk pajama top in the middle drawer. "Crap, you're right. I'd probably hate it, but what the feck else am I going to do?"

"Just because there's mandatory retirement for street work doesn't mean you can't do something else as a cop. Take French's advice and teach."

Lani opens the bottom drawer, which houses winter sweaters and wool socks. "*Pfft.* Barney Fife can bite me. How he made chief at such a young age is beyond me. If I could ship him back to New York, I would."

"Who's Barney Fife?"

Standing up from her crouched position, her knees cracking, Lani stares at her partner. "Seriously? Never heard of *The Andy Griffith Show?*" When Brian shakes his head, her mood sours more.

"You'd be great at teaching cadets," he says.

"Have you met me?"

Brian starts searching the small closet. As gracefully as a mule, Lani drops back down to check under the bed for something useful. Nothing.

When she is once again upright, she makes a face. "Guess what Chief Toddler said to me. Told me I should take a long vacation in Hawaii, visit my *family* there."

"Ouch. What'd you say?"

"Told him my mother's parents were Samoan, not Hawaiian, and that my father's people came from England. Then I may or may not have called him a naïve kid, told him my mom was more native Clevelander than his New York puss would ever be, and recommended he educate himself on the South Pacific."

"Why didn't you just castrate him while you were at it?"

"Yeah, yeah, guess I took it a little far, but having to work under a juvenile stinks, especially one of those ivory-tower types who floats from precinct to precinct and city to city, wanting to change everything up—and not the kind of change we need. Besides, I've already paid my dues, not the least of which was being a female cop in the seventies and eighties." Lani plants her hands on her hips, her body more apple-shaped than pear if she doesn't watch what she eats, and shifts her voice to an annoying Beavis and Butt-Head pitch. "Heh, lookin' good, honey, got any room in those uniform pants for me? Hey, sweetheart, we're out of coffee, can you make some? How about a detective sammich, if you know what I mean, uh huh, uh huh, uh huh."

Brian turns away from the closet with a half-smile. "You seen the color of my skin lately? Don't have to tell me twice." His face sobers. "But you better be careful with Chief French. You don't want him firing you before you retire. Don't risk your pension over pride."

She waves the comment off. "He wouldn't dare."

"Why not?"

"Let's just say I might know a fun tidbit about him he wouldn't want coming to light."

Brian halts his search of the nightstand and stares at her. "Oh yeah? And what would that—"

Lani cuts him off. "You still having problems with that woman? She still stalking you?"

"No, not stalking really. She just doesn't want to take no for an answer. Now what were you saying about—"

Dr. Fry trudges in.

"So?" Lani asks the ME. "Suicide by hanging for sure?"

"Can't say anything for sure yet, but there's no evidence to suggest otherwise at this point. The fingernail scratches could be second thoughts."

When Lani sees Brian is about to gloat, she gives him the stink eye.

"I'll do a more detailed exam once she's on my table," Fry says.

Lani nods and takes in the bedroom as a whole. Aside from the unmade bed, whose pale blue comforter is twisted up in the sheets, the home is tidy. "Doesn't the messy bed strike you as odd?" she asks the two men. "Wouldn't she make her bed before offing herself?"

"Maybe you're overthinking it," Brian says.

Maybe I am overthinking it, Lani muses silently, but she can't help it. She's had too many questionable cases lately, too many unsolvables. If the powers that be are going to boot her out the retirement door, she at least wants to go out with a win. The unresolved cases probably make her look inept to Chief Toddler, proving to him, at least in his mind, that she *is* too old to stay on the job. It doesn't help that he learned about her stained reputation as a rookie, an incident that took place over four decades ago and wasn't her fault, but one she has suffered years of whispers and insinuations for anyway.

Now it looks like she'll be carrying the stain of incompetence on her way out too.

Super.

CHAPTER FOUR

CATHERINE

While the creek burbles to my south and squirrels scratch at my lifeless boughs, the sun drifts lazily to a late-afternoon position. As has been the trend this year, the weather remains fine, with generous sunshine unencumbered by clouds and a light wind that rustles my branchlets.

Although April and its promise of spring will arrive in three days, my mood remains somber. As with every day since the Lockhorn Landscaping truck darkened Mr. Carver's driveway, I wonder if my arboreal death will come soon. The few cars on the road beyond keep whirring past, but my anxiety is no less acute because it's the never knowing that ulcerates the stomach I no longer possess.

With a familiar hitch and then a bang, the sliding door flies opens, and out darts my faithful companion, Iggy, who has been cooped up inside the house while Mr. Carver toiled away at the university. The beagle relieves himself next to the still-dormant maple tree nearest the deck and then bounds around in a flurry of sniffing, snorting, and digging. After a while, he tires out and plants himself on the dirt at my base, unbothered by the new weeds and mushrooms that have sprouted around my exposed roots.

This Friday afternoon, Mr. Carver carries a different drink in his hand, one that comes in a tall bottle and has the amber color of beer. He wiggles into a thin coat, angles his face to the sun, and allows the breeze to caress him.

"What do you think, Iggs? Should we light a fire?" He checks the thermometer on the house. "Could go either way. I'll let you decide."

Iggy tilts his head, as if not understanding what his master wants. I, too, struggle to reconcile this seemingly good-natured man with the unflinching one who bashed in a sparrow's head two days ago. Three times.

Whistling, Mr. Carver disappears behind the opposite side of the house and then reappears with fresh logs. As he sets to starting a fire in the stone pit, his phone rings its melodious tune.

He plops down on the orange Adirondack chair, facing me fully, and answers the call. "Hey, Harrison, how goes it?" He retrieves his beer from the ground and swigs. "What was that? Hold on a sec. I'm going to put you on speaker. No, no, I'm alone in my backyard."

That's what you think, I wish to tell him.

"Just checking in on my favorite researcher," Mr. Price says from the phone that's now resting on Mr. Carver's trousers. Although I have never seen Harrison Price in person, I know he is the oft referred to wealthy investor.

"Thank you for the letter opener," Mr. Carver says. "You didn't need to do that."

"It's nothing. Probably a dumb gift for the twenty-first century, but we still get bills and junk mail, am I right?" Mr. Price allows no time for a response. "Everything still running smoothly on Skinny Z?"

"Not you too."

"Its lab name is too much of a mouthful. Besides, you won't have to put up with it much longer. As soon as we get this to human trials, my pharma team will come up with something brilliant. And let me tell you, they are creaming their jeans to get started."

"I'm sure they are." Though Mr. Carver sounds confident, a shadow crosses his face, one that cannot be blamed on a passing cloud under such a clear sky. "Our plan for phase zero is on track, but remember, these things take time. We need to be efficient but cautious. And there...uh...might be a slight hiccup."

"No hiccups, Mark. I don't like hiccups. Price Industries has given you and your university too much money for hiccups."

Mr. Carver mimes a monkey face to Iggy, who watches his master while scooting back an inch or two closer to me. His rump brushes my bark, and I long to pet him.

"And once this wonder drug is out," Mr. Price continues, "I'll make a fortune, and you'll be the youngest full professor ever, or whatever you academics call it."

"That's what I'm hoping for," Mr. Carver says. "That and helping millions of people lose weight safely, of course." His tone sounds sincere to me, and once again I'm confused by his dual nature.

"Of course. Me too."

"It'll be fine, I'm sure, but Tony Habib—he's one of my PhD students, remember—has found a mouse with liver cancer."

"So? Mice get cancer too."

"I know, and he hadn't found anything up until now, so it might not be related. It's probably not related. But still..."

"Still nothing."

The air grows silent while neither man speaks, and although I can't see Mr. Price, I imagine him pacing an elegant rug in an elegant home with his jaw tensed and his hands fisted.

Finally, through the speakerphone, the investor says, "Listen, of course safety is our number one priority. My entire company and name are at stake, but we need to be careful. Don't do anything stupid. If something like this gets out before we've verified it, my pharma guys will get nervous. I'll lose all the money I've dumped into it, and you can kiss your tenure goodbye. Please tell me your man hasn't blabbed his mouth about it."

"Of course not. He hasn't officially entered it into the data, and he won't without telling me first."

"How can you be so sure?"

Mr. Carver smiles, and with the devious way his lips curl and his eyes crinkle, he reminds me of Curtis Mayfield, a malicious fellow who detested my female presence in class, so much so that I wonder if he is the one who killed me.

"Let's just say Tony likes me more than a friend," Mr. Carver says.

"I don't under—wait, are you gay? I mean, I don't care, but—"

"No, I'm not, but Tony doesn't need to know that."

I can't say for certain what the word "gay" in this capacity means, but I have my suspicions. It doesn't change how I feel about Tony, and I hate to hear them talk about him so callously.

"Use what you've got, Mark, that's what I always say. Just make sure he comes to you first with anything else. Overzealous and foolish researchers are something we don't need."

Mr. Carver squeezes his beer bottle tightly, and his smile fades to irritation. "No, but we don't want to take unnecessary risks either. I'm a scientist above all, and so is Tony."

"If medical innovators didn't take risks, we'd still be bloodletting and thinking infections were caused by bad air."

My branches bristle at this, and I can't help but feel offended by the investor's words, not to mention confused. Do physicians no longer rebalance the body's humors by bleeding? My future partner, Dr. Isaac Fitzgerald (had I not been murdered), would have been pleased to hear that. The progressive doctor had always questioned the treatment and even dared to suggest it would one day be a poorly perceived practice.

"So talk to your student," Mr. Price says from the speakerphone. "Make sure he understands what's at stake."

"Don't worry." Mr. Carver reaches forward and stokes his fire with a stick. "I'll take care of Tony."

———

I'm not sure whether Mr. Carver's comment about taking care of Tony is a veiled threat or an innocent remark, but as I listen to these two influential men spin the world to their whims, my first day of medical lectures over one hundred and seventy years ago flashes back to me. It was a day I, too, received a threat, one that was not at all veiled. Although my recall of the exact conversations may have shifted over the passing years, the events that took place have not.

Back then, becoming a physician required two sixteen-week sessions of classes, along with three years of preceptorship. I had already worked alongside Dr. Samuel Clifton for five months. He had agreed to serve as my educational mentor as a courtesy to my mother, of whose midwifery skills he had heard. He welcomed me into his home, for there was no other way a young woman like me, of modest but respectable upbringing, could have resided in one of Euclid Street's mansions.

After my first day of lectures in the Medical College on St. Clair Street, not far from Cleveland's Public Square, I hurried home to the Cliftons, relieved that aside from a barrage of amused—as well as decidedly unamused—stares in my direction in the amphitheater, it appeared I would be accepted by the male students.

How naïve I was, though, because when I returned to my bedroom in Dr. Clifton's house, I screamed. Screamed not so much over my shock at the gruesome object lying on my bed, but that someone wished me so much ill will they'd dare leave it there in the first place.

Doubtlessly hearing my outburst, my preceptor rushed down the hallway. When he saw the vile thing that desecrated my four-poster bed, his expression was no less stricken than my own.

There, lying upon a colorful quilt sewn by none other than Dr. Clifton's wife, was a severed human foot. Gray in color, wrinkled in texture, and absent of blood, the appendage had likely been removed from a corpse and not a living person. At least for that I was grateful.

"Who?… How?…" I stammered.

Dr. Clifton threw a protective arm around me, as if fearful I might faint, but I shook my head and insisted I was fine. Indeed, lightheadedness was not at all my response. After my initial alarm faded, I felt nothing but anger.

"Who would do such a horrible thing?" I asked my preceptor.

He had no answer, but once assured he could leave my side, he shuffled his stout body to the window near the bed. It opened freely. "I'm afraid your window was not latched, dear. Anyone could have entered."

Swallowing, I edged closer to the bed and lowered my face toward the severed foot. A stench rose with nearly visible fumes. Though hesitant, I was equally curious. "A recent grave robbing, perhaps?"

"Perhaps, but you shouldn't be so close." Dr. Clifton wrung his hands, but after observing me for a spell, he said,

"It appears you'll make a fine doctor if a severed foot causes you no disgust."

My head shot up, and my cheeks heated. "Disgust I feel for sure, but not for the reasons you might think. I feel disgust that someone should wish to taunt me so viciously."

My preceptor's jowled face sagged. "Ah yes, it's likely from one of your foes. Sadly, few men are as progressive as me, and your desire to become a lady doctor is known not only by your teachers and classmates, but by the public as well."

"But having Mrs. Clark in her final year of preceptorship should make me less of a novelty. I've spoken with her in passing. She mentioned nothing of this sort." I bent over the severed foot again and, with interest, examined it from all angles.

"Maybe as the first woman to attend our medical college, Mrs. Clark was a novelty. She's a widow who required physiology studies for her teaching position and had thus been granted the privilege, but you, my dear child, may no longer be a novelty. You may be a…a threat."

"A threat! The only threat posed by me is that I might hit someone with my blasted skirt as I stroll past them. I don't wish to take anything from these men or make them feel inferior. I only wish to be who I am. To be a doctor who looks like the other half of Cleveland's population. I'm merely one small woman taking up the tiniest space on their bench."

Dr. Clifton rejoined my side and eased me away from the bed. Perhaps my fascination with the severed foot unsettled him. "That may be well and good, but maybe they don't see you as 'one' woman. Maybe they see you as a wave of change, a wave they have no desire to join. You must have expected as much. You told me one of your own brothers rails against your medical education."

I puffed annoyed air out of my nostrils and finally removed my wool cape, draping it over the chaise in the corner of the room. "I suppose I did expect as much, but after today's classes went well, at least nothing untoward that I couldn't handle, I hoped I'd misjudged things."

At that point, Dr. Clifton escorted me out of my bedroom and called for Lily the housekeeper to fetch some hot tea. Then he settled me into the parlor.

"I'll have to report this to the constable, but before I go, could you say with any certainty who in your class might have done this? Slipped out during the noon hour or afternoon break? The walk is not far."

"I have no idea," I told him. "But the student who sneered the most whenever I raised my hand or was called upon was Curtis Mayfield, a young man with the face of an ogre."

"And your teachers?"

I couldn't hide my shock. "You think a teacher would do this?"

"I'm only asking to be thorough, my dear. Students aren't the only ones who have a problem with admitting ladies to the college. Quite the contrary, in fact."

I sighed and stared at the Clifton family portrait on the parlor wall. "The professor who displayed the most outward distaste was Dr. Jedidiah Cartwright." A glance at Dr. Clifton's tight lips told me he knew of whom I spoke. "Staring directly at me, he told us, 'I'm here to teach, so that is what I'll do, whether I think you belong here or not.' And yet I possess his class ticket, so he didn't fight me on that. And then there was Dr. William Smith, our surgical teacher, an indignant man who enjoyed pitting me against the men, saying things like, 'Come now, men, are you going to be out-answered by a mere woman?'"

Dr. Clifton shook his head. "I'm sorry to hear that. Anyone else?"

I replayed the day in my mind. "No one beyond a few of the wives who came to have lunch with their husbands. They either looked at me as an oddity, like they might a zoo animal, or shook their heads in disapproval, but I sincerely doubt they had access to a human foot."

"Yes, I'm inclined to believe you're right."

After that, Dr. Clifton left to report the incident to a constable and to the faculty members themselves, but nothing came from it, and no more was learned about the incident. Maybe the revolting foot was placed there by the same monster who killed me.

Nevertheless, as I listen now to Mr. Carver talk to Mr. Price on the phone in front of the fire, I am acutely reminded that there are always men who will do everything in their power to hold people back.

Especially the people who get in their way.

CHAPTER FIVE

LANI

Dressed in her usual Sunday garb of sweatpants and a Cleveland Cavaliers sweatshirt, Lani grabs her watering can off the kitchen counter and holds it under the faucet.

Watching it fill, she is well aware that what she *should* be doing is cleaning out her nightmare of an attic. Find out exactly what her parents have hidden up there. If she does decide to commit to that around-the-world cruise she's put a deposit on, she'll need to rent out the house. She's not about to leave it empty for a year, not with all the crazies out there (and she ought to know—she's arrested buckets of them), but she also doesn't want a stranger, not even one she's vetted, snooping around her family's stuff.

Despite telling herself all weekend she'd get to it before Monday, she has yet to step a slippered foot into that dusty old space of her west-end home.

A few more minutes, Whitaker. Then it's up to the attic you go.

Using both hands to carry the full pitcher, she pads to the living room and bathes the corner ficus until its soil is moist.

Beneath its glossy leaves, the knobby twists of its braided trunk remind her of her own swollen knuckles.

"I'm turning into a troll," she grumbles to the plant. "At least you keep getting better looking each year."

Though she experiences little pain in her finger joints—nothing ibuprofen can't handle—that hasn't stopped them from announcing her age to the world. Same goes for the back of her hands, where her skin looks like crepe paper that's been trampled on the floor of a preschool class.

At least her knees and hips are good, because there's no way in H E double hockey sticks she's giving up her sunrise strolls. Her endomorph body type makes sure of that. A couple times a week she hefts dumbbells too, ranging from five to fifteen pounds, because, according to her egghead doctor and every scary health magazine out there, she's losing five percent of her muscle mass every decade.

Her ex-husband, Doug, whose last name of *Flume* she shed with the rest of him after their bland divorce twenty-nine years ago, often warned her she shouldn't be out walking alone at that hour. "It's not safe," he'd say. She'd give him a *what the feck* look and counter with, "I'm a cop with a gun. Who's going to mess with me?"

Thinking of Doug deflates Lani, not because she misses him—she doesn't; she likes not being under anyone's shadow but her own—but because thoughts of him remind her of what they were never able to have.

She shifts to the row of plants on her window seat and glances out at the picturesque neighborhood she grew up in. Old but clean, it's lined with early-century homes, postage-stamp lawns, and lots of sheltering trees. Moving back to the house after her parents willed it to her was a check in the win column. Despite the work it still needs, it has far more character than her generic townhome did, not to mention memories.

She waters her spider plant, its thin stems tickling her

arms. "You're lookin' good too." To the philodendron next to it, she says, "Better watch out, Didi. Spidey's gonna put you to shame."

After giving the same verbal and hydration care to the rest of the plants scattered throughout the two-story home, including two regal and feathery ferns on the fireplace mantle, Lani realizes she can no longer put off the dreaded attic.

Just a couple boxes. Then your procrastinating rear end can rest for the night.

Besides, she needs something to take her mind off work. It likes to ruminate on cases even on a weekend off, especially now in her dissatisfied state.

She stuffs her reading glasses into the pocket of her sweatpants and finds scissors and a Sharpie in the junk drawer. After grabbing a bottle of Dortmunder beer from the fridge, she shuffles to her upstairs bedroom and enters the walk-in closet where the attic door hides on the ceiling like some sort of horror trap.

At five foot five, she needs a footstool to reach the latch and tug the small door open. Having already brought one up, she grabs it from the corner of the closet, lowers the attic door, and climbs the narrow steps until she spills into the dusty chamber above. When she tugs on the dangling string to ignite the lone light bulb, a shadowy, spider-webbed haze greets her.

Boxes, some piled three to four high, litter the cluttered space in an unorganized fashion. A dress rack with old coats occupies one corner. A torn volleyball net and a broken basketball hoop take up another, and a half a dozen Christmas nutcrackers that haven't seen daylight for years pepper the floor at odd intervals. Ranging from knee-high in height to all the way up to Lani's forehead, they leer at her with painted faces, their rifles at the ready. When the shoulder of one grazes her breast, she nudges it away and says, "Pervert."

Reminding herself she doesn't have to tackle everything

tonight, the task far too daunting, she opts to simply open the boxes and see what they contain. For the next thirty minutes, she slits yellowed tape, pokes around packed contents, and sneezes repeatedly from the dust.

Once all the boxes are unsealed, she starts removing items at random—clothes the Salvation Army could use, a few classic books that might fetch a price, some old Cavs and Browns memorabilia she wants to keep—but mostly she labels the boxes with the marker for more detailed perusal later. She's had enough for one night. The creepy nutcrackers are getting on her nerves.

Stretching her aching spine, Lani spots one more box hidden under the dress rack in the corner. Ignoring the protest in her knees, which want nothing more than an upright position, she crouches toward the missed box and drags it out. Unlike most of the other ones, it's labeled, and she pauses when she reads what's etched on its surface in block letters: Henry Whitaker.

Her great grandfather.

Lani glances up at the nutcracker who tried to cop a feel. "Well, what do we have here?"

As she breaks the box's seal, a rare enthusiasm ripples through her. How weird life is sometimes. She hardly ever thinks about her great grandfather—he died long before she was born—but only two days earlier she was comparing her end-of-career plight to his.

When she flips open the box, her enthusiasm shifts to shock, an even rarer emotion for her considering she's seen all the crap life has to fling. Inside, lying face up on a packing blanket, rests a coal-colored urn stamped with an engraved brass plate near the bottom. It reads: Henry William Whitaker, 1830-1914.

For several seconds, Lani stares at the macabre thing, her mouth hanging open. With a grunt, she pulls the marble urn from the box and holds it in her lap, where it sinks onto her thighs like a concrete block.

She looks up at the nutcracker, his rifle locked and loaded at his side. "Who keeps a dead guy in their attic, for feck's sake? What an awful way to spend eternity." She rests the heavy urn on the floor and brushes dust off her palms. "Jeez, Dad, you didn't exactly think this one through, did you? Doubt the Salvation Army's gonna have much use for Old Henry here."

What in the world is she going to do with the guy? She has no problem with dead people—or in this case, a pile of ashes —but that doesn't mean she wants them on her mantle or coffee table. Talk about a conversation starter. *Hey, have you met my great grandfather? He's not much of a chatterbox, but he's one heck of a paperweight.*

Lani shudders. She removes the blanket that nestled Old Henry and pokes around to see what else hides inside. Hopefully not Grandpa Joe. She knows that can't be the case because she saw his coffin lowered into the ground of Cleveland's Riverside Cemetery with her own two eyes. Still, at this rate, she wouldn't be surprised.

The rest of the box contains an old military uniform and a few medals and plaques. Of more interest to her is a black, leather-bound book, about the size of a five-by-seven photograph.

Lani runs her fingertips over the worn fabric and gently lifts the cover. When she realizes the book is a journal, filled with the dense, no-nonsense handwriting of her great grandfather, another thrill runs through her. She hasn't had this much excitement since the wife-killing doctor she arrested ten years ago pooped his pants in fear when she cuffed him—literally. And the journal comes without the stench.

Forgetting about the late hour, she plucks a big Cleveland Browns foam finger from the floor next to her, places it under her sore butt, and settles back against a box full of old tools.

The lighting sucks, but she has her reading glasses. Besides, she's not blind yet.

The first page of the journal is a family tree of sorts, names and dates connected to other names and dates by imperfect lines stained by ink blots. Lani imagines the nineteenth-century man hunched over a desk, a candle or oil lamp his only illumination as he preserved his lineage for generations to come.

The family tree starts with Henry's great grandparents and ends with him and his wives and children, "wives" plural because his first wife died when he was sixty-one, and they didn't have any kids together. Maybe the woman was unable to conceive, stuck with a runt of a uterus like her own.

Lani downs a long swallow of beer and reads on.

Henry remarried eighteen months after his first wife died, this time to a thirty-six-year-old widow. They had their first child when Henry was almost sixty-four, Joe, Lani's grandfather.

"Go Henry." Lani peers up at the handsy nutcracker who's reading over her shoulder. "Sounds like your kind of guy."

A daughter followed two years later. Henry died in 1914 at the age of eighty-four, which, Lani imagines, would have been long enough to see his son follow in his policing footsteps but not long enough to see the birth of his grandson, Bo Whitaker, Lani's father, who was born in 1924.

The first actual journal entry is dated September 12, 1850, when Henry was twenty years old. The details are clinical— his work plans for the day, what the weather was like, items of significance from Cleveland's newspapers. The sporadic entries continue on in that vein for a while, but gradually, they become more personal. He writes about his desire to be more than a Watchman, and in 1852 it appears he got his wish, because at a mere twenty-two years old, he was named a constable.

Lani grows even more interested at this point because despite her great grandfather's dry prose, reading about the early days of Cleveland policing, before there was a formal police department, fascinates her. Although the previous entries were few and far between, they grow more frequent when Henry starts detailing his involvement in an 1853 case of a young woman who disappeared shortly after her medical school commencement. It was the case Lani's father and grandfather sometimes referenced, although she never knew the particulars.

"A peculiar and sad case," Henry writes in his scrawled penmanship, "particularly as she had just become the third lady doctor to graduate in the country, at least from a reputable college. This made her quite the center of attention in the newspapers and social circles of Cleveland. Did this fascination, which was at times hostile, play a role in the fine lady doctor's disappearance?"

Lani thinks back to her days as a young female cop, one of the first in the department, and feels an immediate connection to this "fine lady doctor."

Despite Henry's analytic writing style, Lani gets the sense the woman's disappearance affected him greatly. Maybe it was their similar ages—both were twenty-three when she disappeared—or maybe it was the sensationalism of the case. Regardless, Lani detects a note of affection in Henry's words, especially as he describes meeting the woman prior to the graduation ceremony, where he was sent by his superior to ensure the event proceeded without discord. Apparently, the Medical Department of Western Reserve College's decision to allow a second woman to graduate sparked a heated debate.

Henry describes Catherine Miller as "a petite young thing, with long wavy locks, fine features, and an air of remarkable respectability for a country girl, albeit perhaps not as cultured as one might find a woman of higher society to be."

Lani burps and then smiles. What would Old Henry have made of her?

Despite her interest in the journal, her eyes blink sleepily, and reading the dense print in the dim light grows difficult, even with her cheaters on.

Okay, maybe I am going blind.

She yawns and figures she better get to bed if she wants to make her sunrise walk.

With a grunt and a groan, Lani rights herself to a stand, stuffs the journal into the waistband of her sweatpants, and hefts up Old Henry's urn. After pulling the string to turn off the attic's light bulb, she carefully descends the steps into the closet, relieved to return to fresh air. Well, reasonably fresh, with the exception of the permanent odor from the toilet across the hallway.

As soon as she's back in the bedroom, her cell phone rings from her dresser. Caller ID confirms it's her young partner, Brian.

"Hey, Einstein, a little late to be calling, don't you think?" Lani sinks down on her duvet and plucks her great grandfather's journal from her waistband, then lays it next to his urn on the nightstand.

"Good grief, Whitaker, it's not even ten o'clock yet."

"Says the kid who's still got time and hormones on his side."

"You do know I'm thirty-two, right?"

"I've got cans of soup older than you. What's up? New case?"

"Nah, nothing like that. Just wanted to let you know I was talking to the ME and—"

"On a Sunday night?" Lani purses her lips in frustration. "French is assigning you cases without me, isn't he? He's already written me off."

"Relax," Brian says. "Don't get your Depends in a wad. I ran into Dr. Fry in the candy aisle at Target. Nothing more sinister than that. But I thought you'd be interested in knowing he's ruling that hanging case we worked the other day a suicide."

"That's bull. Too many things don't add up."

"And many things *do* add up," Brian says. "Her history of suicidal ideation, getting laid off last month, the note the techs found on her computer. Plus, the physical markings fit well enough that Fry is confident calling it a suicide. And since we've found nothing else, I have to agree with him."

"Yeah, well, that's because you're barely two minutes out from getting your braces off. When you've been doing this as long as me, you can smell when something's not right."

"That's just your irritable bowel syndrome."

"Ha. Go feck yourself." She kicks off her slippers and rubs her sore feet over the worn area rug, the joints of her toes having grown as knobby and ugly as those on her fingers. "Ah, well, thanks for letting me know. Maybe I'm grabbing at invisible threads. Just wanna go out with a good solve."

"You've got a string of good solves."

"Whatever. Sorry. Don't mean to be a whiner."

"You're not a whiner. You're just…unsettled. Life changes do that to a person."

"Thanks, Yoda."

"Go to bed, cranky pants. I'll see you tomorrow."

After ending the call, Lani stares at her great grandfather's urn, which, in the bedroom's better lighting, reveals itself to be scuffed and chipped near the base. She thinks about Old Henry inside it. She thinks of his remains buried away in a box next to a pervy nutcracker and a Cleveland Browns foam finger.

Will that be her fate too? Nothing but a mound of forgotten ashes in the attic and a stupid foam finger?

CHAPTER SIX

CATHERINE

It is not yet dusk, but Mr. Carver arrives home later than usual on this early-April evening. I was distracted, struggling with all my energy to move my fractured limb, the one with the bundle of acorns hidden within its crevice, when his car pulled into the driveway with such a squeal that all my branches shook at once. Sadly, no acorns fell for my hungry squirrels, but at least it's not the arborist, and for that I feel momentary peace.

Mr. Carver appears from the side door of the carriage house and stumbles his way toward the home, gripping the connecting trellis as he goes. His swaying movements remind me of my uncle after too many hours in the saloon. Less than a minute after entering the house, the researcher blasts open the sliding glass door. Its panes shake in protest.

"Oops, my bad." He laughs, and his form disappears from view.

Iggy comes bounding out, clearly in need of relieving

himself. The dog wets two smaller trees and a bush before even acknowledging me, but instead of plopping down at my base as usual, he prances around the yard for a spell, giddy to be outdoors after such a long confinement.

Soon I see Mr. Carver again through the kitchen window, dressed in comfortable trousers and a light cloak he refers to as a *fleece*. He rummages around in the cooling box, seems to think better of it, and pours himself a glass of water from its magical dispenser instead. He then grabs a stack of mail from the small desk that's attached to his kitchen's peach wall and exits through the sliding door, his footsteps unsteady. The beagle continues to zoom around the yard.

"Whoa, excited much, Iggs?"

Mr. Carver sits at the clear table on the patio, his preferred breakfast spot when the weather allows. Dinner is usually up on the deck. The glass of water sloshes precariously, and when he sets it down, a few drops sprinkle the mail, on top of which rests the exquisite letter opener from his investor, Mr. Price.

Just as with the last time I watched him open his mail, the angle of the envelopes and my prism-like vision up high prevent me from making out the home address. As always, I remain in the dark about which Northeast Ohio town anchors my roots. Although Cleveland is where I took my last breaths, the wide-open space around me rules out a city environs.

Once firmly settled in his chair, Mr. Carver studies his wobbly hand. "Probably shouldn't have driven home like this, Iggs. One beer too many, methinks. And on a Wednesday night to boot." He belches and then, seeming to enjoy it, belches again. At least he's not full of abdominal wind like the old recluse who built the original cabin. Then again, the codger's fits of flatulence did have their moments of amusement.

After a long exhalation in which Mr. Carver stares off toward the creek, he gulps down half of his water, grips the letter opener, and proceeds to slit open the envelopes with such drunken swipes I fear he might cut himself.

Most of the papers and flyers end up in the trash. In the past, he's said his phone and computer give him all he needs, and he often gripes about wasting paper when an email or text message would do. Although I fail to completely grasp these concepts, I've learned enough from listening to him (and to a lesser extent, the childless couple before him) and from watching the movies he displays on an outdoor screen near his deck to know these electronic wonders seem to magically transport through the air. Once again I marvel at the progress of this evolving world.

I'm so deep in my thoughts that I rustle with surprise and pleasure when Tony bursts into Mr. Carver's yard. He's dressed in the same unkind bike shorts as a week ago, but this time in a hooded jacket as well. His rushed stride makes the trellis shake and the bordering bushes sway. My pleasure shifts to worry. What's happened?

When the young researcher rounds the house, Mr. Carver jumps with alarm. Even Iggy, who has settled against my base and is normally tranquil around Tony, hops up and barks at the unexpected intrusion.

"Jeez, Tony. You trying to give me a heart attack?" Surprise and irritation harden Mr. Carver's tone, his earlier joviality of inebriation gone. He shoves his chair back on the patio with a screech and approaches the visitor. His gait is still unsteady, and the letter opener, along with a sealed envelope, remains clutched in his hand. "I was about to soak in my spa and wind down for the night. We have things called phones, you know."

"Sorry. Mine's charging at home. When I left on my ride, I didn't know I was headed here." Halfway between the house and my tree, the two researchers meet. Tony shifts his weight from one sneaker to the other. "I was just going to clear my head, but then I decided no, this can't wait until tomorrow."

"What's so important it can't wait twelve hours? You look like you ran someone's grandma off the road."

"I didn't see you on campus today."

"Helped my sister move some things around her boutique for an upcoming sale. My TA filled in for me. What's it matter?"

"It doesn't, but before I left the lab this afternoon, I checked on the mice one more time."

Tony's breathlessness has improved and his words are less choppy, but he fidgets incessantly with the zipper on his coat —up down, up down. If such a convenient accessory had been sewn into my own clothes as a child, I would have doubtless done the same thing.

"There's a mouse I've been worried about," Tony says. "He wasn't acting right, so I ran some blood tests." His voice rises in both pitch and volume, enough so that Iggy stops wagging his tail and resettles warily at my base. "The mouse's liver enzymes were high."

Mr. Carver, as if only now realizing he still holds the envelope and letter opener, shoves them inside the pocket of his fleece. "That could mean anything. An infection, a genetic mutation, a stress reaction over seeing you in bike shorts." Though this last remark is clearly a joke, there's no humor in Mr. Carver's tone.

"No, you don't understand. I euthanized him and removed his liver. It's full of cancer, Mark. Another mouse has cancer."

"Shh, lower your voice."

Who Mr. Carver expects to hear Tony's outburst beyond Iggy and me I don't know. The neighboring houses are too far away. Nothing but woods surrounds us.

He rests a hand on Tony's shoulder and offers a reassuring smile I suspect is fake. "Come on, sit down. Let's sort this out."

Tony shakes off both the touch and the smile. "No. No spinning it this time. We have to share this with the team." He pulls out a book not much bigger than a deck of cards. "Look at my notes if you don't believe me."

Mr. Carver obliges Tony and examines the proffered page. "Have you documented this in the records yet?"

"No. I told you I'd let you know first, and that's why I'm here." That same look of amorous pining I saw previously on Tony returns, a look that makes clear he would do anything to please Mr. Carver and detests having to be the bearer of bad news, especially news this disastrous. "You can trust me. Always. But we can't brush this off as another coincidence. We need to slow things down and figure out where the problem is."

Mr. Carver returns the small book to his student, nodding slowly but saying nothing.

"What," Tony says. "What're you thinking?"

"Just sorting some things out in my mind. Wondering how this can be. We found nothing like this earlier."

"Maybe it only happens with prolonged exposure."

Mr. Carver steps back and trips on his own feet before steadying himself against the trunk of a young birch, its springs leaves budding and its surrounding soil sprouting the early stems of tulips planted by the previous homeowners.

"Are you okay, Mark?" Tony moves toward him. "How much have you had to drink? Maybe you better sit down."

Mr. Carver rakes his fingers over his face and looks up toward the darkening sky. "Oh man, Tone, this isn't good. We're supposed to start human trials soon."

"Good to find it out now rather than later though, right?" Tony says hopefully.

A sudden anger seizes Mr. Carver. He shoves away from the birch, startling an unseen creature who scurries away in the grass. "No, Tony, no," he yells. "None of this is good!"

Unlike me, Tony has not witnessed Mr. Carver's rare but knife-like fury, at least I don't think so because he jerks back as if shocked that his superior—and dare I say, his secret love—was capable of such an explosive display.

A sinewy fear spreads through my branches.

"I don't...I don't understand," Tony says.

"Are you an idiot? What don't you understand? Because it's pretty simple if you ask me. We're screwed. We're going to lose everything. Everything we've worked for on this drug."

"You don't know that." Tony reaches for Mr. Carver, but the homeowner pivots away. "We can go back to the chemistry," Tony continues in a soothing manner. "Make some changes, tweak—"

"We've already done that! Two years' worth practically. We're supposed to be well beyond that stage now." Mr. Carver rubs his temples as if they are on fire. "Harrison is going to freak."

"If he wants to be in the drug business, he'll understand."

Mr. Carver snorts. "Yeah, keep telling yourself that, buddy."

As they are programmed to do at this hour, the in-ground lights flicker on. With them comes enough of a shift in the charged atmosphere that Mr. Carver's posture softens, and he seems to relax. Maybe this frightening exchange will now end.

"Look," he says, "don't record it yet. Let me talk it out with Harrison first."

"You promised, Mark. You said if we got another case of cancer, this all goes on the book. You promised."

"Jeez, Tony, what're you, twelve? I need a few days, that's all."

"No," Tony says sharply, making it clear Mr. Carver is not the only one who can make small creatures scatter with a barbed tone. "No more delays. I'm entering my findings in the formal data tomorrow and telling the rest of the team."

"Come on, Tone."

"Sorry. I have to do it. You know it, and I know it."

Tony turns and starts walking away, so he doesn't see Mr. Carver's jaw shift back and forth or his nostrils flare like a demon. But I do. The last time Mr. Carver wore that expression he shattered a glass against my bark, and one week ago, he smashed a sparrow's head into the ground with no hesitation.

Fear floods every arboreal cell I possess. I want to call out to Tony. To scream at him to be careful, that Mr. Carver is not to be trusted, but beyond a disjointed shake of my branches, I can't do anything but stand there like a tethered and mute dolt. Something awful, something unspeakable is about to happen. I feel it as acutely as I feel the night wind in my boughs and the moisture of the creek in my southern-most roots.

Mr. Carver charges after Tony. I howl my silent cry of warning.

But instead of hurting Tony, Mr. Carver seizes him in a full embrace from behind. Confused, I wonder if I've misread his intentions. He spins Tony around, presses his hands against the young researcher's cheeks, and locks him in such a passionate kiss my insides blush.

When he pulls away, he smiles the smile of an angel. "Tony, Tony, Tony," he says. "Work with me here."

It's now obvious what Mr. Carver is doing. Although I haven't witnessed such lustful behavior between men, there was a time I was struck by a similar lightning bolt at the touch of Mr. Mansour Younis. The current within me was so heated I might have said yes to anything that was asked.

Tony, his face impossibly close to Mr. Carver's, illuminated and at the same time shadowed by the in-ground lighting, wears that same expression of desire I once felt as a living woman. The only difference is he doesn't realize Mr. Carver is an impostor with nothing but his own self-interest in mind.

"Just give me a little more time," the senior researcher says, his tone now as soft as a butterfly's wings.

No! I want to scream to Tony. *Don't listen to him. I've seen his underlying nature, what he's capable of. Iggy has seen it too.*

Of course, I cannot.

Instead, I watch Tony pull away with obvious reluctance. "I'm sorry, Mark. I need to disclose this." He turns back around and starts retreating to his bicycle.

Before Tony reaches the trellis, Mr. Carver withdraws the letter opener from his pocket and rushes toward the young researcher.

No! I try again to howl. *Please no!*

Like a crazed devil, Mr. Carver once again spins Tony around, but instead of giving him another passionate kiss, he plunges the blade of the letter opener into Tony's neck.

When Mr. Carver pulls the weapon back out, Tony stumbles forward in shock, hands clutching his neck, blood spurting through his fingertips. He tries to speak, but nothing but gurgling noises emerge.

Iggy, on all fours now, barks madly, and I wail silently in terror and uselessness. Even Mr. Carver, the devil now gone, stares at the letter opener in surprise. But when Tony falls toward the homeowner's arms, his eyes begging for help, Mr. Carver steps away to avoid his touch. He leaves my beautiful Tony to stagger and sputter on his own.

Rage explodes inside me. Like a storm ripping over the land, I try desperately to shift my branches with purpose, anything to reach Tony and keep him from bleeding to death, but in my flustered despair, I cannot. My boughs merely sway as a jumbled mess with the wind, and I must watch as he stumbles to his knees, a look of shock and disbelief on his face. Iggy yips and circles around him.

Tony falls onto his side in the grass.

He blinks rapidly in my direction, his dark eyes tearing.

Then his blinking slows, and soon his eyelids don't flutter at all.

As the remaining life drains from his body, I scream in silent agony, my creaking branches now a disjointed howl.

A blankness fills Tony's eyes, my fractured bark the last thing he sees.

CHAPTER SEVEN

CATHERINE

If I still possessed human arms and legs instead of branches and roots, I would lunge at Mr. Carver and strangle him to death. Squeeze and squeeze and squeeze until his breath is no more.

Or maybe I would snatch the bloody letter opener in his hand and use it to slice open his own neck. That is how horrified and enraged I am by what I witnessed.

Mr. Carver stands there stupidly in the darkening night, staring at the bloody letter opener, the in-ground lighting casting frightening shadows on his face. Tony, lit up by the same beam, lies motionless on the grass, his eyes widened in shock, a tear streaking down his beautiful cheek. Blood pools around his neck and saturates his bicycle jacket and the nearby ground.

Iggy, who was dashing back and forth and yelping around Tony's dying body until a kick from Mr. Carver silenced him, is now whimpering at my base, his body shaking in terror. I yearn to console him, and I pray he takes some comfort from my presence as he presses his small form against my bark.

All around us Mother Nature has quieted. No birds sing their end-of-the-day songs. No frogs croak their night-time pleasure. No snakes slither in and out of the weedy creek. It's as if they, too, sense danger and want to remain hidden.

How could you do such a thing, you vile, despicable man, I yell at Mr. Carver inside my mute consciousness.

So great is my furor that a wave of energy surges through me, and my branches creak and sway in a wild, unexpected shudder, much more forcefully than before.

Mr. Carver must be as surprised as I am by my sudden and emphatic motion because it frees him from his stupor. He whips his gaze toward my branches—in what?...shock? fear? wonder?—and then spins his body in every direction, staring wildly around the yard and then at the letter opener in his hand.

Whether he's looking for witnesses, which there are none beyond Iggy and me, or whether he's wondering how to dispose of the murder weapon, I'm not sure. I only know that every time I see Tony lying in his pool of blood—which, of course, is all the time—a voiceless, soundless wail swells inside me, unable to escape its confinement.

Mr. Carver wipes a nervous hand across his mouth. The other hand clutches the letter opener. "Wow, Iggs, I didn't mean to do that. Not like this. Anger first, payback later, right?" He takes a deep breath and squeezes the weapon, his frenetic movements quieting. "What'd you think I should do with it?"

Although his voice carries a slight tremor, it holds none of the horror, remorse, or temporary madness it should. Wouldn't I be babbling idiotically and tearing my hair out had I committed a similar act as a woman?

In fact, Mr. Carver calms so quickly that when he strolls to my tree and squats down to pet Iggy, apologizing for the cruel kick, I can only guess this is not the first time he has acted so violently toward another person. This realization freezes my insides more starkly than any Ohio winter could do.

"Can't put it in the creek," he mumbles, staring behind me at the rippling water, his drunkenness seeming to wear off. "That'd be the first place they'd look, don't you think? Probably not a big enough stream to be carried away."

The beagle whimpers and presses more firmly against me.

Still on his haunches, Mr. Carver studies the expanse of his yard and the wooded acreage beyond. "Bury it maybe?" He answers his own question with a shake of his head. "A metal detector could find it. They might sweep the whole grounds." Ruffling the dog's fur more deeply, he smiles and adds, "Not that I intend to get caught."

If that amicable grin is meant to reassure Iggy, it has grossly failed because the dog's alarm—and my own—only heightens. Iggy is shaking so much I feel it in my trunk. The disconnect between Mr. Carver's smile and Tony's bloody body a few yards away is too ghastly to comprehend.

Mr. Carver rises, moves back to Tony, and stares down at him from above. "Why did you have to keep pushing me? This is honestly the last thing I need."

The murderous researcher strides toward the unlit fire pit and pauses in front of it, no doubt contemplating whether he should burn the letter opener. He twirls it in his hand as if it were no more than a stick or a hairbrush. He must know as well as me that although the wooden handle would ignite, the steel blade would not.

He grabs a rock from the darkened ground and sits on the orange Adirondack chair that faces me, maybe not wanting his back to the carriage house and the driveway beyond it, though a visitor at this hour seems unlikely. With the rock, he vigorously scratches at the mahogany handle of the letter opener, trying to scrape away the personal engraving Mr. Harrison Price had etched upon it. Moments later, he tosses the stone across the yard, rises from the chair, and examines the letter opener in front of one of the in-ground lights.

He curses. "It's not working."

Then he contemplates the trash can on his patio.

"No way, Iggs. It's not like I can just throw it away. What if it's found? Something this fancy could be traced back to the buyer, even if I could scratch out my name."

As abruptly as his mood shifted earlier, it does so again, and he stomps back to Tony and hisses, "What am I supposed to do now?" He rubs his head with the hand not clutching the bloody letter opener and paces as if in deep contemplation. "One wrong step, and they'll get me," he says to my poor dead Tony, whose vacant eyes and horrified death mask remain cast my way. "Why couldn't you have just given me a little more time? Now what am I supposed to do?"

Mr. Carver's audacity to blame Tony for his own inability to hide a murder weapon revolts me, and another wave of fury swells in my veins, rattling the tips of my aged boughs and the few leaves that sprout there. Although it's not the same forceful quake as a few minutes ago, the branch harboring the acorns within its deep fissure cracks and shifts. The nuts don't fall, but it doesn't matter because no squirrels remain to fetch them. Mr. Carver's violence has seen to that.

The motion of my branch is enough to direct the madman's gaze to me. So disturbingly cold and calculating is it that it's a wonder my bark doesn't splinter into thousands of wooden shards.

Mr. Carver trudges toward me. Iggy darts away to keep a safe distance between him and his master. The researcher stops in front of my trunk.

Oh no. What have I done? Oh no, oh no, oh no.

"Huh, check this out, Iggs." Mr. Carver pulls out his phone and makes it light up.

Shining the beam at my lowest branch, he inspects the area above his head, which is where the deepest crevice in my fractured bark lies. It wasn't but a week ago I mused that if an item were lost inside the fissure, it would likely never be found. If only I'd known how prescient I was I would have never conjured the energy to shake my branches just now and draw Mr. Carver's attention my way. I would have stayed as silent and still as an oak is expected to do.

But it's too late. Mr. Carver grins at Iggy, who stares uncertainly at him from across the yard and seems ready to dart again. "I think we found the golden ticket, boy."

With the hand not holding the murder weapon, Mr. Carver reaches up toward my split bark. Before he touches it, he hesitates, his hand hovering in the air, his expression wary. Does he think I might bite him? Oh, if only I could. Finally, he pokes around inside the deep crevice, which is just off the crook of the branch but not in the branch itself. With an extended arm above his head he's able to bury his hand all the way to the wrist.

"Plenty deep," he murmurs. Grimacing, he tosses out rotted leaves, putrid acorn shells, and other foul debris from the fissure.

Once it's cleared out to his satisfaction, Mr. Carver wedges the bloody letter opener into the crevice. Deeper, deeper, deeper, each thrust causing me more agonizing pain than if he had sliced me repeatedly with the arborist's saw. It's not the same type of pain I felt as a woman. It's a deeper pain, a pain unlike anything I have ever experienced, a pain worse than the blow to my skull that led to my human demise, because not only was I powerless to help Tony and protect him from death, I'm now an involuntary accessory to it.

When the weapon is wedged deeply enough to satisfy Mr. Carver, he uses the light from his phone to guide him as he refills the crevice with the same debris he removed from it. He then gathers weeds and twigs from the ground near the creek and stuffs them in as well. Finally, as if to be sure of his hiding place, he pushes on the branch itself. It creaks but doesn't break, and the actual crevice is far enough away from the crook that if the branch should fall off—or be cut off as it will be soon—the weapon will not be exposed.

"I think this might actually work, Iggs." Mr. Carver pumps his fists in the air and performs a vulgar shimmy of a dance that is completely at odds with the heinousness of the evening's events. "Talk about a lucky break."

Iggy stares at him with sorrowful eyes. It's evident the dog wishes to return to me but doesn't dare trot past his master to do so.

Mr. Carver shifts his attention to Tony's lifeless body, the student's frozen eyes and mouth too much for me to bear.

"Now, what do we do with you?" he says, his tone as casual as if he were asking about the weather or the evening meal.

He strolls back to where Tony lies, and as soon as he does, Iggy hurries back to my base. Standing over his student's corpse, Mr. Carver seems to be considering his options, just as he did with the letter opener. Abruptly, he darts off to the carriage house, but for what, I'm not sure. He can't intend to bury Tony here in the yard.

But then I wonder, would that be so bad? Although I don't know how I became a tree, I remember a conversation the childless couple once had. They were not social entertainers like Mr. Carver, but on summer nights, the two of them would occasionally sit out on the patio and converse. As engineers, they had a quiet intelligence that appealed to me, and they seemed to have a good deal of knowledge on a variety of topics. One evening, after a typically long day at work and armed with a glass of wine each, they discussed a subject that captivated me. Even the foraging squirrels could not steal my attention away.

They mentioned a strange kind of burial. A person, before they die, chooses what type of tree they would like to become. Then, after death, their body is placed in the fetal position into an egg-shaped pod which is then buried. Above this pod, a tree is planted. The decomposing pod then nourishes this growing tree, such that a transformation of molecules occurs so one might, quite literally, become a tree.

Had I raised this idea to my classmates back in the mid-nineteenth century, they would have carted me off to the asylum, thinking me quite mad. Even for me the concept is difficult to imagine, and I can't pretend to have understood all of the couple's words. Yet I couldn't help but wonder, is that what happened to me? Is my human body buried somewhere deep beneath my roots? Did I decay into the earth, my molecules fusing with the seedlings of a tree, and together we developed into one respiring, thinking, conscious being? A blending of woman and nature, the likes of which seem too incredible and impossible to contemplate?

If that is indeed the case, could it not happen again? If my Tony were buried next to me and soon became one with the earth, we could be together forever, at least our earthly forms. How lovely that would be. The thought alone softens some of my angst.

As soon as I feel that morsel of hope, it vanishes because Mr. Carver returns from the carriage house with two large black bags, the kind I've seen him use to dispose of leaves and other debris. He's also donned a pair of work gloves.

Carelessly, as if Tony were no more than that very yard refuse he carries away in the fall, Mr. Carver stuffs the lower half of Tony's body in one bag and the upper half in another. He then secures the two bags together with the sticky silver binding he's referred to in the past as duct tape. Although I was intrigued the first time I saw it, imagining all sorts of useful applications the tape might have, I never foresaw its use for this. Iggy, who finally seemed to calm down, shivers anew.

When Mr. Carver hefts Tony's lithe body over his shoulder and lumbers toward his car in the carriage house, I understand my unrequited love is not to be buried next to me.

Never will I see him again. Nevermore will I feel the spark his presence gave me. Yes, I too am dying and am not long for this world, but what is to say I won't come back? I did once before. Could I not again?

I would loathe such a rebirth now, though, because I would rather be a nonexistent nothing than endlessly endure the painful memory of tonight.

Instantly, my rage surges back, but oh what useless rage it is. What can I, a tree, do to avenge my Tony's death? And how can I, a rooted, voiceless, dying mass, see to it that this hateful and wretched Mr. Carver never kills again?

CHAPTER EIGHT

LANI

Lani and Brian lead the skinny perp into the station. On their way back from a coffee run in Lani's department-issued Crown Vic, they spotted him trying to break into the side window of a split-level home. He hasn't stopped hollering about his rights since.

"Quit your bellyaching," Lani says to him on the way to the holding cell. "Your shenanigans are what got you here, not us."

"Shenanigans?" The feisty twig, who reeks of alcohol, laughs. "What're you, eighty?"

"Just for that I'm gonna tell them to make you wait extra long before processing."

"Hey, you can't—"

"You got this?" Brian asks her, raising his phone. "I have to take this."

"Of course. Is it your stalker-not-stalker girlfriend?"

Brian steps away to answer the call, and Lani guides the boozy perp toward the empty cell. No sooner has she opened the barred door than he wrestles out of her grip and tries to flee. Where he thinks he's headed in handcuffs and a building full of cops, she has no idea, but she grabs his arm to stop him. Apparently not ready to give up, he whips his skull down toward her own, as if to head butt her. She ducks out of the way before impact and shoves him into the empty cell with a grunt.

The commotion causes Brian and a few other cops to come running, including the chief, Warren French.

"You okay?" Brian asks her, closing the cell's door and glaring at the drunk before removing his handcuffs in the space between the bars.

"I'm fine," Lani says, more breathlessly than she would like. She zeroes in on French. "See? I'm not dead yet. Still some use in this old gal, at least until...what day is it, Einstein?"

"Friday."

"Right. At least for another five weeks."

French groans. "Not that again, Whitaker. You act like I'm the one forcing you out. You're not the first cop to face mandatory retirement, and you won't be the last. We're just not as sharp as we get older. Deal with it, or you'll go out with a mark on your record just like you ca—" Chief Toddler cuts himself off.

"Go ahead," Lani says. "Finish your sentence. Like I came in with? Is that what you were going to say?"

"Forget it." French walks away.

Unable to stop herself, Lani trots behind him to his corner office, his stride twice that of her own. Inside the glass-fronted room, multiple framed photographs of French standing alongside important-looking people hang on the back wall, which probably explains how he made chief so early.

"Not sure who you've been talking to," Lani says, "but that cop getting killed wasn't my fault."

"Let it go, Whitaker."

"What was I supposed to do, lie to IA? Not tell them what I really saw? I was a scared rookie, and they'd figured it out anyway." Lani feels her cheeks flush, and as annoyed as she is at herself for letting Chief Toddler rile her (*what's happening to me lately?*), she can't let it go. "It's not my fault Dunn froze up and couldn't use his gun like a real cop. He's the reason the other officer got shot, not me. Forty-two years on the job, and I still have the fecking stink of a snitch on my back? Is that what you're telling me?"

Brian puts a hand on her shoulder. She wasn't even aware her young partner followed her into the office.

Chief Toddler, who is still standing behind his desk, gives her a patronizing look, the kind of look reserved for older women to make them feel less-than simply because of their gender and age. He's about to say something when a junior officer marches in and plants his calloused hand against the doorframe.

"Got a call about a body," he tells the chief. "Male, extensive damage from animals, cause of death unclear. Was found by a hiker taking a leak near the towpath trail north of Hillside Road. Says his dog sniffed it out. Broke away from his leash and ran off toward it."

French nods. "Dupree, he's yours."

"Sure thing," Brian says as the junior officer leaves. "Let's go, Whitaker."

"No, Dupree." French cracks his knuckles. "Work it with Johnson. He's in between cases."

"What the heck?" Lani's face heats even more. "Last I checked I'm still on the job."

French plops down on his leather chair. "Does everything have to be a battle with you? Why do you want a fresh case so close to the finish line? Most detectives would be happy to get out with no lingering headaches. Why don't you spend these last few weeks focusing on the cases you *haven't* been able to solve."

Lani grinds her teeth. Behind her, Brian mutters for her to drop it, says he'll consult her on the new case, but instead she steps closer to French's desk. With her middle finger, she traces the outline of his cast-iron paperweight of New York City's skyline. The hometown memento isn't exactly the best way to endear himself to Clevelanders.

It's clear by the way the chief taps on his keyboard that he's dismissed her. Lani stands a little straighter. "Been spending any time down in Peninsula lately?"

French's gaze shoots up from his computer screen. His mouth opens, but he says nothing.

"Could've sworn I saw you there a few weeks ago."

The chief remains still, as if knowing but not knowing where she's headed.

Lani shrugs. "Eh, maybe I was mistaken. How's your wife doing, anyway? Julie, isn't it?"

Dropping this line of talk makes Lani feel like a sleazy drug dealer, but she's learned a thing or two about playing in a man's world, and no way is she going to let Chief Toddler dismiss her like some useless old housemother.

From the way he flips his pen and chews the inside of his lip, she can tell he's trying to piece together how much she knows. *He's wondering if I saw him kissing that woman outside that little café.* A woman who most definitely wasn't Julie French, whom Lani met at a department Christmas party the previous December.

Lani winks at the chief. *Oh yeah, I saw you,* the wink says.

She was visiting a retired cop friend at the time, a guy who owns a good piece of property near Peninsula. He's an ornery old cuss who's alienated everyone but her. Lani recognizes his demeanor as loneliness, so she stops by every now and then to play a few rounds of poker and put up with his dumb jokes. Although he acts like her visits are no big deal, she doesn't miss the gratitude in his handshake when she leaves. It was on the drive back from his ranch house that she spotted French with the woman. While Lani's Crown Vic was idling at a red light on State Route 303, she glanced at the cafe on her left. There, at a tiny outdoor table for two, was French frenchin' a woman he shouldn't have been frenchin'.

Chief Toddler clears his throat. To Brian, who isn't in a position to have seen Lani's wink but is no doubt smart enough to read the subtext, he says, "Oh for God's sake, Dupree, go ahead and work the new case with Whitaker then. She'll never quit whining if you don't. You'll save us both five weeks of nagging."

Lani lets the veiled sexism go. She knows when she's won a battle and is polite enough not to gloat.

"Let's go, Einstein," she says to her partner, her focused professionalism back in place. "Some poor guy's waiting for us to find his killer, which is about the only thing we can do for him now." She glances back at Brian as they make their way out. "At least it's something."

On her second trek back into a dense thicket of trees within the Cuyahoga Valley National Park, Lani starts to wonder if forced retirement is really so bad after all. The early spring branches, still mostly devoid of leaves, launch a prickly attack on her face and windbreaker, and the scent of human decay makes cleaning out her attic seem like a trip to Disney Land in comparison. At least she's grown accustomed to the smell over the years. Brian's earlier gags and throat-clearing suggests he hasn't.

Lani already directed the boundaries for the crime scene perimeter when they got there an hour ago, and a small crowd of essential bodies—some uniformed, some not—now occupy the area.

"Sweet freaking Fanny, that's awful." She squeezes her

nose as Brian holds a thick branch out of her way so they can return to the body.

"Welcome to my world." Dr. Fry, the medical examiner, crouches near the victim. Dressed in protective garb, he arrived a short time ago, along with the crime scene techs. Now that the body has been photographed, he can get to work. He glances up at Lani behind his face shield, wiry gray hairs poking out from his eyebrows like the steel-wool fibers of a kitchen scrubber. "Be happy it's fifty-four degrees and not ninety-four. He'd stink even worse if it was a hot mug of July."

The *he* in this scenario is the dead man, lying in a mess of twigs and pebbles in a dirt hollow between the trees, his torn-up corpus a horrid tableau of death. Shreds of duct tape and black garbage bags stick to parts of his exposed skin and intestines and flap around in the wind. Dried blood coats his face and neck, as well as what remains of his jacket.

After decades of homicide work, Lani still cringes at how casually they all refer to cadavers, but she also knows it's a defense mechanism. Much easier to depersonalize the process, make it seem less than it really is. Otherwise they'd all end up on pills or booze. A lot of them already have. But as she stares at the victim's face, scratched up and ravaged by animals, the eyes black pits where the scavengers have enjoyed their feast, every fiber of her being is well aware this man was somebody's son, or somebody's brother, or maybe even somebody's husband or father. Sadly, she'll find out soon enough.

With the back of her hand still covering her nose, she asks Dr. Fry if he's learned anything yet. Other than getting a close-up whiff of her own drugstore hand cream, her attempt at odor-dispersal is futile. A crow tries to land for another meal, and she kicks the air until it squawks away.

"I've only done a cursory examination so far. Might not be easy to pinpoint things with all this animal damage."

"Find any ID on him? We haven't touched anything yet."

"Nothing. No wallet. No phone. And as you can see,

getting fingerprints probably won't be possible." The ME points to the victim's chewed-up hands, the fingers that remain nothing but mangled nubs of scavenger leftovers. "We'll have to hope for dental records. Can't even narrow down his age yet, though I'd guess well under forty."

Judging by the dead man's lean body and full head of dark hair, albeit matted with blood, dirt, and twigs, Lani agrees.

"How long you think he's been here?" Brian asks.

Lani is impressed by the kid's fortitude. He hasn't worked all that many homicide cases yet, and none quite with this stench, but he wears the discomfort well. He isn't even covering his nose and mouth anymore. With a grunt, she lowers her hand from her own face. She'll need it to take notes, anyway. Even though she has an officer recording everything, she likes to keep a detailed account herself.

"Was about to check his body temp," Dr. Fry says, "but judging by the state of decomp, which is still pretty early, and the mild temps we've been having, I'd say no longer than a couple days. Much of what you're smelling is from his exposed bowels. Animals look like they've gotten to it."

Lani glances at the extruding entrails plastered against the shredded garbage bag. *That's putting it mildly*, she thinks.

"He's wearing bike shorts." Brian scans the area. "I don't see any bike."

"Well, look at you, Einstein. Continuing to prove you're more than just a pretty face."

Brian ignores her. Rightfully so, she figures.

"With the garbage bags and the absence of blood on the ground," her partner continues, "it looks like he was dumped here. Whoever did it was probably hoping it'd be far enough off the towpath trail that no one would find him. Guess they hadn't counted on a dog sniffing him out."

Lani noticed all these things the moment they arrived, but she held back comment because, in just a few months, Brian has picked up far more than most new homicide detectives. Maybe even more than she did when she first started.

Well, let's not get carried away.

Regardless, with his talent, he'll move up the ranks quickly. *And if he doesn't*, Lani thinks, *something is severely wrong with the system.*

"You're right," Dr. Fry says. "And the bites and abrasions all look to be postmortem from the animals. I haven't found any gunshot wounds or obvious stab marks yet, but of course, I'll know more once I get him on the table and take a better look."

"Given the blood, he must've been stabbed," Lani says.

"Agreed," the ME replies, "but again, with all the dried blood and scavenger damage, it's difficult to tell where the weapon went in. His jacket is saturated, especially up here on the left, so maybe he bled out from a neck wound. Seems most likely." Dr. Fry peers up at Lani and Brian. "But don't quote me on that. You know I don't like speculating. Wait until I finish the autopsy."

On the drive over, Lani told Brian about finding her great grandfather's journal—"and feckin' ashes too, for God's sake"—in her parents' attic, so she knows he'll understand when she turns to him and says, "Well, at least we've got a body. That's more than Old Henry had."

CHAPTER NINE

Catherine

Since murdering Tony two days ago, Mr. Carver's distraction has been great. Last evening, he slipped in his hot tub and hit his head, and earlier this morning after his sunrise run, he dropped a plate of fried eggs onto the kitchen floor, spattering porcelain bits and runny yolk everywhere. Even through the closed sliding door, his violent cursing reverberated off my bark.

I don't know what he did with Tony's body, but I do know he burned the small book of notes Tony had shown him that night. Right there in his fire pit, after he returned from wherever it was he took my beloved researcher. Following that, he entered the carriage house and brought out that long green tube he calls a *hose* and bathed Tony's deathbed with water, washing away the young researcher's blood from the grass and soil.

I, too, have been addled, beyond which can be explained by my advanced age and numbered days. My thoughts flit from here to there, and though I try to focus on the sprouting leaves of the beeches and birches or the wildflowers who, like mischievous sprites, pop up out of nowhere near the creek, my mental images always return to Tony. I see him just before Mr. Carver stabbed him, when he was still vibrant and beautiful and alive, and then I see the awful moment he died, his face shifting from shock and terror to eternal death.

How very tired I am. Over the past decade my energy has dwindled, but in the last two days it's plummeted to depths I've never felt before. Perhaps my horror and powerlessness over Mr. Carver's actions have assured my demise more swiftly than any arborist's saw could do.

Today, a Friday, Mr. Carver returns from work before noon, at least according to the wooden clock that hangs above his calendar. He's dressed in dark trousers, a button-down shirt, and a wool jacket he calls a *blazer*. It was a gift from his sister last Christmas, and it's all that's needed in this mild spring weather.

Since killing Tony, he's been going into work by eight o'clock, which is early for him. When he let Iggy out this morning to pee, he grumbled at the beagle to hurry. "Need to check on the mice before anyone gets there," he said.

One doesn't have to be a sage to know why Mr. Carver wants to be alone with the mice. If another case of cancer develops, he wants to be the first, and likely the only, person to know.

At this moment, the deceitful man sits down on the green Adirondack chair and rests his feet on the ledge of the unlit fire pit, most of his back to me. He brought poor Iggy with him and restrains him in his lap. Iggy's stiff posture indicates his desire to flee, but Mr. Carver, who rarely shows such sustained interest in the dog, will not let him depart. Around them, birds flutter and chirp, their memory of the homeowner's wretched deed apparently short.

"I don't know, Iggs." He ruffles the beagle's tri-colored coat. When the dog glances back at me and whimpers, Mr.

Carver must misunderstand because he says, "Don't worry, they won't find it there. That weird-ass tree is the perfect spot. And it's supposed to rain tonight, so that should wash away anything I missed with the hose. It's his body we need to worry about. What if it doesn't stay hidden? Maybe they've already found him."

He shakes his head and continues to knead Iggy like a loaf of bread.

"Wasn't easy to move him, that's for sure. You'd have been impressed. Buried his wallet and keys in a different spot but didn't dare risk taking the time to bury him." Mr. Carver drops his head and raises Iggy's snout until they are nose to nose. "I dumped his bike in a sketchy part of Cleveland. Pretty smart, huh?" He lowers Iggy back down but still doesn't release him. "Yep, I think we'll be all right. He didn't have his phone with him, and I left him far enough away from here to avoid suspicion."

In the ten months Mr. Carver has lived here, I've witnessed these types of conversations with his dog many times. Not talks of disposing human bodies, to be sure, but general day-to-day concerns. It's as if the man is incapable of remaining silent for long. Up until now, I've enjoyed his one-sided chats, even if I did suspect his blood of circulating bad humor. They've improved my modern vocabulary and lessened my loneliness and boredom. Again, if not for the home-owners over the years, I would have grown quite mad.

Now, however, as I listen to this human-to-canine exchange, I realize it's not me who's mad. It's Mr. Carver. What used to seem merely an unusual penchant for voicing his thoughts out loud appears to be more of a symptom, like the patients I cared for at the asylum with Dr. Clifton. At least with those forlorn souls—some of whom, I'm ashamed to admit, frightened me with their incurable shrieking and laughter—I felt compassion.

I don't feel a shred of compassion for Mr. Carver. He is

too well contained, too well functioning to blame his actions on a sick mind alone. With him, an element of enjoyment seems to accompany his cruelty. A smile on his face after crushing a bird's skull. A disregard for Iggy until he requires the beagle's company, at which time he speaks to the dog like a best friend. And what of his sadistic betrayal of Tony? He allowed the young researcher to believe the two of them might one day be lovers, only to stab him in the neck instead.

Mr. Carver curses forcibly, startling me from my thoughts. Iggy trembles in fright, and when Mr. Carver raises his hand to scratch at his own hair like a deranged monkey, the beagle jumps free of his master's hold and rushes to my side. Mr. Carver seems not to notice. He pulls out his phone, sighs, and mutters, "Gonna have to do it."

After pressing some buttons on that miracle device, he waits a few seconds and then transforms his face from scowl to innocence. "Hello, is this campus security? This is Dr. Mark Carver. I'm a pharmaceutical scientist at the university, and I thought I better call you guys to let you know one of my PhD students didn't show up for work yesterday or today. None of us have been able to reach him, and when I stopped by his house to check on him, no one answered. Normally I wouldn't be too concerned, but he takes care of the research mice, and it isn't like him not to show up. Should I call the police instead and— Oh, you will? That'd be great. Thanks so much." A pause. "No, I'm home right now, but I'm happy to come back to campus if you need me." Another pause. "Okay, well let me know if you do. I'll stay by the phone. Thanks. Take care."

Mr. Carver disconnects from the call and rises, brushing Iggy's hair off his trousers and blazer. "Guess the mice are my job now." He stares off at Iggy and, by default, me. "Can't risk putting someone new on it yet. I'm out of letter openers, know what I mean?"

He laughs, and the wicked bark of it reminds me of Curtis Mayfield, my horrible classmate from so long ago. The memory that surfaces is from a social gathering that included students' and teachers' wives. One of the few supportive women among the group raved that my presence in the college could revolutionize medicine. To that, Curtis Mayfield barked the same laugh as Mr. Carver just did and said, "Ha! It shall revolutionize nothing but ridicule and folly."

When Mr. Carver orders a reluctant Iggy back inside and departs to the carriage house to leave for who knows where, my thoughts drift back to that medical-college banquet. Curtis Mayfield's hostility was the least of my worries that night. A far more sinister encounter occurred, this time at the hands of a man as charming on the surface as Mr. Carver but every bit as dark and cruel.

Near the end of our first class session in February 1852, in which my studies had gone so well no one could declare me incapable of mastering the curriculum, our progressive dean invited the students and faculty, along with their wives, to a lively dinner in a tavern near Public Square.

Within the rich oak walls of the establishment, tables over-flowed with platters of food and bottles of drinks, and a piano player plucked spirited tunes in the corner. My surgery professor, Dr. Smith, attended with his wife, and although he had been neither supportive nor ridiculing of me up to that point, he chose that evening to berate my nemesis, Curtis Mayfield. "I expect a better showing from you these last two weeks," he said to the brash student. "Miss Miller here has proved herself more competent with a lancet than you, and she is only a woman."

It was at that point Dr. Smith's wife made the comment about my presence revolutionizing medicine, which was then followed by Curtis's caustic reply of it revolutionizing nothing but ridicule and folly. Regardless of Curtis's vitriol and my surgery professor's insinuation that because I was a woman I should not excel at anything medical, I was in a gay mood for much of the festivities. Even Dr. Jedediah Cartwright, who detested my presence in his class as much as Curtis Mayfield did and who had yet to offer me anything beyond a grunt and a scowl, couldn't dampen my spirits. Indeed, that was the evening I met my future partner-to-be, Dr. Isaac Fitzgerald.

He and his awkward but kind wife, Ruth, had been guests of the dean, who had served as a preceptor to Dr. Fitzgerald five years before. As the piano entertained in the background, Dr. Fitzgerald spoke of his busy practice and his work with Cleveland's destitute populations, including the fallen women who few other doctors would treat. He mentioned how useful a female physician at his side might be. "Wouldn't that be splendid, Ruthie?" he asked his wife who smiled in agreement.

As the evening went on, I mingled with the rest of the guests, imbibing in one glass of wine too many. As such, desperate to loosen my corset and catch my breath, I retreated to a storage room at the end of a hallway.

Sadly, I didn't go there alone.

Dr. Frederick Morrison, who was my greatest supporter among the faculty—"Ignore those ignorant buffoons," the Pathology and Obstetrics teacher would often say of my male critics. "They are merely envious of your considerably greater talent."—slunk quietly into the room when my back was turned.

With my gown still unbuttoned halfway down my front, the loosened corset granting the breaths I craved, Dr. Morrison crept up behind me, his footsteps drowned out by the pelting piano in the banquet room. At the puff of warm air on my neck, I nearly jumped into the rafters.

Spinning around, I let out a startled cry. My teacher stood only inches from me, his brown hair dipped over a still-youthful face and his suit stretched at the buttons over his expanding girth. How long had he been lurking there?

Although the chamber was dark, illuminated only by an oil lamp in the corner, had he seen anything untoward?

"Dr. Morrison," I sputtered, trying to collect my composure, the combination of surprise, modesty, and wine doubtlessly flaming my cheeks. "Is there something you need?" When he failed to respond, unease tightened my throat. I glanced at the bottles of spirits on the shelf to my left and the plates and cutlery on my right. Would I need a weapon?

Finally, he spoke, his breaths heavy and his eyes drunken. "You are quite fetching, Miss Miller, quite fetching indeed."

My fingers fumbled to redo the gold buttons on my dress, their ridged contours a challenge. "I'm sorry, but I must go. They'll be expecting—"

Dr. Morrison stepped toward me and touched my pinned hair. "How silky your hair is." His fingers sank within it, and when several strands fell loose to my shoulders, his breathing deepened and his expression grew lecherous. This was a Dr. Morrison I'd yet to meet and one I'd never in a million years wish to.

"Please, I must go." I detested how small my voice sounded, but I wasn't prepared for such forwardness.

When I tried to move past him, he pressed me back against the shelf holding the wine and spirits, their bottles rolling and clacking together. The whiskey on his breath warmed my face, and the coarseness of his suit scratched the flesh over my exposed clavicles.

"I should wish to know you better, Catherine." He nestled his nose against my neck and inhaled deeply.

"Please," I cried, finally finding the strength my mother had instilled in me. "If you touch me again I'll scream."

He clamped a hand over my mouth, and I could feel my eyes grow wide.

"You will not scream, Catherine, and you will not refuse

me, for if you wish that I sign off on your class ticket, you will accept what I have to offer."

With that his moist, fat lips were on mine, and no matter how hard I struggled to free myself, his body was too heavy against my own. Before I could stop it, his tongue wriggled between my lips and teeth, and if a snake had slithered its way into my mouth, it couldn't have been more revolting. No man had ever been permitted such entrance, and I refused to have my first true kiss be from a fat teacher who smelled of mold and whiskey. That tender intimacy was meant only for Mr. Mansour Younis.

I chomped down on Dr. Morrison's tongue until I tasted his vile blood. With a yelp he shrank back, and in that loosening of his grip, I bolted from the supply room, ran down the dark hallway, and hurried out the back door of the tavern, holding the bodice of my dress together in the cold night air. Like a wild woman, without even my cloak, I ran the four blocks to Dr. Clifton's Euclid Street home. I didn't care about the snow dampening my fine dress. I didn't care about the surprised looks from carriage passengers and their snorting horses. I didn't care about the February air chapping my exposed skin and freezing my hands.

I only cared that I reach home before my tears started flowing.

Would Dr. Morrison really withhold his signature from my class ticket as he'd threatened? What would become of my studies if he did? How would I explain such a shameful encounter to Dr. and Mrs. Clifton?

Once safely ensconced in my bedroom and buried under the quilt on my four-poster bed, I berated myself for not seeing it sooner. His frequent words of encouragement. The smile that lit up his eyes whenever I entered the amphitheater. He had been buttering me up for his own lascivious needs. And really, how foolish could I be, for surely there must be something suspect about a man who chooses to study the delicate areas of women as his career.

Fortunately, he didn't withhold my valuable class ticket. Maybe he worried our progressive dean would not take kindly to his harassment of me, should it be revealed, or maybe he worried my preceptor, Dr. Clifton, who held much sway in the medical college, would force his ouster. Regardless, Dr. Morrison no longer treated me special. He treated me with nothing but disdain.

If anyone wondered about this sudden chill in our professor-student relationship, they said nothing, but I felt it every day, forced from that moment on to suffer his sneers and snubs in our every exchange. Maybe he was the one who murdered me on my graduation day, his bruised ego still stinging. I shudder to think it.

It doesn't matter that between my human life and my arboreal one, I've lived almost two centuries because one needs very little time on earth to see there are evil men who wear all sorts of fancy sheep's clothing. And just like Dr. Morrison and Curtis Mayfield, Mr. Carver lopes among them.

Despite my tremendous fatigue, my fury floods back. How dare men like them think they can steal our spirits, our future, our lives? Who are they to control our worlds?

In a brief fit, my branches shake and rattle all the way to their brittle tips. I'm pleased this ability of mine remains, even if in a lesser form, but the acorns trapped inside my fissures do not budge.

More tragically, neither does the blood-stained blade that murdered my Tony.

CHAPTER TEN

LANI

For a twenty-seven-year-old man, Tony Habib's townhome is the cleanest bachelor pad Lani has ever seen. Not just *tidy*, but *clean*, from the spotless granite countertops and sparkling stainless-steel appliances in the kitchen to the brushed nickel faucets and streak-free shower glass in the primary bathroom. Well, at least they *were* spotless, before the team came in last night and checked for fingerprints and other evidence and left their powder and messes behind. Lani joined them at the time, but since Brian was unavailable, she agreed to meet him at the townhome again this morning.

Dressed in Saturday-appropriate clothes of jeans and a zippered jacket, her partner enters through the front door. As always, seeing him elevates Lani's mood from grumpy to tolerable, and she marvels at how quickly she's taken to him. Her fondness grew even deeper when she learned he lost his mother to lupus when he was thirteen. With two younger sisters and a father working two jobs, a whole heap of responsibility landed on young Brian's shoulders. A shrink might say

Lani and Brian filled a void for each other, him motherless, her childless, but she's no shrink. All she knows is she enjoys being around him. And that's saying a lot.

He shuts the door with his elbow and gives her a ridiculously cheery hello. Thanks to the two cups of coffee he totes, she lets it slide.

"These arc some nice digs for a graduate student." Brian pauses in the foyer as if listening for something. "And quiet too."

Lani nods and accepts the sleeved cup he offers, the coffee black with only a splash of milk. Her doctor preaches enough about the perils of sugar and artificial sweeteners, and Lani figures there's no need to tick off her pancreas any more than she needs to, especially considering she loves a strong brew.

"Fry ruled Habib's death a homicide." Lani tests the coffee with a small sip. Finds it cool enough to drink. "No surprise there." Hoping it doesn't trigger Brian's own painful memories, she adds, "Background check shows his parents died when he was twelve. Semi-truck crossed the median and smashed right into them. Totaled six other cars and killed five people."

"God, that's awful. Was Tony with them?"

"No. This was back in Chicago. His mom was a pharmacist and his dad a sanitarian with the health department. No siblings. I've been trying to locate family in Lebanon to notify them, but apparently there's some bad blood. When his parents died, their will stipulated that Tony be raised here in Cleveland—well, Winston, to be exact—with his great aunt, who used to be an accountant. She's the only family member in the U.S."

"Is she the one who reported him missing? Is that how you and Fry ID'd him?" Before Lani can answer Brian's questions, he shakes his head and says, "By the way, boss, thanks for covering for me yesterday. Playing hooky from an investigation is no way for me to move up the ladder."

"No need to thank me. What Chief Toddler doesn't know won't hurt him. My greatest wish fulfilled will be to see you in his chair someday. And for feck's sake, I'm not your boss. Everything okay, by the way?" She makes fleeting eye contact before heading into Tony's den to look around his desk one more time. "Was it that woman again?"

Brian follows her into the room. "It's fine. I got the usual 'I have to see you now' and 'I can't live without you' stuff."

"She suicidal?"

"No, nothing like that. At least I don't think so. Just… really persistent. It's not like we even spent that much time together. She was busy. I was busy. Didn't talk much about our personal lives."

"Is that a euphemism for 'we were just in it for the sex'?"

Brian smiles modestly. "Our hook-ups weren't exactly full of conversation, no. I'm too focused on the job right now. But it didn't…feel right. So I told her it was over. That's when she was on me like cellophane. I don't do well with the crying. Couldn't just shove her out my door like that."

"That's 'cause you're a decent human being."

"Whatever. But thanks again for covering for me." Brian readjusts his belt holster. "Is this the Dr. Phil show or what? Let's move on."

Lani smirks. "And just when we were getting to the juicy stuff. But to answer your question, it was a colleague who reported the PhD student missing. Some pharmacy researcher at Cardon University named Mark Carver. When he ID'd the John Doe last night in the morgue as Habib, we had our answer. Habib's great aunt is in a nursing home not far from here. Been there for two years. Alzheimer's, I guess. The center told me she doesn't recognize her nephew anymore, so his death will likely mean nothing to her."

"Could this case get any sadder?"

"Yes, it can, because although Fry ruled it a homicide, all he can pinpoint for cause of death is exsanguination. Said the postmortem animal damage is too extensive, makes finding the exact wound difficult. No bullet holes or obvious stab marks, and no signs of natural death, so at least we have that, but his assumption is the guy's neck was sliced or stabbed. Aside from his clothes, that's where most of the dried blood was. No foreign hairs or other trace evidence to point to his murderer." Lani, her hands gloved, pulls a plastic box out of the top drawer of Tony's desk. Nothing but unused index cards inside. "The only thing Dr. Fry *did* find for sure was a small nick in a cervical vertebra that *might* be from the tip of a dull blade, but he said it could be animal teeth too. The scavengers destroyed too much tissue to tell."

"So we gotta find the murder weapon."

"We can't even find his bike."

"Yeah, I noticed the empty bike rack in the garage on my way in," Brian says. "Given the bike shorts he was wearing when he died and assuming that Accord out there is his only car, he was probably out riding when he disappeared."

"Maybe so," Lani replies. "According to the receptionist at his great aunt's nursing home, he was an avid cyclist. I've got patrol units keeping an eye out for a bike that looks like this." Lani lifts a framed photograph off Tony's desk. In it, the PhD student is straddling a black road bike.

Brian snatches it away and whistles. "Whoa, that's a Rochelle. Very expensive. If this was the bike he was riding when he was killed, our guys aren't gonna find it just lying around. Someone's got it by now."

"If it's that fancy, maybe we can track it down. Serial number or something?"

"That can be filed off. It's possible he's got a tracker device on his phone for it or some other security tool, but those are only as effective as the ignorance of the thief. A smart bike thief will post the thing online right away and sell it outside our area. It's already been three days since Habib died."

Lani studies her six-foot partner, his tawny eyes intelligent, his angled jaw like a fecking actor's. No wonder stalker-woman is clinging to him. "Well, look at the newbie teaching the oldie moldy new tricks. If Chief Toddler wasn't kicking me out, I might just keep you around."

"Your mandatory retirement is not French's doing and you know it. It's a department policy, from here to Cleveland and beyond."

"Whatever. And don't you go planning a retirement party for me either. I don't want any of that crap." Lani waves her hand over the clean desk. "Where's all the junk? Receipts, bank statements, bills? Hardly anything in the drawers either. Very little to tell me who Tony Habib was."

Brian holds up his cell phone. "It's all in here, boss. No one uses cash or banks the old-fashioned way anymore. You gotta get with the times."

She scoffs. "Right. Wait 'til there's a big cyberattack and your whole life is erased in a heartbeat." She snaps her gloved fingers, which, damn it, makes her knuckles hurt. "Then who'll have the last laugh? Hopefully, the tech geeks will find something in Habib's laptop or cell to point us to his killer. They hauled the electronics away last night. Crappy luck that the phone was here charging." She points to the oak night-stand where the mobile sat before the team confiscated it. "No way to track his location when he died."

"So you *do* understand some tech."

"I understand it. Doesn't mean I have to like it."

"Is there much you do like?"

She ignores him, but on the inside she smiles. "You up for a trip back to college, Einstein? Let's talk to the research professor who reported Habib missing. His team too. I asked them all to meet us there this morning."

"Lead the way, boss."

They exit the beige-paneled townhome and veer off toward their separate cars, one parked in front of the other in the driveway. The returning sun has dried up last night's rain.

"You figure out what you're going to do with your great grandpa's ashes yet?" Brian asks, his hand on his door handle.

"I wish. It's weird having him in my house. Can't exactly dump him out in my vegetable garden. Kind of cool reading his journal though. That 1853 case really got to him."

"Wait. 1853? You didn't mention the year before. How's he your great grandpa and not your great great?"

"He had my grandpa Joe when he was sixty-four. Remarried some young woman after his first wife died. Some things never change, huh?" This time she does smile on the outside, and the two of them climb into their cars, a Prius for Brian and the Crown Vic for Lani. "I'll follow you to your place so you can drop your toy car off," she tells him from her open door. "Then we'll head to the Cleveland campus and see if we can find something that might've gotten this poor kid killed."

With each of the three young researchers Lani and Brian interview in the university lab an hour later, Lani feels less and less optimistic about getting leads on Tony Habib's killer. From Montell Riggs, a PhD student in chemistry who's involved in the development of ZM6635, a weight-loss drug, they learn Tony was a quiet, conscientious man who didn't hang out with them much socially but who was "a solid guy."

From Alice Chang, a postdoc in pharmaceutical science, also involved in ZM6635's development, they learn the victim was responsible for creating the genetically engineered models and for monitoring the drug's pharmacokinetic and pharmacodynamic effects in the mice.

Whatever that mouthful means, Lani thinks.

And finally, from the bubbly Chloe Sampson, a PhD student in biomedical science who handles the computational analysis and statistics, they learn more of the same, with the added tidbit that Tony Habib did not have a girlfriend.

"In fact," the auburn-haired student says, tipping on her stool toward Lani as if they share some female insider trading, "I'd wager that if he had anyone close to him, it was a guy."

"So he was gay?" Lani asks, frowning at Chloe's gossipy tone. Unless it helps her find his killer, Lani doesn't care what Tony's sexual orientation was.

"Well, it never came up. He kept to himself, but I kind of think he had a crush on Dr. Carver."

Now, *that* gets Lani's attention. "Your professor? What do you mean?"

Chloe makes a rush to defend herself. "No, no, nothing official. Dr. Carver isn't gay, and Tony never said anything about liking him. It's just a sense I got from how...well, you know...how Tony looked at him."

From the way Chloe keeps flipping a pen on the smudged lab counter and twisting her stool back and forth, Lani suspects her bubbliness may be more from anxiety. Not necessarily out of guilt, although Lani won't rule anyone out until there's a good reason to do so, but from the stress of talking to detectives about a dead colleague. Over the years, Lani has witnessed all sorts of reactions from people put under a detective's microscope, and Chloe's doesn't seem out of the ordinary.

Regardless, Lani and Brian will confirm the students' alibis, but if their claims of having drinks and dinner together at a Mexican restaurant three nights ago check out, then none of these three are Habib's killer. The ME narrowed the time of death down to Wednesday evening. The grad students all seem enthusiastic about their colleague and are happy with how well their research is going. His death appears to have left them stunned.

Unfortunately, their professor and lead researcher, Dr. Mark Carver, who reported the victim missing, hasn't come to the university as requested. He left word with Montell to let the detectives know he had a water leak at his house and would be in touch with them later.

Which annoys the heck out of Lani.

"Come on, Einstein," she says. "Let's go pay the boss-man a visit. He lives on the outskirts of Hudson."

Thirty minutes later and twenty miles south, Lani is surprised to find such a large lot. "This has to be three or four acres at least." She pulls up on the driveway of the two-story, reddish-brown home. "Who wants this much grass to mow or mulch to lay? I'll take my quarter-acre and pocket-sized garden any day."

"It's more woods than lawn. Looks like tall fescue grass too. Doesn't need much watering."

"Doesn't your brain ever run out of facts?"

"What? I know something about vegetation the plant lady doesn't?"

"Ah, quit your gloating."

Brian opens his car door, leaving his jacket behind on the seat. "Decent-sized house too. Would you call it a mid-century?"

"Looks a little newer than that." Lani digs for her sunglasses in the glove compartment. "Eighties maybe? Suppose that's old enough for a water leak."

"Always so suspicious, Whitaker."

"And what? You aren't? You wouldn't be such a good detective if you were a Pollyanna."

Brian waits for her to drag her old bones out of the driver's seat. Given it's at least seventy degrees in Hudson, she ditches her windbreaker too.

"So you're admitting I'm a good detective then?" Brian says with a grin.

Lani makes a *pfft* sound and waves him onward toward the house.

A pretty white trellis about ten feet long separates the main residence from the garage. Lani imagines it will be even more gorgeous in a few weeks when the lilac and rose bushes bloom on either side of it. Still, if she had an unattached garage, she'd spend a chunk of her retirement money to remedy that. It might be sunny and seventy now, but it sure as shih tzu isn't in January.

She's about to follow Brian onto the stone pathway that leads to the front door when a man dressed in a T-shirt and basketball shorts rounds the back of the house and stares at her from the other side of the trellis. He seems as surprised to see her as she is him. A beagle trots after him, and upon noticing the guests, it starts barking.

"Iggy, shush." To Lani and Brian, the man says, "I thought I heard someone out here."

Lani points to the beagle, his fur brown and white with a black splotch on top. "Not much of a watchdog if he's just barking now. What keeps him from running off? An electric fence?"

The man smooths his dark hair, and a smile lights up his attractive features. His shorts are wet and stained and his kneecaps smudged with dirt. "Yeah, and Iggy here is more a lover than a fighter. Can I help you?"

"You Dr. Mark Carver?" Lani asks.

"I am."

"I'm Detective Lani Whitaker, and this is my partner Brian Dupree." The dog approaches her, and she kneels to give him a pet, her knees cracking in protest. "Hey boy, how's it going?"

When Dr. Carver nears them, the beagle darts off. "I'd shake your hand, but as you can see, mine are dirty."

He holds up two soiled palms, and Lani realizes the water leak might not have been an excuse after all.

"I hope you got the message I couldn't come to the university," he says. "A pipe burst in my basement. Been trying to clean it up all morning. Just stepped outside for some fresh air, and that's when I heard you. Come, come." He waves them into the backyard.

Lani makes her way behind Dr. Carver under the trellis, followed by Brian. Even without her windbreaker, her cable-knit sweater is too warm for the day. At least she has her sunglasses on. She likes knowing people can't see her eyes while she's questioning them.

"Thank you for identifying Mr. Habib's body last night," she says. "If you hadn't reported him missing, we might not have put two and two together so quickly."

"It wasn't like Tony to miss two days of work, not without telling anyone, so my students and I agreed we better call it in. He took care of our research mice as if they were kittens."

The back of the house is as impressive as the front, with dense trees in all directions, most still showing the barren branches of early April. A variety of shrubbery and flowering plants line the home, and patches of tulips spring to life around the yard. In addition to this impressive display of nature, a stone patio abuts the near end of the house, a richly stained deck the far end, and a stone fire pit sits in the middle of the yard, surrounded by a rainbow of Adirondack chairs. Completing this outdoor entertainer's dream are a hot tub on the deck, a massive grill and bar on the patio, and an assortment of cushioned furniture that puts Lani's big box-store set to shame.

Despite all this natural and manufactured beauty, what strikes Lani most is a majestic Northern Red Oak fronting the small creek at the edge of the backyard. Iggy the beagle lounges in front of it.

"This is an incredible set-up you've got." Lani means it, too. No false flattery there.

"Thanks. I love being outside, winter or summer. It's my oasis."

Lani strolls toward the huge oak in front of the creek. "And this one here is incredible, but it looks like—"

"Can I get you a drink?" Dr. Carver asks.

Glancing back at him, Lani notes a change in his expression.

"We can go inside," he says, smile returning, gaze shifting from Lani to Brian—who is examining the fire pit—and then back to Lani.

"Sure, in a moment." She rests her hand on the tree's bark. A sudden, unexpected breeze sways its brittle branches. "You poor thing. Looks like you're dying."

Dr. Carver hurries over. "Shame, isn't it? I'm getting it cut down before it hurts someone. Iggy here is going to be sad though, aren't you, Iggs? He loves the thing."

"Seems like a great dog. You get him from a breeder?"

"Nah, a local shelter." Carver looks back at Brian, who's now poking around the fire pit with a stick. The drug developer seems none too comfortable having two detectives in his backyard.

Then again, Lani supposes, *who would?*

She caresses the oak's trunk. A sheet of dry bark breaks off in her hand. The tree might be older than her grandpa. Realizing Brian is asking Dr. Carver a question, Lani pulls her attention away from the massive oak, gives the beagle another pat, and follows the men toward the house. Once they're inside, the researcher seems more relaxed, and while sipping sparkling water at his breakfast table, with a beautiful view of the yard through the sliding glass door, Lani asks about his PhD student.

"It's awful. Who would want to kill Tony?"

"That's what we're here to find out," Lani says. "Got any ideas?"

"Me? God no. Everybody liked him. I mean, sure, he was quiet. Didn't socialize much with the others, but he always came to my parties here."

"So he's been to your house?" Brian asks.

Dr. Carver leans back in his chair. "Several times. I've

lived here less than a year, but I host a lot of get-togethers. Inside and outside."

"One of your colleagues suggested Tony had a crush on you," Lani says.

Dr. Carver's eyebrows shoot up, but whether his startlement is because he didn't know Tony liked him or because he's surprised the others knew, Lani isn't sure.

"I have no idea about that, detective," he says. "I mean, if he was gay, no worries, but that's not how I roll."

They talk a bit more, mostly about Tony's part in the drug development, and Dr. Carver's responses line up with those of the others.

"So who'll take over the mice now?" Lani asks.

"I will."

"You? Wouldn't you assign it to a new student?"

"Kind of late in the research to bring someone else on board, and the others are busy enough as it is. I know every detail about their work, and we're almost to human trials, so it makes sense I take over."

"Any problems with the research?" Brian asks.

"None. Everything's going beautifully. There are always hiccups and bumps along the way, of course, but we've got all the kinks worked out now."

"A drug that'll make people lose weight. Talk about a boon for science," Lani says. *Not to mention your pocketbook.*

"Minimal side effects too." Carver is clearly proud of his drug. "At least in the mice so far."

Lani wipes condensation off her water glass but keeps her gaze pinned on Dr. Carver, sunglasses now perched on top of her head. "So where were you Wednesday evening?"

"I was meeting with my investor, Harrison Price, of Price Industries."

Carver didn't hesitate to respond, and for some reason that bothers Lani. Wouldn't he at least ask her, "Why?" or, "Was that when Tony was killed?"

"Right, Mr. Price," she says. "Your students mentioned his name. Mind giving us his number?"

"Sure." Dr. Carver recites the investor's phone number, and both Lani and Brian jot it down.

She gazes around Dr. Carver's kitchen and into the living room beyond. "This is a nice place. Looks remodeled."

"It was. Had the work done before I moved in." Dr. Carver laughs. "You look like you'd like a tour, detective."

With the way his dimples pop up and his eyes sparkle, Lani understands why a young researcher—male or female—would be smitten with him. In some ways, he reminds her of a Caucasian Brian, only Brian doesn't make the nerve endings in her hair follicles tingle uneasily like this guy does.

"You're free to look around if you'd like," he says.

Lani can't tell by his tone whether these are the words of a man who has nothing to hide or a man who knows there is nothing to find. In her experience, those are two very different things.

She takes him up on his offer. Who doesn't like to look at pretty houses? But other than stroll through three bedrooms, three bathrooms, an entertainment room, and the unfinished basement, which does indeed have a half-inch of water on the floor and a wet-vac propped up in the corner, Lani does little else but murmur admiringly at the home. For the places she likes to look, they'd need a warrant.

When she and Brian depart and are back inside the Crown Vic, Brian says, "Looks like we can rule out any work-related problems. I say we try to find out if there was more to Tony Habib's love life than anyone let on. Or maybe he had a gambling problem or some enemy no one knows about. Doesn't it always come down to love, money, or revenge?"

"Usually." Lani rolls down her window, the sun having heated the car's interior to an uncomfortable degree. "But something feels off."

"There's always the possibility it was a robbery gone wrong."

"But then why dump him in the national park? You'd take more risk being seen than if you'd just mugged him someplace and left him to die."

"True. So what feels off to you?"

Lani cruises the old car down the rural road. "Don't know, but that's what years of working this rankness will do to you."

CHAPTER ELEVEN

CATHERINE

With scuffed knees and stained shorts, Mr. Carver paces the stone path around his unlit fire pit and holds a small phone I don't recognize. I've seen little of him this morning, maybe because of his basement's water leak, but my restlessness matches his own. Every sinusoid of my arboreal form pulses with excitement. The constables were here!

At first I thought I was dreaming. Well, not so much a dream. Sleep is a requirement I no longer need. More like a trance. It would not be the first time my thoughts drifted away to a nothing-land.

But this was not nothing. This was a very real something.

What brought the lady constable and her partner here, I don't know, but when she approached me? When she laid her hand on me and spoke to me? I have never felt such a human connection, not even with my Tony. Her touch upon my bark was every bit as electric as the lights that illuminate Mr. Carver's yard come nightfall.

But with my excitement comes frustration and worry

because the lady constable seemed unaware Tony's killer stood inches from her in this yard. Worse, she had no knowledge the murder weapon was a mere arm's reach away.

Hello! I wanted to shout. *Hello, yes, I am here. Check inside my fractured trunk. See what this vile man has hidden within me. Get justice for poor Tony.*

Of course, I could articulate none of these things. I managed nothing but an uncoordinated shiver of my branches which could have been attributed to the wind. Maybe my emotions were too scattered to corral my dwindling energy into a fluid motion. When the lady constable walked away, after being so close to the weapon that would ensure justice for Tony, my hope sank faster than a stone tablet.

Once they retreated into Mr. Carver's house, I heard no more of their conversation. I only know the constables left a short time ago, and Mr. Carver remains a free man. Not confronted, not arrested, not taken away for trial and judgment.

And yet something brought the law man and woman here. Something roused the lady constable's suspicion. I sensed her heightened vigilance as plainly as I sense the decay of my aging roots.

Mr. Carver begins speaking on his phone, and I shift my attention his way. Iggy, too, stirs and pricks up his ears, his rump pressed against my bark.

"There you are," the murderous homeowner says. "I called you four times." A pause. "Yes, I know, sorry, this is a different phone. I—" Another pause. "I'll explain later. I just need you to come here, and if a detective calls you before then, tell her you were with me Wednesday night at my house, discussing my research progress." A longer pause. "No, I don't want to say anything else by phone, not even on a burner. Just come here now please."

Mr. Carver returns the phone to the pocket of his loose-fitting shorts, the ones with the big, curved check mark near the hem, and resumes his pacing. At various intervals he performs jumping jacks and then drops to the grass to push his body up and down with his arms. He then flips over onto his back and folds his body into an accordion. Up, down. Up, down. Up, down. I recall his sister reminding him he was no longer that chubby little boy, and I suppose some of his energy stems from not wanting history to repeat itself.

Or maybe the constant movement is a way of releasing his worries and sorting out thoughts in his mind. As a woman, I used to take long strolls to do the same thing, and I loved a good round of sport. When we were children, my younger brother and I, along with our friends, would play Annie Over for hours, tossing the cloth ball over the old shack in our yard. How quick I was at catching it and sneaking over to the other side to tag one of the boys.

But that's where the similarities between Mr. Carver and me end. I don't hurt people. I don't lie and charm and then kill them to get what I desire. I don't use strange things called burner phones, which I can only suspect signals nothing good. No matter his title of doctor, he is nothing but an evil murderer, like those awful characters in the movies he shows for his friends on his giant screen.

A short time later a car pulls into the driveway. Mr. Carver hurries to the trellis. Iggy darts off to join him, his curiosity over the caller perhaps greater than his desire to keep a distance from his master.

"I'm back here," Mr. Carver calls out.

A short, trim man with chestnut hair slicked back from his forehead and casual clothing of cream-colored trousers and a short-sleeved shirt comes into view beyond the trellis. He appears to be in his fourth or fifth decade of life and struts into the backyard with the confidence of a peacock in full plumage. Iggy barks for good measure and sniffs around the man's polished shoes. When the beagle's attention isn't recip-rocated, he trots back to me.

"What's going on, Mark?" the visitor says. "I was just leaving my daughter's ballet recital." He puffs out his chest. "She's really talented. One of the best. And now I have a pizza celebration to get to, so this better be quick."

Recognizing his voice from previous phone calls on speaker, I assume this is Harrison Price, the investor.

"We've got a problem," Mr. Carver says, offering no comment on the gifted ballerina. He directs Mr. Price to the clear-topped table on the patio, where the slope of the roof provides a triangle of shade. Ever the fine host, he offers the investor a drink.

"I don't need a drink," the man says. "I need to know why I'm here. I don't like hearing the word 'problem.'"

Mr. Carver plops onto a chair next to Mr. Price. Even from across the yard, I see the researcher chew his bottom lip, as if trying to find the right words. "I guess it depends on how you define 'problem.' Tony Habib found a second mouse with liver cancer, but...well...Tony won't be finding any more cancer. He..." Mr. Carver takes a big breath. "I'm going to need you to say you were with me Wednesday night. Around seven thirty, after I got back from dinner with my sister. You came over to talk business, had some drinks, and stayed for a few hours."

"And why am I doing that?"

I spot no remorse on Mr. Carver's face, only the uncertainty of a dilemma. "Tony...Tony's dead. He was murdered, and—"

Mr. Price holds up a hand adorned with a thick gold ring. "Oh my God, did you kill him?"

"Of course not." Mr. Carver looks affronted, and his ability to lie so effortlessly disgusts me. "But the police are investigating, and I don't have a good alibi. Things could get dicey."

"Well, I want no part of this."

Mr. Carver thumps the tabletop. "You *are* a part of this. I made Tony keep quiet about the cancer findings because you wanted to be a hundred percent sure about them before we derailed our progress."

The investor shoves back his chair as if to leave, the metal legs scraping over the stone patio tiles, but he doesn't stand. "Did he tell anyone else about the mice? Write it down anywhere? Enter it in the data?"

For a man who seconds ago blustered in alarm over learning of Tony's demise, he seems to have moved on swiftly from the horror of it to his own self-interest. He asks nothing about the murder itself.

"No. I've checked the data. There's nothing there, and I know he hasn't told any of my other students. They would've said something."

"Did the two of you ever talk about it by voicemail or text? Email? Anything that could be accessed from a device?"

"No. Everything's been face-to-face. I'm not stupid."

Mr. Price's posture seems to relax. "Don't worry. You'll get your alibi. We can't have anything slowing this down. My wife was at my daughter's rehearsal Wednesday night, and my two boys were with their grandparents, so no one will be able to counter otherwise." Then, shaking off Tony's death as if it were nothing more than a crumb on his trousers, he adds, "I'm sorry the kid's dead, of course, but you have no idea how much I have riding on this. Everything I've got and then some."

"Come on, you're loaded. The drug's failure would be a tiny blip in your bank account."

The investor squeezes the sides of the table with both hands. Although he's a slender man, his sinewy arm muscles bulge from the strain. "Everything. Everything I have I've put into your drug."

From the angry red hue of his cheeks, I fear this man could have stabbed my Tony as easily as Mr. Carver did.

"Okay, okay." Mr. Carver wipes his chin. "I get it. But instead of spitting on my face you should be thanking me for getting Tony to withhold the results." Now it's the researcher's turn for ire. "If more mice get cancer, though, I'll have to bring things to a halt and figure out what's going on. Start back at square one." When Mr. Price says nothing, simply maintains his grip on the table, Mr. Carver adds, "No matter how badly we both want this, I won't put a dangerous drug out there."

Won't you? I wonder. *You already killed a man to hide it.* If only Mr. Carver would have thought this reasonably before he plunged the letter opener into Tony's neck.

"It was smart to monitor things a bit," he goes on. "Tony could be a little eager. But if there's a link between liver cancer and our drug, we can't advance it to clinical trials. I want to help people lose weight, but I don't want to give them cancer as a result."

"Oh, look who has ethics suddenly," Mr. Price says in a mocking tone.

"I've always had ethics when it comes to my research. Don't you dare paint me otherwise."

Once again, I struggle to believe Mr. Carver's words. If he's sincere, then maybe he's delusional. Or maybe he simply says these things in hopes of convincing himself of their truth. If given the chance, I'd be terrified to enter his mind to find out.

"As much as I want full tenure and a major drug discovery," the researcher continues, "I want my scientific reputation more. Academia can be a dog-eat-dog world, but there are limits to how far I'll go."

Like aggressive wolves, the two men stare at each other, jaws tight, breaths heavy. I wonder if Mr. Price truly believes Mr. Carver is innocent of Tony's murder. Or if he even cares.

The investor releases his hold on the table. "Of course. I feel the same. I can't have Price Industries behind a drug that causes cancer. But your mice are getting mega doses of Skinny Z. It won't be the same for humans. It's like saccharine, right? The study rats got far bigger doses than people get from a few sprinkles in their coffee. Maybe you need to decrease the dosage."

A lively melody erupts from Mr. Price's shirt pocket. He plucks out his phone and answers it. "Hi sweetie, I'm on my way. You were awesome up on that stage. Daddy was so proud of you. Give your mom a kiss for me and tell her I'll be there soon." He replaces the phone in his pocket and stands. "So we're good here?"

"As long as you give me an alibi, we are."

"You have my word."

As I watch the short man strut back to his car, I question how much his word is worth. Surely not more than the penny price of a licorice whip from my father's store.

These men appall me. Anyone who met them would find them charming, pleasant, and no doubt upstanding citizens, but once the layers of their onion-like selves are peeled back, one would find nothing but rot. Have morals changed so much in the past century and a half?

A bullfrog plops up from the creek and belches a guttural tune. Its warty skin undulates in the weedy growth.

Yes, I respond to him. *You are correct.*

Since the beginning of time, men with questionable morals have hidden beneath kindly exteriors. Dr. Frederick Morrison is a fine example of that. Led me to believe he had nothing but unconditional support for my presence in his lectures, when in truth it was quite conditional, foisted upon me in the form of his fleshy lips and roving hands.

A shudder creaks through my branches at the memory.

And what about Dr. Jedediah Cartwright? His morals were equally questionable, not in the form of unwanted advances, but in allowing—perhaps even *assisting*—Curtis Mayfield and his friends to rob the grave of a recently deceased mother he had treated only two days before.

I remember it as if it were yesterday. Her distraught husband had carried her into Dr. Cartwright's small infirmary near Trinity Church and laid her onto the exam table. Upon seeing her skeletal state, Dr. Cartwright demanded his nurse fetch his bloodletting kit while I, along with three fellow students—Curtis Mayfield, Zachary Horton, and Joseph Bridleman—observed with wide eyes, our minds eager to learn.

After bleeding the deathly ill mother, her eyes and skin bearing the yellow stain of jaundice and her hair patchy and dull, Dr. Cartwright sent her home with nothing more than a bottle of opium drops. He warned her tearful husband she might not survive the night. Indeed, she died in the early morning hours of the next day and was buried later that afternoon, the November soil not yet frozen.

Sorrow over her passing pinched my heart. She left five young children behind and a husband with little money. I knew I would need better control of my emotions if I wanted to survive the heartbreaking realities of medicine. If not, my own grief might prevent me from providing the best care I could. Therefore, I tried to push the case from my mind, but on the dawn following her burial, the entire matter resurfaced in the most dreadful way.

In that early morning hour, with the businesses and residences of St. Clair Street still quiet, I arrived at the medical college to visit the top-floor library for materials I needed for my Medicine and Jurisprudence assignment. Being in the building alone at dawn didn't bother me—it would soon be light enough for my studies—but when a noise from above startled me, I questioned my judgment. Footsteps and muffled voices filtered down from the attic.

Were some of the teachers preparing lectures up there?

The idea made little sense. Maybe it was students, studying together in hopes of improving their skills. If so, why wasn't I invited? Must they exclude me from everything? And why, of all places, in a dingy garret?

I departed the library and marched up the narrow staircase toward the attic, determined to let my fellow students know I was not a fragile flower. I could tolerate an overnight session of studies as heartily as them. They must have heard my laced-up boots clomping on the wooden steps and the swish of my skirt and cloak, because their voices fell silent. Near the top of the stairwell, an unpleasant smell like a dead mouse trapped inside a wall reached me, but I stomped on.

When I flung open the attic door, my breath caught in my throat. There, surrounding a rectangular table, stood Curtis Mayfield, Zachary Horton, and Joseph Bridleman, garbed in stained aprons and gripping dissection tools. Lying on the table in front of them was the mother of five who was buried the afternoon before, her body splayed open, her chest wall nailed to the table, and her face peeled back. So hideous was the scene in the shadowy light of oil lamps and creeping dawn that I nearly lost my supper from the night before. I refused, however, to give them the satisfaction. I swallowed my revulsion and the coppery taste that went with it.

"How dare you," I sputtered. "Robbing graves now, are you?"

The act of grave robbing by medical students was nothing new. Neither were stories of the trap door in the cupola where the corpses were sometimes hidden. Students—and even practicing doctors—were eager to hone their dissection skills. Unfortunately, few bodies were available. But learning my classmates had participated in the desecration of a mother's grave filled me with disgust. Where was her soul now? How would it return to her body in the afterlife?

"How dare you," I repeated.

Curtis Mayfield, who resembled the bullfrog who croaks in

the creek beside me now, spat a thick wad of mucus onto the attic floor. "You know right well how few bodies the college receives for our learning. Have to take them where we can." He sneered at his two classmates. "Told you medical school wasn't a place for a woman."

Zachary Horton's ensuing laughter didn't surprise me. From day one of our class sessions, he had shown barely concealed resentment toward me. What I hadn't expected was the shrug and smirk from Joseph Bridleman, a quiet young man who had seemed to accept my presence from the start.

The four of us glared at each other, oil lamps flickering, wind howling outside the lone garret window and rattling its pane. Although the scholarly part of me wanted desperately to participate in a dissection—I hadn't yet had the opportunity—I couldn't do so at the expense of this woman's soul. Yet I was unsure how to proceed. Keep quiet about my discovery or report it to the dean?

Finally, I said, "What would Dr. Cartwright think of you desecrating his patient's mortal body?"

Curtis laughed and stabbed his blade into the wood table, inches from the woman's splayed flesh. "Who do you think told us to grab our shovels and a potato sack?"

This information should have surprised me, but given Dr. Cartwright's malignant disposition (*malignant enough to be my murderer?*), it didn't. It disturbed me though, not only from the knowledge that an esteemed physician would have such low morals but also—and this part I'm ashamed to admit—because I, who had been present with the three male students in Dr. Cartwright's clinic when this woman was treated, was not similarly encouraged to further my education with a dissection. Not that I would have done, but the exclusion stung nonetheless.

As if reading my mind, Curtis said to his friends, "You see? This is why Dr. Cartwright said not to tell her. Women like her, ripe with sensitivities and silliness, can't be trusted with such complicated matters." He constricted his eyes into slits. "And you best not be saying anything about it either, for that's just what a woman would do."

"And if I do?" I asked, my voice carrying more confidence than I felt.

Curtis grinned. "Then maybe we'll have us *two* bodies to be a-cutting."

CHAPTER TWELVE

Lani

Six days after interviewing Tony Habib's colleagues, Lani sits in Chief French's office and waits for him to finish his phone call. Her foot bounces in annoyance, especially since he was the one who summoned her. It's Friday afternoon, and he wants an update on the murder investigation before he leaves for the weekend to play ball with his kids or cheat on his wife or maybe both.

The mature and reasonable part of her knows her dislike of Chief Toddler is probably unfair. After all, he must have some hidden skills to be named chief at such a young age, albeit in a Cleveland suburb and not his native New York, and it isn't like he's always an arrogant prick. When Mature Lani sticks around, she even acknowledges that his pushback on her might have a little something to do with her pushback on him.

Then again, the man is an ageist and a philanderer, and he's keeping her from new cases, so an ounce of childish insubordination seems called for.

If he's worried she'll blackmail him again about his affair

to land another case, he doesn't show it. Maybe he's calling her bluff. No wonder she always loses in poker to the old cuss in Peninsula. The chief seems to sense she won't use his infidelity against him a second time—and she won't; it's not in her nature to be cruel—and now he simply appears to be counting the days until she's gone, throwing off nothing but waves of indifference her way.

When he finally hangs up the phone, Lani attempts a smile. "Only four more weeks and you'll never see my apple cheeks again." She picks up his New York paperweight and plops it back and forth in her hands.

"You're a good detective, Whitaker. I know that, you know that, the whole department knows that. Regardless of what might have happened all those years ago."

Just had to slip that in there, didn't you? Lani thinks.

"But taking your retirement out on me doesn't do either of us any favors. You're not being treated any differently than anyone else who's been in your shoes. Most detectives are thrilled to see the finish line. Some find a new job, others enjoy the peace and quiet they've earned." He raises his palms and smiles in a condescending way rather than an encouraging one. "After all, you're in your golden years now."

"Sweet almighty, that's supposed to make me feel better? Like I'm just toddling on a golden chariot toward death?"

At least on some level he's right. She's had some great solves in her career. Even won a few medals and honors. Why can't she focus on the wins instead of the losses? Her colleagues are already calling her *Let-It-Go Lani.* Even singing that song from the kids' movie. And why is it so hard for her to separate retirement from death? Logically she knows the two are not one in the same, and yet to her entire core being they are.

But Chief Toddler isn't her therapist. He isn't on a need-to-know basis with her feelings. So she simply points to his partially full coffee mug and says, "Some see half-full. Some see half-empty. I see, 'wait, shouldn't there be more?'"

He surprises her by laughing, his chair squeaking as he swivels it closer to his desk. "So, are you going to whack me in the head with that paperweight or update me on the Habib case?"

Lani returns New York City's skyline to the corner of French's desk. A part of her hesitates to discuss the case because after nearly a week of investigation, they have a box full of nothing. No doubt the chief will interpret that as confirmation she's getting too old to be effective.

She sighs. "You probably already know most of it. There's nothing new. We've talked to everyone we can find but have learned zilch. His colleagues have alibis that check out. Dr. Mark Carver's is the weakest, but he claims he was home talking shop with his investor, Harrison Price *the Third*." Lani voices the suffix with a queen's accent and an eye roll. "Price confirms it. If the ME's time-of-death estimate is off by a couple hours though, there might be some wiggle room."

"I know Harrison Price," Chief Toddler says.

Of course you do.

"He's a venture capitalist and a huge donor and supporter of the Winston PD. A lot of our body cams and vests are thanks to him. Other equipment too."

Terrific.

"I'd take his word as solid," French adds. "What about Habib's family? Didn't find anyone else here in the U.S.?"

"Nope. Just the great aunt who raised him after his parents died."

"The one with Alzheimer's."

"Yep. We paid her a visit, but she spoke only of her deceased husband in rambling sentences and seemed to have no knowledge of her nephew."

"And his friends?"

Lani flutters her lips. "People think *I'm* a loner? Tony

makes me look like a party animal in comparison. Kept to himself a lot, and the only evidence I can find of him socializing is parties at Carver's house or occasional video-game jams with two techies he went to undergrad with, Landon and Arjun. Both were stoned when Brian and I interviewed them a couple days ago, so yeah, that was fun."

"Did they know he was dead?"

"They did. Saw it on a local news app. Seemed genuinely surprised and remorseful but didn't have much to offer. They didn't think he had any girlfriends. Or boyfriends, for that matter."

"And no one with any motive?"

Lani shakes her head. "Everyone claims he was a great guy. His gamer friends called him an 'awesome dude.' Nothing weird on his computer or phone. Didn't appear to have a will, despite his inheritance from his parents. Not sure where that will end up. The lawyers should have fun with it. And of the few extended family members back in Lebanon who could be tracked down, no one wants the body. Guess there was family discord when Habib's parents married—clashing religions, pregnancy out of wedlock, that kind of thing. The families disowned them, so they moved to Chicago and started a new life."

"That's awful."

"Isn't it, though? First his parents die, then him, now just a maternal great aunt with Alzheimer's is left. The aunt's husband, who moved here with her decades ago, died when she was in her mid-twenties. Never had any kids." Complete strangers or not, the whole situation weights Lani with sadness.

"Poor guy," the chief says. "Makes me want to go home and hug my wife and kids."

For his empathy, Lani raises him a notch on her likability scale. But only a notch.

"He wasn't involved on social media much either," she

adds. "Nothing beyond LinkedIn and a couple academic sites where he shared egg-head stuff about research, drug development, that kind of thing. Was active on an online gamer site with the username SkinnyZ though. That's the nickname for the drug he was working on, but again, nothing weird or helpful for us to find. Not even porn."

"Was he a practicing Muslim?"

"Had a prayer rug in his townhome but not his office, and none of his colleagues saw him take prayer breaks, so I don't know. His stoner friends claim he never touched drugs, but he did have an occasional drink at Carver's parties. Everyone says he was quiet, loyal, kind. Pretty much the kind of guy you'd want for a son, a husband, a brother, whatever." The sorrow on Lani's chest grows heavier.

What's the fecking point of life if we just end up dying alone? she thinks.

"He has no family here to keep pushing for answers, and meanwhile, other cases are piling up on our desks. Or at least Brian's desk." Lani raises an eyebrow at Chief Toddler for her lack of new work but holds back a comment. Instead, she steels her jaw and says, "I can't sleep at night knowing his killer might get away."

"Don't beat yourself up. You know as well as me that some murders never get solved. It's awful, of course, but it happens, and it has nothing to do with the detective."

Lani shrugs in response.

"It could very well turn out to be a random killing," French says. "A mugging gone wrong." When Lani starts to protest, he raises his hand. "I agree, it's odd a mugger would move the body, and that's why you guys are still going hard at this, but you need to prepare yourself that we might never have an answer."

"Nope. Not good enough. I *will* have an answer. We're going to question everyone again. Something about the head researcher, Dr. Carver, rubs me wrong."

French bristles. "We need a little more than being *rubbed* the wrong way."

"Like I don't know that, for crying out loud?" And just like that their brief lovefest is broken. "But there's something about him. Everyone responds to grief differently, I get that. As a beat cop, I once had to knock on a mother's door to tell her that her son died in a car accident. She stared at me for a few seconds and then went back to sweeping her house, too stricken to do anything else. So I understand that everyone responds differently. But Carver?" Lani frowns. "When I asked for his alibi, he had it at the ready. A little too quick with it, you know? And he didn't display any shock over Habib's death."

"That's probably because he'd already ID'd the body at the morgue after he reported Habib missing."

"Yeah, but wouldn't you still show some residual disbelief? Say something like, 'I can't believe he's really gone.' That type of thing?"

"Bring me some concrete evidence, and we'll talk. Until then, don't tick anyone off with your gut feelings. We don't need any more bad publicity than what already comes with the territory."

With that, Chief Toddler stands and signals their meeting is over.

Fine by me, Lani thinks and steps out.

Having little more to do on Tony Habib's case for the time being, Lani devotes most of Saturday and Sunday to yard work. Mid-April is always a good time to tidy up her landscaping and ready her small garden for planting.

She prunes evergreens, trims dead foliage from perennials, removes old mulch and other debris, and even plants a row of onions in her vegetable garden, the staple hardy enough to withstand a few days of residual cold should they get them. And Northeast Ohio *would* get them. The rest of the vegetable seeds—tomatoes, peppers, cucumbers, squash—will see their turn next month.

So productive is Lani that she also manages to finish cleaning out the attic, taking most of her parents' old things to the Salvation Army. The rest she puts out on the berm—junk nobody needs but someone will take. A few items she keeps for sentimental purposes, which for her means they barely fill a single box: an old gold-framed photograph of the Whitaker family back when her father was a boy; a handful of sports jerseys her dad used to wear when the three of them went to a game—Browns, Guardians, Cavaliers—it didn't matter, they loved them all; a few yellowed and dog-eared cookbooks her mother once used; and a couple of old history books Lani flipped through as a child, one about her mother's ancestral land of Samoa and the other about England, the Whitaker family's country of origin.

Good grief, I was even weird as a kid.

Everything else, she gets rid of. Well, everything but her great grandfather's ashes and journal. Last week, the urn somehow managed to find a temporary home on her mantle, sandwiched between the two stately ferns, both plants probably furious at Lani for giving them such an appalling roommate.

And now her reward for all the hard work is to grab a beer and some pretzels, light a ginger spice candle, and settle in for more of Old Henry's dry prose. She'll deal with his ashes later. Once she knows where to put them.

In a recliner that feels like a little piece of heaven on her overworked muscles and joints, Lani savors a mouthful of a local pilsner and cracks open the journal. Slipping on her readers, she picks up where she left off when she found the book two weeks earlier.

In an entry dated April 2, 1853, Constable Henry

Whitaker documents his investigation of Catherine Miller's disappearance in great detail, mentioning that he interviewed everyone tied to her in some way, including the other graduates of the medical college, her teachers, her preceptor, her future work partner, her male suitor, the family members present at her graduation ceremony, and any other guests he could find who attended the social hour of tea and cake that had followed.

"Her family from Pennsylvania," Old Henry notes, "including her father, mother, and eldest brother, Charles, were as distraught as one might expect a family member to be over the disappearance of their daughter or sister. The last they saw of Catherine was when she whispered to her mother that she wanted to take a stroll to catch some fresh air and calm her nerves. Although her mother offered companionship, Catherine declined, desiring a moment of solitude.

"Her heartsick mother now wishes she had insisted on accompanying her daughter. From our conversations, I concluded that Charles, a pastor, was not happy about his sister's decision to become a doctor and the perceived embarrassment to the family it brought. 'I urged her not to attend the medical college,' he told me. 'Its chambers are no place for a woman.' As I detected a hint of jealousy mixed with the man's sorrow, I am including him in my list of suspect persons, however unlikely."

As Lani reads Henry's words, she chugs a quarter of her beer for the uptight pastor's benefit.

The next page in the journal is more clinical, with Henry making a list of people he wanted to reinterview. Lani can only surmise that the CMU he writes about stands for Cleveland Medical College, which an earlier Google search told her was also known as the Medical Department of Western Reserve College, the main college being located in Hudson. The Hudson campus is still around but is now a boarding school, and Cleveland's medical college has become the Case

Western Reserve School of Medicine. Unfortunately, the original building on the corner of St. Clair Avenue and E. 9th Street has long since been destroyed. Lani wishes she'd been able to visit it. Stroll the same corridors as the missing young "lady doctor" with whom her great grandfather was so obsessed.

As if she herself is working the case, Lani scans Henry's scrawled list of suspects and non-suspects. According to his notes, the ones he felt deserved "special scrutiny" are marked with an X:

X Curtis Mayfield
    —Fellow student at CMU and outspoken critic of admittance of women
    —Believed by classmates to be responsible for depositing a severed foot on Catherine's bed
    —Grave robber, whom Catherine caught dissecting a recently deceased woman
    —Departed the commencement celebration early to visit a tavern with Zachary Horton, but no witnesses beyond Horton to confirm this

X Joseph Bridleman
    —Fellow student who confessed the aforementioned grave robbing to me out of worry that Curtis Mayfield might have harmed Catherine
    —Genuine concern for the lady doctor's disappearance or merely deflecting suspicion from himself?
    —Was present for most of the commencement celebration during which Catherine disappeared, witnesses confirm

X Zachary Horton

—Fellow student and third grave robber

—Departed the commencement celebration early to visit a tavern with Curtis Mayfield, but no witnesses beyond Mayfield to confirm this

X Dr. Jedediah Cartwright

—Teacher of Theory and Practice of Medicine

—Implicated by J. Bridleman as encouraging the three students in their grave robbing for educational dissection

—Denies any involvement in grave robbing and thus stands in contrast to J. Bridleman's testimony

—Told me the idea of lady doctors is 'pure madness'

—Did not attend commencement celebration but instead returned home, confirmed only by his wife

X Dr. Frederick Morrison

—Teacher of Pathology and Obstetrics, who, on the word of several sources, initially seemed enamored with young Catherine

—Did he make untoward advances toward the lady? Did she rebuff his efforts and pay the harshest price?

—Did not attend commencement celebration, but his alibi of traveling by carriage to Hudson could not be confirmed

X Mansour Younis

—A lawyer and Catherine's companion on Sunday strolls

—No talk of marriage yet, but he'd hoped for more serious courting

—Seems distressed by Catherine's disappearance, but there is an arrogance to him as well

—No reliable alibi, was home alone preparing a case when she disappeared

—Strikes me as peculiar he didn't attend the commencement ceremony

Dr. Samuel Clifton
 —Non-suspect person
 —Catherine's preceptor
 —Critical resource for future inquiries
 —At commencement ceremony during the time Catherine disappeared, witnesses confirm

Dr. Isaac Fitzgerald
 —Most likely a non-suspect person
 —Offered Catherine a position in his clinic, a fine chap supportive of lady doctors joining the profession
 —Was the last person to see Catherine before she disappeared, so must be kept in mind

Four more names made Henry's list, all teachers, one of whom enjoyed the flask hidden away in his coat pocket a little too freely, but evidently, none stood out to Henry because he made few notations about them.

In the next paragraph, he jots, "When I questioned Dr. Frederick Morrison, the obstetrics teacher, about his views on women attending his lectures, he told me it was lovely to see a girl playing make believe, but that the demands of doctoring were not suited to their gender's weaker constitution and inferior intellect. When I suggested Catherine might have been killed by someone who thought very much the same way, Dr. Morrison claimed the notion of Catherine being murdered was ludicrous. He stated, and I remember his exact words, 'The poor girl probably hopped a train home to Pennsylvania, her pretty little tail between her legs.' His tone grew less condescending when I asked if he had acted improperly toward Catherine. He stammered a hearty denial, but I daresay I fail to believe him."

Lani rests the journal on her lap and pops a pretzel in her mouth. Her early policing days flood back to her. *Someone's gotta pave the way*, she thinks, staring at the spider plant on the window seat, *but that road definitely takes guts to travel.*

The next few paragraphs of the entry discuss Catherine's future partner, Dr. Isaac Fitzgerald, as being the last person to see her at the post-commencement celebration. Henry writes: "The good doctor informed me he kissed his wife goodbye outside. She had to leave the celebration early to deliver one of her dresses. He then planned to return to congratulate the graduates on his own, but before he could, a foot messenger called him away to tend to a patient on Euclid Street. When Dr. Fitzgerald once again exited the college, Catherine was hurrying down St. Clair Street in the opposite direction. He called out to her, but she didn't hear him, so he continued on his way toward Euclid. He suspected she needed to clear her head. 'It was a very exciting day for her, constable,' he told me."

Henry then goes on to note: "Although I have no reason to suspect Dr. Fitzgerald of wrongdoing, I find it unusual he wouldn't go after Catherine to make sure she was all right. So although I put no X in front of his name, he's not far from my thoughts. Neither is Mr. Mansour Younis. The wealthy lawyer has no alibi during Catherine's disappearance, and although his sorrow over her absence seems perhaps genuine, his attitude of superiority over a young constable is unmistakable."

Henry closes the entry by saying: "Although some believe the lady doctor fled because she was unable to face what was now expected of her, I, and many others, believe that to be pure folly. Her love of medicine seemed quite obvious. My problem lies in having too many suspects and no evidence to yield an arrest. Could one of the men I questioned be responsible for her disappearance? Indeed. Could a random stranger have murdered her, or maybe an ill-tempered patient from her preceptor's clinic? Indeed. Could she have gotten lost in the woods beyond Cleveland's edge and perished at the hand of Mother Nature? Indeed. But I'll make no inferences without proof. A false and rash accusation will help neither Catherine nor my future career."

A final statement completes the entry. "But this I know with no uncertainty: I will not stop investigating her disappearance until the answer finds me."

Lani, who's hunched over in rapt attention at Old Henry's words, straightens in the recliner and rubs the back of her stiff neck. The police apple didn't fall far from the tree. Four generations between them, and her great grandfather seems like he was every bit the obsessive stickler she is.

A glance at the digital clock near the TV indicates she better get her butt to bed if she wants a solid eight hours before her dawn walk, especially with all the physical labor she's done these past two days, but when she scans the opening sentence of the next entry, she's tempted to keep reading. Henry writes of a "horrific act committed against Catherine during her second round of class sessions, making me believe the killer is someone close to her."

Before Lani can read further, her phone chimes louder than the old church bell down the street. She jumps at the sudden interruption, and the journal drops to the floor.

Why in the world did I choose that ringtone?

With one hand over her pounding heart, she uses the other to snatch the phone off the end table. She doesn't recognize the number and debates answering, but considering how many business cards she's passed out over the past several days, hoping to find a lead on the Habib case, she figures she better.

She isn't disappointed.

CHAPTER THIRTEEN

LANI

At first, when the caller identifies himself as Arjun Shah, Lani can't place him, but then she remembers a small apartment, enough electronic equipment to fill a Best Buy, and two gamers trying to hide the fact they were smoking pot.

"I'm sorry for bugging you on a Sunday night," he says, his tone cautious and shy, "but you told me to call any time if I remembered something about Tony, and, well, I just remembered something."

Lani fumbles with the wooden arm on the side of the recliner and scrambles back into an upright position.

Relax, Whitaker. It could be nothing.

"You're not bugging me," she says. "Do you have an iPhone?"

"Um…yeah. Why?"

"Mind if we FaceTime? I prefer to see the people I'm talking to."

He laughs. "You know how to do that? Wish I could get my grandma to figure it out."

What a little fecker.

"There," she says, once his dopey face is on the screen. Then again, he's not exactly getting Angelina Jolie on his end. "So what do you remember?"

"It's probably stupid, but I was thinking about something Tony said a few weeks ago. We were playing Call of Duty here—"

"Where's *here*?"

"My apartment."

Arjun rotates the phone so Lani can see his living room on the screen. The flash tour includes grimy takeout containers on the coffee table and a pair of Batman boxer shorts on the floor. It's similar to how the place looked when she visited it in person.

"Well, Landon's apartment too," Arjun says. "We're roommates, remember."

"Okay. And?"

"And Tony seemed a bit out of it. Kind of down, you know? He ended up leaving early. I figured it was because he was playing so bad, kept getting himself killed, and it's not like he was much of a talker anyway. Not about anything personal at least. But now I'm wondering if it was something more, something about his research."

"Why would you wonder that?"

"Because when I asked him if something was wrong, he said no, he was fine. Just had a glitch in his research to work out."

"He used that word? Glitch?"

Arjun's lips purse in thought on Lani's phone screen. "No, I don't think so. I can't remember exactly what he said."

Because you were stoned, Lani thinks with a smirk.

"Honestly, I didn't make much of it, and when we played the following week, he didn't mention it again. So maybe I'm wasting your time."

"You're not wasting my time." Lani ponders what Arjun

has told her. What might seem like nothing at first glance can end up being crucial. Any detective knows that. "Anything else?"

"No. Like I said before, we mostly played video games and talked crap. Landon and I are best friends, but Tony never seemed interested in joining the ring. Still, I feel awful about his death. Kind of having trouble sleeping at night, you know?" The young man's cheeks sag like a puppy's.

"That's understandable, Arjun. You want me to give you some resources? People you can talk to?"

"I'm good, but thanks. My company has a counselor on staff."

Lani nods and thanks him for the call.

Once they disconnect, she sits very still, staring at her plant companions on the window seat, the blinds closed behind them. Then she picks Old Henry's journal up from the floor where it fell, empties the rest of her beer, and glances at the digital clock near the TV once again. Nine thirty on a Sunday night might be late for her, but it's probably not for a PhD student. Or three PhD students, to be exact. She'd like to talk to Dr. Mark Carver's team again. None of them reported problems with the research. In fact, they said everything was going fine.

But was it?

She pulls up their contact info on her phone. She typed it into her Notes app when she interviewed them. *See, Einstein? Lani Whitaker can handle a little technology.* Calling them can wait until morning, of course, but patience has never been her strong suit. "Hold your horses, kid," her dad constantly told her, and not just when she was a little girl.

She'll wait on Carver though. She wants to question Mr. Handsome and Charming face-to-face. In person, not on a phone camera.

In starting with Chloe Sampson, the auburn-haired stats whiz whose anxiety Lani initially mistook for bubble-headedness, Lani scores a trifecta. Not only does the PhD student answer, she's at a bar playing pool with the other two researchers. On FaceTime, Lani speaks to Chloe, Montell Riggs, and Alice Chang as a group.

As before, none report a problem with Skinny Z's development and early testing, at least nothing significant. Chloe recently reviewed everyone's progress, including Tony's records, and ran the details through her fancy stats program. She claims everything is going "fantastically well." Their excitement over being at the forefront of something so important, a drug that could help millions of people lose weight without serious side effects, is infectious, so much so that were Lani not a collection of tired muscles and knobby joints, she might just drive to the bar and join them.

Satisfied with this interaction, she says goodbye and heads to her bedroom to call it a night. Sleep will fight her though, no doubt about that. Whenever she gets the first hint of a lead, her mind explodes into a minefield of *what if*s and *maybe that*s and *how does it fit in*s. Even if Arjun's research "glitch" turns out to be a red herring, which it probably will, her mind won't stop firing until she rules it out. Given her earlier reservations about Mark Carver, following up on that herring, no matter how red, seems important.

As she brushes her teeth and changes into pajamas—a Browns T-shirt and knee-length shorts—another thought surfaces. What about Carver's former universities and jobs? Should she check them out too? It might lead nowhere. *Probably* will lead nowhere, but what harm is there in a couple emails? Besides, what else is she going to do in her countdown to retirement? Chief Toddler is biding his time with her. Come tomorrow, he'll probably stick her with a missing-cat case, anything to keep her grumbling mug out of his office.

After slathering on moisturizer, Lani pads her slippered feet into her study, which holds a desktop computer, a loveseat sofa, and no less than five plants, although the tiny cactus might not count. She reawakens her sleeping monitor and, with the help of Google, reads Dr. Carver's bio on Cardon University's website. Prior to becoming an assistant professor in their pharmacology department four years ago, he did two post-doc fellowships there. Before that, he completed a PhD in pharmaceutical sciences at the University of Southern California, and prior to that he spent three years working at a pharma company after receiving a master's degree in medicinal chemistry with an emphasis on obesity. His undergrad was in chemistry. Both of those degrees were from Northwestern in Illinois.

Wow. The man is no slouch.

Lani sinks back against the desk chair. Carver's bio is a lot to unpack and contains a lot of people to contact. Definitely *not* an activity for a Sunday night.

And yet she is too wired to sleep. That rumble of a hunch burns in her belly and ignites the only type of passion she knows: catching the bad guys and getting justice for the good ones.

Okay then. One more thing.

She searches the pharmaceutical science department at the University of Southern California, finds the chairwoman's name and email address, and fires off a message identifying herself as a detective from Ohio who'd like to speak with her about a case. After supplying her phone number, she does the same with the communications director of the pharma company where Carver worked, as well as the head of the medicinal chemistry program at Northwestern. None of the three people she emailed might have anything to tell her, but maybe they could direct her to some of Carver's former colleagues and friends.

Figuring that's a good start, Lani stands and stretches. Before she can even power off the desktop, her inbox flashes a new message. The chairwoman at USC, a Dr. Sally McDaniels, has emailed her back.

Holy heck. Doesn't anyone escape work anymore?

But this downside of the internet is Lani's upside because when Dr. McDaniels asks what time would be good to contact her, Lani types back: How about now?

Within seconds they're chatting. Not by FaceTime. Lani has a limit to what she'll expose callers to, and a stretched-out T-shirt and a face full of Pond's cream is it.

What she learns from the chairwoman gets her tingling all over again. Once their call ends, she immediately phones Brian, who's probably nose-deep in one of his brainy nonfiction books.

"Whoa, Grandma W's up past her bedtime," he says.

"Be ready early. Like at 6:30. I'll pick you up." She doesn't want Carver talking to his PhD students before she has a chance to reinterview him.

"And why would I want to do that?" Brian asks. "Some of us need our beauty sleep, you know."

"Because, Einstein, you and I are going to pay a certain researcher a good-morning visit."

CHAPTER FOURTEEN

Lani

Brian must be watching out the window for her because at six thirty, when Lani pulls her Crown Vic into the driveway of his two-bedroom home on a quiet residential street in Winston, he hurries outside and jogs to her car, his overcoat flapping against his suit. Thanks to Ohio's let's-see-how-we-can-mess-with-them-today weather, the spring temperature has nose-dived to a nippy forty degrees.

Once Brian is inside the vehicle, Lani hands him a cup of coffee. "Don't say I never gave you nothing."

"Morning to you too, sunshine." He smiles and gets right down to business. "She really said she had reservations about him?"

Lani knows he's referring to her phone call with Sally McDaniels last night. "Those very words."

"No way to prove it wasn't an accident though. Some of those California roads can get pretty dicey."

"Probably not, at least not now, but knowing that six and a half years ago Carver's PhD colleague drove off a cliff to his death gives *me* a major dose of reservations too, especially since he and Carver had an argument over whose idea a new drug was."

"How did Dr. McDaniels know they'd argued?"

"Overheard their conversation when she was in the women's bathroom. They were in the men's on the other side of the wall, and the old building carried the sound right through the vent. A little muffled, but she got the gist of it."

"Did she know what the drug was?"

"Nothing concrete, just a sprout of an idea, but sounds like it was a weight-loss drug. Obesity was Carver's focus there."

Brian raises an eyebrow.

"Exactly," Lani says. "But to be fair, the chairwoman also had good things to say about Carver. Said he was a strong researcher, a stickler for details, and seemed to have a genuine interest in helping people manage their obesity. Guess he used to be overweight as a kid. He included that morsel in his personal statement when he applied for the PhD program. So yeah, I've gotta be fair to the guy. You don't want tunnel vision, or you'll feck up the job." Lani taps the steering wheel. "Still, something feels off about him, and the more I think about it, the more I'm convinced he created that water leak on purpose. Hoped we'd bypass him altogether in our questioning, but in case we didn't, he had proof of the leak in his basement."

"Well then," Brian says, "you're going to be interested in this."

Lani shoots a glance his way before entering the on-ramp for I-77 south. "Oh yeah, what's 'this'?"

"After hearing about your extra-curricular activities last night, I felt like a slacker, so I called Chloe Sampson. Figured of Carver's three remaining PhD students, she'd give me the most juice. Met her at the pub just as her friends were leaving. She was happy to stick around and chat."

Lani takes in Brian's trim, muscular frame and good looks. "I bet she was."

"Are you objectifying me, boss?"

"You wish. And I'm not your boss. So what'd you learn from Chloe that I didn't? Pretty sure I'm about to be shown up."

"I'm just happy that for once I get to tell you something you don't already know. For an old person, you can be pretty sharp."

Lani snorts. "Yeah, yeah, get on with it."

"I asked Chloe a little more about Carver in general. Kept it light. Didn't want her to think we had an interest in the guy. That might put him on alert before we had a chance to talk to him again, you know? So I ordered her another glass of wine and said I wanted to get a better feel of the department. Said it might help us learn more about Tony. In fact—"

"Crap on a cracker, you're killing me with the suspense. What'd ya learn, already?"

"Carver's former girlfriend committed suicide two years ago."

Lani swerves onto the shoulder. "You're kidding me." She jerks the Crown Vic back in the lane.

"I'm not. But before you get your granny panties in a wad and kill us with your driving, according to Chloe, the woman and Carver had already broken up. Apparently he was shocked by her death and seemed 'super sad.'"

"Chloe really said 'super sad'? Maybe she's a bubblehead after all."

"Nah, she's cool. Clearly smart. Statistics? Whoosh." Brian makes a sweeping gesture over his head, as if the concept of numbers and probabilities sails over him.

"Yeah, right. You're like a walking Google. You probably do calculus in your head for fun." Lani feels Brian staring at her. "What?"

"I see that look on your face. The way you're chewing

your lip and breathing like a bull. You think we've got our man, don't you?" When Lani doesn't respond, he adds, "Just because two people Carver used to know are dead—one by a car accident and the other by suicide—doesn't mean he killed Tony. I understand stats well enough to know that doesn't prove causation."

Lani slows her bull breaths and pulls her lip out of her teeth. "I know, I know, I know. Sheesh, wasn't I the one lecturing you about tunnel vision? I'm keeping an open mind, I promise. But I'll say this: my focus on Carver just got a whole lot sharper."

When they reach Mark Carver's house, Lani finds him up in his hot tub, peering down at her through the wooden slats of the second story deck. Her presence clearly surprises him. Truth be told, he surprised her too. She wanted to snoop around out back a bit while Brian was in the front ringing the doorbell.

"Detective Whitaker." Carver scrambles out of the hot tub.

"No, no, don't get out." She stares up at him from below. "Don't want you to freeze to death. You always sit out here at seven in the morning?"

"You always make house calls at seven in the morning?"

"Touché," she says.

"I went on an early run." Carver sinks back into the hot tub. "I like warming up in the spa before I shower and get ready for work."

Spa, Lani thinks. *Well, la-di-da.*

She notices the beagle sitting near the dying tree at the back of the yard. He jumps up and gives her a tepid bark. When she heads his way, he wags his tail and sinks back down.

"It's Iggy, right?" Not waiting for an answer, Lani squats

next to the beagle. "You cold out here, bud?" He seems to welcome her touch and licks her hand. When she glances back, she sees Carver standing rigid in the hot tub, watching her with the intensity of a tiger, his body dripping water.

For feck's sake, does he think I'm going to steal his dog?

Lani pushes herself back to a stand. When she does, the oak's massive branches shake noisily. The motion surprises her. She didn't feel a gust of wind. She studies the tree, but when Brian calls out to her, she turns her partner's way.

He strides under the trellis, palms raised in question. "You coming or what."

Lani rubs Iggy's dog hair off her hands and points to the deck. Together she and Brian make their way to the far side of the house and climb the wooden steps to join their person of interest, who is once again submerged in the bubbling water. Chlorine fumes open Lani's sinuses and steam warms her face, and dang if she doesn't want to join the researcher for a soak. Instead, she zips her L.L.Bean coat higher and drags a heavy wrought-iron chair away from the table and over to the hoity-toity *spa*. Brian remains standing but leans against the nearby railing.

Carver looks back and forth between them. "Help me out here, guys. I'm a little confused. You sure you don't want to go inside?"

"Nah, this won't take long," Brian says. "We know you have to get to work." He continues with some light banter and innocuous questions about Tony Habib, putting Dr. Carver at ease.

When he tapers off, Lani takes over. "Hey doc, one of Tony's friends said there was a problem with his research. Know anything about that?"

A brief hesitation from Carver. "Not that I'm aware of. If Tony hit a snag, I'd be the first to know. What friend mentioned that?"

"So everything's hunky-dory with your weight-loss drug?"

Carver smiles. His wet shoulders glisten above the steaming water. "Everything's going great. We'll have it ready for human trials soon. Maybe Tony was running behind on some tests for the mice. Or maybe he was referring to a project for one of his classes. He could get pretty stressed out."

"Maybe," Lani says, as if no longer interested. She looks over at Brian. "Did I forget anything?"

Playing along, he shakes his head. "Nope. I think we're good to go."

Lani plops her hands on her thighs in a "let's roll" fashion and stands. She notices Carver's posture relax, his shoulders sinking deeper into the water. She thanks him for his time but then turns back. "Oh, wait, sorry, there was something else. I wanted to ask you about a former colleague of yours, back in California. Drove his car right off the road. That must've been awful for you and the other students."

A muscle in Carver's jaw contracts. Brief but there. Or is Lani simply seeing things she wants to see?

"His name was Keith, and you're right, detective, it was awful." The researcher tugs at his chin with a sudsy hand. "He was a friend of mine. His death traumatized our department."

"Were you two working on a drug together?"

"Me and Keith? No, not at all. We both had our own separate research."

"Dr. McDaniels mentioned you two fought over whose idea a weight-loss drug was. Is that the one you're working on now?"

With a splash, Carver bursts up from the water and climbs out of the hot tub, his torso sleek and firm, his toned legs hairy. He snatches a bath towel from the table and wraps his dripping body in it. When he turns to face them, his lips are dusky from the cold, and his expression looks fierce.

"I don't know what you're driving at, detective, but no, we were not working on a drug together, and I guarantee you

ZM6635 was entirely my creation. Now, I have to ask you to leave. I need to get to the university."

"Sure, no problem." Lani gives a thumbs up. "But first, I also wanted to ask about a former girlfriend of yours. Committed suicide. Must've been another tragic loss for you."

"Yes. It was," Carver says through clenched teeth. From cold or from fear, Lani isn't sure. "And I felt responsible, so yeah, thanks for bringing it up."

"Why would you be responsible?" Brian asks.

"Because I broke up with her a couple weeks before."

"Wow." Lani widens her eyes. "You must've been really special."

Carver has clearly had it. "Listen, I don't understand your little game here, but I can see you're somehow trying to implicate me in Tony's death, and that's insulting. Tony was a good friend and a valued researcher." Carver reaches for the handle on a set of French doors that appear to lead to a second-floor bedroom. "I'm going to shower and head to work. My job is doubled now that I have to take care of the mice. I'd like to say that if you have any more questions, you'll have to talk to my lawyer, but that'll only make me sound guilty." He glances toward the backyard and calls sharply for Iggy.

The dog bounds up and trots toward the house and then up the deck stairs. Lani swears he shoots her a take-me-with-you look before darting into the bedroom. Without another word, Mark Carver enters behind the beagle and slams the door shut.

"Oopsie," Lani says to her partner. "Methinks we made Dr. Prissy Pants mad."

As they make their way back to the car, Brian asks, "You believe him?"

"Not sure yet, but something's going on with him. Even his dog doesn't trust him."

"So what's our next move?"

"*My* next move, you mean. Today you should work on

some of those other cases Chief Toddler assigned you. Carver will be a long shot in French's eyes, and he won't want both of us wasting our time on that angle. But since he and the rest of the department are just waiting for me to crawl off and die, I'm going to call the families of Carver's former PhD buddy and former girlfriend. See if I can learn anything more about their deaths and about Dr. Carver himself."

"That's going to open up some old wounds."

"Yeah, it will," Lani says with genuine remorse. "But if we find out he's somehow involved, it'll also help heal them."

CHAPTER FIFTEEN

Catherine

Anguish floods my arboreal pores. If I could scream, I would wail until the crows and frogs and rushing creek all fell silent. The lady constable stood mere inches from me. She felt the shudder of my branches, a shudder that in my dying state took enormous strength to muster. Yet it was not enough to crack the most important of my boughs, the one that flanks the weapon buried deep within my bark.

It was all for naught. Her attention was drawn to her partner. And now the blood-stained letter opener remains tucked away inside me like a festering sore, the likes of which I haven't seen since working alongside Dr. Clifton.

My sorrow is so great that were it not for my ongoing hope (*folly* might be a better word) of somehow avenging Tony, I would be content to die at this very moment. Two deaths for one soul, first as a young doctor full of life, and second as a withered tree of no use to anyone beyond a source of shade for a beagle.

Yet even in my exhaustion and decay, Tony's spirit keeps me going. I'm not ready to surrender in defeat.

The lady constable seems highly intuitive. To me, to Iggy, to the earth around her. Even to Mr. Carver himself. I think she senses a bad air about him, just as I did before he confirmed my suspicions.

He must realize this, too, because the moment the constables left his deck, he was on his phone. The glass door leading to his bedroom was closed, and I couldn't hear his conversation, but my intuition tells me his call was to his investor, maybe to inquire about a lawyer. A man as rich and powerful as Mr. Harrison Price could hire the finest attorney around.

Could Mr. Carver really be responsible for the two deaths Constable Whitaker mentioned? And if so, are there others? Who would ever believe this social and accomplished homeowner could be capable of murder? Certainly not his sister.

I, on the other hand, have seen his evil side. With whatever inexplainable sensory tools I possess, I've seen it. And I believe the lady constable has seen it too.

Considering my own experiences as a student of medicine, it's lunacy for me to assume men like him are few and far between. I had hoped with the passage of a century and a half, humankind's depravity would pass. After all, hasn't civilization seen significant progress? A woman constable alone shows it has.

I wonder how she might have fared back in my day, with her strange, blunt hair and unflattering—but enviable—male-style clothing. Would she have found my murderer? Did anyone find my murderer? Perhaps my disappearance was never solved, my body never found. If it was, would I have metamorphosed into a tree? Knowing my parents might have spent their remaining days never learning the truth of my whereabouts squeezes my trunk with heartache.

A wood thrush lands on a branchlet and picks at my

failing buds. As it warbles a mournful trill, I wonder which one of us is sadder.

Like a fisherman's line, my state of despondency casts my thoughts back to another painful memory from my days as a woman, back when I suffered a terrible spell of illness after being poisoned.

It happened during another social gathering at the medical college, this time almost halfway into our second session of lectures. On a cold January day, with fireplaces crackling inside the community hall and stoves burning coal, a light meal of dumplings and tea sandwiches was served to the guests, topped off with cakes and pies from a bakery on Superior Street.

It was within one of my sandwiches or dumplings that someone sprinkled arsenic. Who or when, I'm not sure, but I'm convinced I was poisoned. Less than an hour after eating my meal, which fortunately I didn't finish, I left the building. As I pulled my cloak tightly over my dress, the wool fabric insufficient against the winter chill, an odd taste formed in my mouth. Nausea crept over me, and an acute cramp seized my abdomen, doubling me over in pain.

At the bottom of the building's steps, I vomited into the snow, one convulsive retch after another. After that, my muscles spasmed, and I fell to the icy ground. A handful of men—I was too overcome by pain to see who—ran to my aid and lifted me into a carriage. The driver snapped the horse's reigns and rushed me to the hospital.

After a few days in the infirmary, the retching passed, but the abdominal cramping and diarrhea persisted. My preceptor diagnosed an acute case of food poisoning. When I broached the possibility of arsenic, a chemical I well understood given it was my area of study for a Materia Medica assignment, Dr. Clifton frowned and, as if speaking to a child, said, "My dearest Catherine, that seems unlikely."

I held up my arm, its flesh the color of a flamingo's feathers. "Look at my pink skin. Isn't that a sign? And what of the rest of my symptoms?"

"I hate to say it, but if it were arsenic, an acute attack like yours would have killed you."

"It might have if I had finished my meal."

Thick with feverish emotion, I explained to my preceptor that while I was eating, Dr. Fitzgerald called me away to discuss our upcoming partnership. When I returned to my table, my plate had been cleared away, only half of my meal consumed.

"So you see, Dr. Clifton, there could have been arsenic in my food, placed by any number of men who resent me. Fortunately, I didn't receive the full dose."

"But Catherine, the Arsenic Act has restricted its sale, and you would have noticed its indigo color."

"You know as well as me that plenty of the older form still exists."

His response was a patronizing frown, and it was the only time I felt irritated with my preceptor. He was treating me as if I were a naive girl and not a doctor in the making.

My poisoning was never proved, but the incident nearly derailed my dreams. After six days in the hospital, I took to my bed for another two weeks, forcing me to miss three weeks of classes. As such, Curtis Mayfield, the lecherous Dr. Morrison, and the scornful Dr. Cartwright all insisted I withdraw from the class session. Doing so would make me ineligible to attend the commencement ceremony in March. I would have to apply for another session the following year, and who knew whether they would readmit me then? Rumors abounded that our progressive dean might soon leave his post.

"She has missed far too much material to catch up," Dr. Morrison said with an insufferable grin, probably still angry over my rebuff of his lewd advances one year prior.

"I'm in total agreement," Dr. Cartwright added, incensed over having a woman in his class, even though I hadn't mentioned his involvement in the grave robbing to anyone. "She must leave the college. It was madness to admit her."

Even Joseph Bridleman and Zachary Horton spoke up against me. Prior to that, aside from mocking me when I caught them performing their illicit dissection, they mostly grew neutral to my presence. Most likely this newfound animosity was because both men coveted the employment position Dr. Fitzgerald offered me. Although Curtis Mayfield had not similarly applied for the job, having his own father's clinic to join, he found it preposterous a "silly woman" would "steal" such a highly sought position away from more qualified men.

With hard work, determination, and the leniency of our sympathetic dean, I was able to regain my footing in my classes once I recovered enough to attend, but it was not without pain. An additional four weeks passed before I was free of stomach cramps. Dr. Clifton felt I had developed an ulcer as a complication. I spent days in the amphitheater and nights in my bed twisted in misery. Doing my best to ignore those gnawing clutches of an invisible poison, I fought to focus on my studies. I wouldn't grant my naysayers any excuses to wield against me and force my dismissal from the program.

To this day, even as a rooted tree, I'm convinced one of those men poisoned me, acting either to advance his own goals or to seek revenge over my audacity to want the same educational privileges as him. Men like Mr. Carver, who, unless the lady constable can prove his guilt, will walk away as freely as my poisoner and my murderer did, who perhaps were one and the same. It infuriates me that I'll never know who killed me. Like a tongue probing an empty socket, my mind endlessly digs at the mystery.

As for Mr. Carver eluding justice, unless I can find the strength to break the heavy branch that hides the deep crevice in my trunk and thereby draw Constable Whitaker's eyes my way, I can do nothing but let it happen.

My focus returns to the branch above it, where the acorns remain trapped. If I can control the act of snapping this smaller limb and free the acorns, then maybe, just maybe, I'll be able to do the same with the heavier branch should the lady constable return. No matter how impossible the task, I can't give up. I can't let the last of my arboreal breaths slip away—and with every passing day I'm aware this will happen soon, either at the hands of the arborist or Mother Nature herself—without fighting with every molecule I still possess.

I will not give up.

I will keep fighting for Tony.

CHAPTER SIXTEEN

Lani

Monday evening, after a long day of tracking down leads and putting the finishing touches on old case files before she gets booted out the detective door, Lani settles into her recliner with Old Henry's journal in her lap, reading glasses on her face, and a cup of tea in her hand. Maybe there's a finger of Jack Daniels in there as well. Who's around to tell her otherwise?

She found contact information for the sister of the PhD student who drove off the road in California and the mother of Carver's ex-girlfriend who committed suicide. She arranged by email to speak to each of them in the morning. No one wants memories of their loved ones' deaths stirred up before bed. Over the years, Lani has lost enough sleep of her own— regurgitating unsolved cases, brooding about getting older, distressing over her solitude which, during the day, suits her fine but at night sometimes comes with a vulnerable loneliness —so no, she doesn't need to make someone else lose sleep too.

Besides, letting things percolate for another day isn't a bad idea. Nothing tangible connects Carver to Tony Habib's murder. A personal hunch and the word of a gamer that there *might* have been a glitch with Tony's research that *might* have upset him isn't much to go on. Carver has a solid alibi from his philanthropic investor, and Chief Toddler will burst an aneurysm if Lani stirs up trouble for Harrison Price *the Third* without a shred of evidence.

She'll be leaving the department for good in less than four weeks. Why not slide toward the finish line like Chief Toddler is encouraging her to do? Why risk leaving with an embarrassing—and given Price's generosity to the Winston PD, costly—stain on her back? If she's smart, she'll make the final payment on that cruise she reserved, shop for a swimsuit that doesn't ride up her crack, and get ready to sip margaritas by the pool while the cruise director and a bunch of drunk people dance in a conga line past her.

Because she carries Old Henry's blood, that's why. Like scorpions, they need to go out stinging. Murder victims have nothing to look forward to six feet under. The least Lani can do is give them justice.

She stares at Henry Whitaker's marble urn on the mantle. "You made it to eighty-four in a century where you'd have been lucky to see sixty," she tells him. "Let's hope you weren't stingy with those longevity genes."

Shoving her unrest over Tony Habib's case aside, Lani turns her focus to the journal. She left off at a pivotal point. Her great grandfather had mentioned a "horrific act" committed against Catherine, making him think the person behind her disappearance was someone close to her. Lani picks back up at that point and starts reading.

"To investigate the possibilities," Henry writes in his minute scrawl, "I requested a meeting at the home of Dr. Isaac Fitzgerald, who was to be Catherine's employer had she not disappeared. I also requested the presence of her preceptor, Dr. Samuel Clifton. These two men were the least likely to want her dead and might be able to offer valuable insights.

"When I arrived at Dr. Fitzgerald's handsome abode behind Public Square, both men were waiting for me. Ruth Fitzgerald was also present, but after settling us in with tea and pound cake and affectionately tending to her husband, the gangly woman bade us adieu. Behind her, she toted a homely trunk on wheels, one with plaid flowers sewn onto its pink straps. She said her husband had added the wheels so she could transport the dresses she designs for local society women. Her spirit of independence made my heart ache over the loss of the lady doctor, whose disappearance I yearn to solve. I hold nothing but admiration for fellows (or ladies, in this instance) who are forced to swim against the tide of public opinion."

Lani can't help smiling. Old Henry was a progressive. She's proud to carry his DNA. Plus, his prose is more interesting when it offers personal insights, including his obvious crush on the "lady doctor."

She reads on. "Upon Ruth Fitzgerald's departure, we three men discussed Catherine's disappearance. I relayed to them that Joseph Bridleman, one of Catherine's classmates, had later admitted he suspected Catherine had been poisoned with arsenic at a school event.

"'Poisoned!' Dr. Fitzgerald exclaimed. Dr. Clifton, too, looked surprised. It appeared he had something to say on the matter, but then he shook his head and confirmed Catherine had indeed been violently ill and missed nearly three weeks of classes as a result. He then asked me why the now-graduated student, Joseph Bridleman, would make such a claim. I told him the young man approached me out of guilt. He felt he had not treated Miss Miller properly. He confessed she had endured both ridicule and hostility during their lecture sessions, even though she was clearly the best diagnostician in the class. It was those very skills that made him believe her when she told him she had been poisoned. He said he owed it to her to come forward. He had not come to her defense as a gentleman should, and for that he felt remorse.

"I then asked Drs. Fitzgerald and Clifton who they thought might have planted the poison, and as has often been the case during my investigation, Curtis Mayfield's name was among the first offered. According to Dr. Clifton, Mayfield despised Catherine's presence in the classroom and believed no woman was fit for the title of Doctor of Medicine. When I reminded Dr. Fitzgerald that both Joseph Bridleman and Zachary Horton had desired the position in his clinic, Dr. Fitzgerald felt neither of these students would commit murder to attain it. Given that Bridleman had come forward to me about the poisoning, I am inclined to believe the same, although this altruistic action could be a clever ruse on Bridleman's part. He never mentioned the incident the first time I questioned him.

"We also discussed Dr. Jedediah Cartwright, who was opposed to Catherine's attendance and had encouraged three male students to participate in a grave robbery (of which he has denied) and Dr. Frederick Morrison, who seemed smitten with Catherine in an impolite way. Despite these unprofessional displays, neither Dr. Fitzgerald nor Dr. Clifton could imagine the teachers guilty of murder.

"Unfortunately, after lengthy conversation, neither could they offer anything that might aid my case. Dr. Clifton, who seems bereft over Catherine's disappearance, asked me if Catherine could have met an accident in the woods. Dr. Fitzgerald had caught sight of her hurrying away on St. Clair Street, and her mother had mentioned Catherine's desire of a few moments alone.

"I assured him that was a possibility and could not be ruled out, although to this date no body has been found, making the theory less likely. I should also think her suitor, Mr. Mansour Younis, seems a less sure suspect, since he was not present at the banquet where she was poisoned. In my conversations with him (and despite my own personal feelings about him), his bereavement appears to be ongoing. Of course, appearances can be deceiving.

"Alas, as I close out this journal entry, I fear I am no closer to the truth today than when I started this investigation six months ago. There are many possible suspects and yet none I can prove, and with each passing day the trail grows colder. Meanwhile, my commander grows restless and wants my efforts placed elsewhere. 'You can't wrestle with this forever,' he tells me, but I should think nothing is further from the truth. Should I fail to discover what happened to Catherine Miller, my heart and conscious shall wrestle with her disappearance for years to come."

Lani gently closes the old book and removes her reading glasses. She rests her head back against the recliner and closes her eyes, her spiked tea long since gone cold.

I feel you, Great Grandpa Henry. I feel you.

CHAPTER SEVENTEEN

LANI

Wasting no time on Tuesday morning, Lani bursts through the double doors of the Winston police station, eager to make her scheduled phone calls. With her coat halfway off and her Glock pressing into her waist beneath her blazer, she ignores the ache in her knee joint and strides toward her desk in the left corner of the room.

The air in the open floor plan is already a nose-tingling mix of men's cologne and Anderson's farts. Anderson, a crude bulldog of a detective who does his best to grasp the Me Too movement but typically falls far short, has IBS that dwarfs her own and has no qualms about proving it. And yet, God help her, she loves the guy. If ever an extra hand is needed, whether following up on leads or making mind-numbing calls, Anderson is there.

Currently, he's on his phone two desks away. He flips Lani the bird in greeting, and she flips it back. Around her, personnel click on keyboards or shuffle like zombies as they try to wake up. Her partner is out checking a lead on a case that her retiring bones were ixnayed from, but the hope of finding something useful on Mark Carver keeps her resentment at bay.

Once she confirms Chief Toddler is tucked away in his glass playpen, bloviating at a young officer who stands rigid before him, she picks up the receiver of her desk phone and calls Fiona Bishop, a teacher in Ann Arbor who agreed to talk to Lani before her first class. She is Keith Bishop's sister, Keith being the former PhD student and colleague of Carver's who drove off a treacherous California highway six and a half years ago. While Lani waits for the woman to pick up, she swivels her chair and stares out the window at a nearby redbud tree, its sprouting rosy-pink blooms filling her with a rare sense of lightness.

After Fiona Bishop answers, they exchange a few pleasantries—small talk that Lani has worked hard over the years to improve.

"I do remember Mark Carver," Fiona says, "but only vaguely."

"So you met him?"

"Once. At a bar when Keith was out with some classmates. I'd stopped by for a drink because Keith, as usual, was trying to set me up with one of his friends."

"Mark?"

"No, someone else."

"How'd that work out?"

"Not great." Fiona laughs. "We dated for a few months but then split up. I'm thinking I'll be single forever."

"Nothing wrong with that. Eat when you want, sleep when you want, and no pee on the bathroom floor."

Fiona chuckles again. "I suppose that's true, but I don't remember much about Mark Carver, other than he was smart, good-looking, nice. Seemed like a cool guy all around."

Not exactly what Lani wants to hear. "Do you know if Carver and your brother ever fought?"

"Fought? As in a physical fight?"

"No, more like an argument."

"Not that I'm aware of. Like I said, I only met him that one night, and Keith never said anything to me about a falling out. The only reason I remember Mark is because he and my brother shared an interest in developing a weight-loss drug, one without all the side effects."

Lani stops fiddling with the stapler on her desk. "They were working on it together?"

"No, not really. They both had separate dissertations and research focuses. I think Keith's involved a medication for high blood pressure. It wasn't until their final year they started thinking about it. It didn't get far though." Fiona's voice softens. "Keith died a few months later. That was over six years ago now."

"I'm sorry for dragging it up," Lani says. "I wouldn't if I didn't think it was important."

"It's fine, but why are you asking all this? Has Mark done something?" Suspicion creeps into the teacher's tone. "To my brother?"

Lani hesitates. "My apologies if I gave that impression." Chief Toddler would kill her if he thought she was stirring up trouble for the Bishop family when she has zero evidence Carver had anything to do with Keith's death. "I'm just… uh…working out something with Dr. Carver on my end. Need a bit more information."

"Oh. Okay." Fiona doesn't sound convinced. "Well, that's really all I can tell you."

"No problem. I appreciate you taking the time. I'll let you get back to your classes now."

When they end the call, Lani stares at the blooming tree and the cloudy sky beyond. She thinks about Carver's weight-loss drug. Was it actually Keith's idea? Did Mark run the guy off the road out of greed? After all, a drug like that would sell faster than Oxy, and maybe Carver didn't want to share the benefits or the prestige.

Lani swivels away from the window. To her surprise, Chief Toddler is standing two feet away, arms crossed, jaw hard. Lani jumps, and her knee bangs the desk leg.

"Jeez," she yelps, rubbing the sting out of her joint. "You almost gave me a stroke." She wonders how much of her conversation with Fiona he overheard.

"You don't have enough loose ends on other cases to tie up?" French asks. "You have to go and call the sister of some guy who has nothing to do with Habib's case?"

Guess he was there long enough to hear me say 'brother.'

The chief smooths his gelled hair, which Lani has to admit looks perfect on camera when he preens for the masses. No chance in the world he uses her barber up in Edgewater.

"I should've never assigned it to you," French says.

Lani doesn't reply, but they both know why he did. No need to remind him about the lip-lock with the woman who wasn't his wife.

"Mark Carver has lawyered up," Chief Toddler says. "Honestly, I can't blame him. Claims you went to his house yesterday morning, snooping around, spying on him in his hot tub."

"Only two of the three are correct. I never spied on him."

"You think this is funny? You have nothing on Dr. Carver, and he has no motive, so how can that not be seen as harassment?"

"One of Tony Habib's friends said—"

"Yeah, yeah, Dupree filled me in. One of Habib's gamer friends mentioned there *might* have been a problem with his research—a problem his co-researchers say doesn't exist, mind you—and suddenly Dr. Carver is guilty of killing him? And because a couple people Carver once knew died from explainable causes? Do you realize how desperate that sounds?"

"Yeah, well, what else've we got?"

"That's supposed to be your job, right? To find out?"

Lani points to her phone. "What the feck do you think I'm doing?"

"I think you're reopening old wounds for people who don't deserve it. Guess who Carver hired for his lawyer."

"No idea."

"Your old buddy, Quinton Dunn." French emphasizes the word *buddy*, knowing full well Dunn is anything but Lani's buddy. "Dunn's a friend of Harrison Price, Carver's investor, and I have no doubt that played into it. He probably told Price about your troubles with him as a rookie, and now he'd like nothing better than to get back at you for going after Carver."

"Holy mother of murder, it really is an old boys' club out there, isn't it?" Lani says.

"Don't play that card with me. You seem to have done just fine in this business."

"Yeah, and what an easy road it's been." Lani lets her sarcasm linger in the air but grits her teeth to keep her ire from exploding all over the squad room. "And it wasn't *my* troubles as a rookie. It was Dunn's inability to do what was expected of him as a cop. I get it. Much easier to blame the rookie instead of the former chief of police's son. But it's not my fault he couldn't handle the job and slunk off to be a lawyer instead. For God's sake, you'd think this ancient book could finally be shelved."

French works his jaw back and forth, his hue the color of the redbud blooms outside. "Just stick to what's relevant to this case, that's all I ask. Don't go after Carver just because he reminds you of some jerk you used to know—or whatever your motive is. We don't need him suing us."

Or his investor cutting off the flow of green to the department, right, big guy? Lani thinks.

She salutes him. "Aye aye, chief."

As soon as he returns to his office, she picks up her phone and calls the next person on her list: Susan Walker, a librarian in Buffalo whose daughter, Cindy, once dated Mark Carver and then killed herself. Does Lani relish reigniting the woman's grief? God no. But does she feel she's onto something with Carver? Yes with a capital Y, and she won't let the philandering chief tell her otherwise.

As with Fiona Bishop, Lani already arranged a time to call Mrs. Walker. The woman answers on the first ring, and during their difficult conversation, Lani learns Cindy, a bakery manager who lived in a rented house west of Cleveland, swallowed a handful of sleeping pills two years ago and never woke up. When nothing more follows, Lani worries Chief Toddler might be right. Maybe there's nothing new to learn from these women. Although Mrs. Walker never met her daughter's boyfriend, she says Cindy was enamored with the university researcher and devastated when he ended the relationship.

"You see, detective, my daughter was…well, she was quite clingy. Needy really, especially after her father and I moved to Buffalo four years ago. And I imagine that neediness led to Dr. Carver breaking up with her."

When Mrs. Walker's weeping comes through the cellular airwaves, Lani feels fouler than the onion roots sprouting in her garden. She soothes the still-grieving mother as best she can and apologizes for the call. "I didn't want to upset you. I was just following up on some information."

"It's okay," Mrs. Walker says, seemingly collecting herself. "It's just so hard. Do you have any children, detective?"

Lani bites the inside of her cheek. "No." Feeling she owes this woman a little of her own pain, she adds, "Was never able to. Malformed uterus, or so I've been told. After a few miscarriages, I considered adoption, but my husband wasn't up for that." Four miscarriages to be exact, each one ripping out her heart and stomping on it.

"Oh, I'm sorry. That must've been difficult for you."

"It was." Lani clears her throat. "Okay then, Mrs. Walker, I'll let you go now. Thank you—"

"You know what still eats at me?"

"What?"

"My daughter was insecure, sure, but she also had a big heart, and she loved her dog as much as she loved her family. That's why I was surprised she would take her own life and leave him behind, especially without making sure he had a good home first. Not that we could take him, of course. We live in a condo with pet restrictions. But still, someone would have welcomed him in."

Lani's hand tightens around the receiver. "What happened to the dog?"

"That's just it. I don't know. I never saw him again. By the time a coworker found Cindy's body..." a pause while Mrs. Walker steadies herself again, "there was no sign of him. We assumed Iggy slipped out the doggy door and under the fence where he'd dug a hole, but we never knew for sure if—"

"I'm sorry, what did you say the dog's name was?" The hair on the back of Lani's neck stands up.

"Iggy. Oh, he was such a lovely beagle. About three years old at the time. Mostly brown and white, but he had the cutest black mark on his back. It looked like a saddle. My husband used to joke that..."

But Lani hears little else.

A beagle. Same breed as Mark Carver's dog.

With the same name.

She glances over at the chief's office. *That ain't nothing, chief. That ain't nothing.*

Did Carver take the dog as a parting gift right after he overdosed his clingy ex-girlfriend with sleeping pills?

Lani tries to remember if the marking on Iggy's back resembles a saddle. Can't. But what are the odds Carver would have the same breed of dog with the same name as that of his ex-girlfriend?

Pretty. Fecking. Slim.

CHAPTER EIGHTEEN

CATHERINE

On this late and cloudy afternoon, two compelling conversations take place at the same time at Mr. Carver's home, one inside the sliding glass door and the other in his driveway. Rattled, I'm unsure where to direct my focus. Just like in a massive storm, where the stimulation from the many elements overwhelms my senses, I struggle to catch it all.

Mr. Carver stands inside his peach kitchen, the sliding door still open. He speaks with emotion to someone on the phone while aggressively waving Iggy inside. The beagle, up on all fours at my base with his tail on high alert, doesn't obey. He, too, seems unsure where to turn his attention.

On the back portion of Mr. Carver's driveway, which I view above and through the trellis, Constable Whitaker stands next to her car and chats with Melissa, who's just left her brother's company. Melissa's own vehicle is hidden from my sight by the carriage house. A chilly wind blows the women's dark hair into their faces, and while the constable's locks are short and manageable, Melissa has to swipe hers out of her eyes and mouth.

Constable Whitaker introduces herself as a "friend" of Mr. Carver's and starts asking general questions, nothing sinister. She learns Melissa's married name is Taylor and that she has two children whose ages make them want nothing more to do with their mother and a husband who's too busy to care. Both women laugh at this, so I assume it's a joke, but it seems a sad one. I return my attention to Mr. Carver in his kitchen, his form shadowy behind the screen door.

"No, she's here now," he says. "Talking to my sister." A pause. "I have no idea, but it's the third time she's come. I need you here like ten minutes ago. That's what Harrison gave you the retainer for, right?" Mr. Carver ends the call. His elbow bangs the wood frame along the sliding door, and I feel his cursing as much as I hear it.

I return to Melissa, who's just started her car. She backs up in the driveway, careful not to hit the lady constable's vehicle, and waves as she departs. Constable Whitaker, dressed in a shapeless coat and unflattering pants that fall shy of her manly shoes, makes her way toward the stone pathway that leads to the front door. Before she disappears from my view, she pauses and ventures into the backyard instead, admiring the trellis and its flanking flowering bushes as she walks beneath it. Maybe she wants to surprise Mr. Carver again, just as she did yesterday morning when he was taking a soak in his steam tub.

She looks my way, and as she strolls toward Iggy and me, a rush of excitement jolts my branchlets into a disjointed shake.

"Hey, beautiful girl." She pats my dry bark, her fingers showing the swell of arthritis. "Still here, I see. You're a real fighter."

At her touch, every one of my senses alights, and a childish hope runs through me. Surely this time she'll notice my deep fractures. Glance up and discover the crevice that hides the weapon that killed Tony. Her round cheeks are pink from the cold, and her nose runs a clear stream that she wipes away with the back of her hand, but it doesn't matter. To me she's a fortress of beauty and strength, albeit a rather short one.

She leans down to pet Iggy. He wags his tail and sniffs at the laces of her thick shoes.

"Hey, Iggy, how're you doing?" Constable Whitaker's tone is playful, and a smile forms on her normally impassive face. "Let's take a look at you, shall we?" She rubs her hand over the dark patch of fur on his back. "Well, whaddaya know. Looks like you're wearing a saddle." For some reason this seems to delight her.

"Oh, crap," Mr. Carver says loudly enough from his kitchen to draw my attention back.

He hurries out through the sliding door and rushes toward us, phone still clutched in his hand. He wears pants he's referred to as *jeans* and a thick shirt with a hood and a zipper.

"Detective, I'm starting to think you've got a thing for me." His words sound jovial, but his tight smile suggests otherwise.

Constable Whitaker stands and rubs her hands on her trousers. "Forgive me, Dr. Carver. Just admiring your dog. Got a chance to meet your sister too."

Mr. Carver's pretend cheer fades. "And?"

"And nothing. She's nice. Says you two have always been close. She's what, two years older than you?"

"Yes, and we *are* close. I'm lucky to have her. Life wasn't much fun as a fat kid."

"That why you got into the pharmaceutical business? To make a weight-loss drug?" The lady constable glances at her watch and raises an eyebrow. "And apparently to finish work early?"

"I like research. And four thirty isn't that early."

Their conversation is stilted and awkward. Mr. Carver's

gaze flits nervously back and forth between the lady constable and me, but only he and I know why. As they verbally dance around each other, I try to move the thick branch that hides the letter opener. I manage nothing but a general rattle of my smaller limbs, an act which, given the wind, draws no attention. Even that trifle attempt tires me.

"I imagine there's a lot of pressure on you to get a drug like that right," Constable Whitaker says, Iggy's snout resting on her shoe. "Your investor is probably chomping at the bit to sell it to the highest bidder."

"Why are you here, detective?" Mr. Carver waves a hand toward the house. "Why don't we head inside? It's going to rain soon."

Oh no. I'll lose my chance if I don't act quickly. I muster another round of strength and direct all my energy onto my lowest branch. With the amount of effort required, it feels as though I'm trying to squeeze an ocean through a hollow reed. An unfamiliar pressure builds inside me. To my delight, I invoke a respectable arboreal contraction, enough to make those troublesome acorns trapped in the higher limb shift and clatter against each other. Sadly, they don't fall, and neither does the lower branch that shields the bloody weapon.

The lady constable shakes her head at Mr. Carver's invitation to go inside, and if she noticed my branches rustling she gives no indication. She probably assumed it was the wind.

"No need," she tells Mr. Carver. "I won't keep you long. I just wanted to ask you about Iggy." At the sound of his name, the beagle's snout pops up from her shoe, and his tail wags anew.

"Iggy?" At first Mr. Carver seems perplexed, but then he stiffens. "What about him?"

"Remind me how you got him again?"

With a feverish intensity, I work once again to compel the branch near the letter opener to crack and fall.

"From a shelter," Mr. Carver says.

"Oh, right. I remember you told me that. I'd like the name of that shelter, please. It's funny though because Cindy Walker? Your former girlfriend who committed suicide? She had a beagle named Iggy too. What are the odds of that?"

At this canon-ball piece of news, my focus on the branch stumbles.

"Her dog disappeared after she killed herself," Constable Whitaker says. "Did you know that?"

"I had no idea." Mr. Carver sounds convincing, but I've heard him lie enough times to know he does it with little effort. "I figured her family had him. But I loved her dog. That's why I got one like him. Named him Iggy as a way of memorializing Cindy, you know?"

If I could scoff aloud, I would. His pathetic explanation reminds me of the male classmates who taunted me one moment, only to pretend it was all in fun the next.

"Well, see, Dr. Carver, that's confusing because Mrs. Walker told me her daughter's dog had black fur in the shape of a saddle on his back, and sure enough, so does he." The lady constable points to Iggy's marking, the same saddle shape I myself have noted. "It's as if yours and Cindy's dogs are twins."

Mr. Carver shivers in his light clothing. Time is not on my side. I must hurry. I must break that branch, or at least crack it widely enough so she notices the deep crevice next to it. With a ferocity I thought I no longer possessed, I pour all my energy and thought into breaking the telltale branch. Once again, I push that ocean through the hollow reed. Everything else fades. Their voices. The rush of the wind. The darkening clouds that will soon spill rain.

A branch snaps. Forcefully. A splattering of acorns falls to the dirt and grass below me. Mr. Carver whips his head in my direction and then at the acorns on the ground. It was the wrong branch, but I pray it's enough to make the intuitive constable examine my concealed nooks and crannies.

But to my chagrin, she doesn't. Instead, she maintains her keen gaze on Mr. Carver, her attention focused only on the accusation of a stolen dog.

"Maybe your Iggy and Cindy's Iggy aren't twins at all," she says. "Maybe they're the same dog. Which would mean you were there when she killed herself. *If* she killed herself, that is."

Like the marionettes my father used to display in his store window at Christmas, Mr. Carver opens his mouth, closes it, and opens it again. Before any lying words fly out, an older man dressed in a suit and overcoat comes running into the backyard. His thin hair lifts in the wind, and his voice carries over the rain that has just started splattering my branches.

"Detective Whitaker, quit harassing my client," the newcomer hollers.

Despite his shivering, Mr. Carver's posture relaxes. With his sleeve, he wipes raindrops from his face.

The lady constable plants her man shoes in a wide stance and curls her lip. "Right on cue, Dunn. Heard the doc's investor hired you. Must've known what great pals we are. But really, with all those millions Price has, you're the best he could do? A has-been cop turned inept lawyer?"

If only I could have spoken to Curtis Mayfield with such boldness, maybe he would have left me alone. But although my admiration for Constable Whitaker climbs higher, anguish overwhelms me because the last opportunity I will likely ever have to expose the murder weapon has passed. My strength is depleted. This lawyer will no doubt make sure Constable Whitaker never sets foot on Mr. Carver's land again.

Then poor, beautiful Tony will never see justice.

And my incessant, inexplicable existence will have been for nothing at all.

CHAPTER NINETEEN

LANI

Three hours after Lani paid Dr. Mark Carver his third surprise visit, she still itches with restlessness. Worry, too, because she hopes she didn't show her cards too early by mentioning Iggy. Might have been a rookie mistake, but she assumed her knowledge of Cindy Walker's missing dog would rattle the researcher enough that he'd let something slip. He might have, too, if Dunn hadn't shown up and zipped his client's lips.

Will Carver get rid of Iggy now? Lani hopes not. That sweet dog doesn't deserve to be dragged into this.

Nah. Carver is smart enough to know doing so would only sharpen Lani's focus on him. But she might have given him the chance to cover his tracks and somehow prove ownership of the dog.

To distract herself from the endless rumination, she waters her plants, plucks weeds from her vegetable garden despite the brisk weather, and makes a pot of chili that in an hour will no doubt give her gas like Anderson's. The more time that passes, the more confident she is that Mark Carver is a murderer. Not just of Tony Habib, but possibly of at least one, if not two, other people.

The hurdle to leap is finding the evidence to prove it. Is a stolen dog enough? Because really, same name, same breed, same fur pattern? It's enough for her, but will it be enough for the judge she sent a request to earlier? She crosses her knobby fingers it will be.

Even reading the rest of her great grandfather's journal and sipping Jack-Daniels-laced tea doesn't calm her antsiness. If anything, it worsens it because Old Henry was as unsatisfied in his remaining days as she's proving to be. He never learned what happened to Catherine Miller. Even though his journal entries grew years apart and his notes less detailed, he never stopped obsessing about the "fine lady doctor with a bright future who disappeared somewhere off Cleveland's St. Clair Street." It's now called St. Clair Avenue but still very much around.

Did Catherine wander off and suffer an accident as some suggested to Old Henry? Or did she run away, fearing she couldn't handle her new role as a doctor? It's clear Old Henry didn't think so. In the last entry dated May 3, 1905, at which time he would have been seventy-five years old, he remained convinced the young medical-school graduate was murdered.

At least Old Henry put some things to rest. He deduced Curtis Mayfield (whom Lani now pictures as Mark Carver in her mind) poisoned Catherine at the school social event. On further questioning, "the disagreeable lad" finally copped to it, but only after realizing it was better to be charged with poisoning the woman than to be charged with killing her, which was what Henry had threatened to do.

Curtis also admitted to planting a severed foot in Catherine's room after their first day of class sessions, but he adamantly denied killing her. "I only did those things to scare her off. Medicine is no place for a woman. But with God as my witness, I didn't kill her," he pleaded to Henry.

Sure, Curtis boy, sure, Lani thinks. *You're as sweet and innocent as Ted Bundy.*

But even if Old Henry suspected Curtis Mayfield was the culprit behind Catherine's disappearance, he had no proof the young man was guilty of anything beyond arsenic poisoning, for which he was later punished. Like Henry, Lani suspects Curtis was the murderer, but given the number of women killed by their boyfriends or husbands, Mr. Mansour Younis remains high on her list too. Without a body or a confession, though, Henry's nineteenth-century hands were tied. Much like Lani, he struggled to find something tangible, and it's clear from his increasingly disgruntled words he never did.

She ponders her great grandfather's situation, her tea warming her throat, her plants silent in their motionless observation. Then she shakes her head and brings her recliner to its upright position with a thud.

"Nope," she says out loud. "Henry might not have had a body, but I do. That and the dog of a dead woman. One way or another, I'll get this guy."

She retreats to her bedroom for the night, hoping sleep will come.

Miraculously, sleep does come, and the next morning Lani enters the station with a full cup of coffee and an even fuller cup of enthusiasm. Something good is about to happen with the Tony Habib case, she feels it. Even her still-burning chili gut can't break her buoyed sense of expectation.

In a rare display of sunshine, she smiles and says hello to everyone she passes in the corridor, including the annoying public service officer who works the front desk and nibbles her afternoon Snickers bar like a rabbit.

Lani greets the cops in the squad room with the same cheer, some hunkered over their messy desks, others loitering around and shooting the breeze. She even tosses a nod to Chief Toddler inside his glass castle. His return greeting is far less congenial. Good thing he's on the phone.

"Well, well, well," Anderson says, slipping into a sportscoat that hides the bulge of his Glock but struggles to contain his shoulders. "Look who got laid last night. Hope you *rode* him his rights good and hard." Then, like a child realizing he's just said something he shouldn't, he covers his mouth and offers a sheepish, "Oops."

After a career full of similar comments, albeit less frequently in the new millennium, Lani knows how to stomp them out. Her days of putting up with innuendos and double entendres are behind her. But for Anderson, who's a hell of a detective but slow on the sexual-appropriateness uptake, she makes an exception.

"Yep," she replies. "And your brother said he's never had better."

A boisterous laugh erupts from the man, followed by amused chortles from her colleagues, most of whom she likes and all of whom she respects.

Her partner, Brian, enters from the back hallway, probably having just whizzed away his Venti Starbucks and the energy drink he chases it down with. Given his explosion of morning caffeine seems to be his only vice, Lani holds back her opinion. Usually. She wonders if that woman is still bothering him.

"Hey boss." He joins her at her desk.

She removes her coat and drapes it over the back of the chair. If she gets what she requested from the judge, she'll need the jacket again soon. "I'm your partner, not your boss, Einstein."

"Did you know the word *partner* comes from the Old French word *parçonier*?" he asks. "It means coheir."

"Shut up or I'll demote you."

He laughs and shoves her potted philodendron out of the way so he can perch on the corner of her desk. "Did you really go back to Carver's place last night?"

"Guilty as charged, but it was more like four thirty in the afternoon. How'd you know? I was planning on surprising you with something juicy." Lani rubs her hands together and licks her lips, which still carry the sting of jalapeño from last night's chili.

Brian flicks a sideways glance toward Chief Toddler's office. Although still on the phone, French is eyeing them, a pen flipping back and forth between his fingers like the tail of an angry cat.

"Guess he's heard I went back again too, huh?" Lani says.

"Yep."

"Whatever. He'd have found out soon enough because guess what? You know Carver's dog? That little beagle named Iggy?"

"Yeah."

"Cindy Walker, the ex-girlfriend who supposedly committed suicide because she couldn't get over the marvelous Dr. Carver, had a beagle named Iggy."

Brian cocks his head. "You're kidding me."

"And guess what else? I talked to Cindy's mom—that's how I learned about the dog—and she claims her daughter's Iggy ran off after Cindy killed herself. Everyone assumes he snuck out the doggy door and burrowed his way under the fence, never to be seen again."

"Man, I picked the wrong day to be working a different case."

"Nah. I'm glad you were off doing something else. You don't need my stink on you. Chief Toddler's wrath should be on me alone."

"You're grinning like an evil warlord," Brian says. "Why do I get the feeling you're about to toss me another bombshell?"

"Because Mrs. Walker also told me that Cindy's Iggy had a patch of black fur in the shape of a saddle on his back. And—"

"So does Carver's Iggy," Brian finishes for her. He shoots up from her desk. "So that's what you went to his place to confirm."

Lani nods and returns her plant to its rightful place. "There the dog was, sitting by that massive dying oak, a big ol' saddle mark on his back. No wonder Carver nearly fell out of his hot tub when I went by that tree. He was worried I'd look too closely at the dog."

"How did he justify it?"

"Says he got the dog at a rescue and named him Iggy as a tribute to Cindy."

"Bull. That's easily confirmed with a call to the shelter."

"That's why I like you, kid."

"Oh, you like me now, do you?" Brian wiggles his eyebrows.

"Unfortunately, by the time I asked Carver for the shelter's name, his lawyer showed up. Quinton Dunn, can you believe it? Carver says he doesn't remember the rescue's name. Some farm-based set-up a couple hours away that's since closed."

"Bull again."

"Exactly. I imagine Carver wishes he would've said he got Iggy from an old girlfriend, back when I first asked him about the dog. Cindy Walker wasn't on my radar then. I was just making small talk. Would've made things a lot easier for him."

"Probably didn't want anything to draw our attention Cindy's way, not realizing we'd get there ourselves," Brian says. "But as incriminating as that dog is, it's not proof Carver killed Cindy, and certainly not proof he killed Tony Habib."

"No, but hopefully we'll have something else soon."

Brian narrows his eyes. "Why? What did you do?"

"I'll tell you what she's done," Chief Toddler bellows, storming toward them in a well-tailored suit that probably set him back a couple grand. "I got a call last night from Quinton Dunn. He says you're still harassing his client. And this morning?" French points toward his office. "I had the wonderful pleasure of listening to the mayor berate me over the fact that one of my detectives—a *seasoned* detective who should know better, by the way—is hassling a university researcher who's funded by the same guy who might've paid for that Glock in your holster and that computer on your desk."

French takes a breath but, to Lani's misfortune, continues. "He says you just popped up at Dr. Carver's place again, berating him about his dog of all things. You're barking up the wrong tree here, Whitaker, and you're wasting everyone's time. Not to mention Carver's lawyer has a personal vendetta against you, so yeah, that should turn out great. He's already threatened to sue the department. I should've never given you this case. Why can't you just coast to the finish line like a normal cop?" French pauses his tantrum, but if he expects a response from Lani, he doesn't get one. His nostrils twitch, and he adds, "Redirect your investigation or I'm pulling you off."

With a bit of drama, Lani rises to a stand and pushes her desk chair back with her legs. Because her mood is a Teflon Shirley Temple this morning, she explains in a calm and courteous manner to Chief Toddler what she learned about Iggy the dog. When she sees the shift in his expression, as if he, too, finds the same-name, same-breed, same-fur-marking thing a *taaaaad* suspicious, she figures there might still be some cop left in him after all. The room falls silent, and she feels everyone's attention on them, save for those who have to answer their ringing phones.

After a long beat, French grunts his acknowledgement. "It's weird, I'll give you that, but it proves nothing. Maybe it was her dog, maybe it wasn't. Has nothing to do with Habib's case."

"It does if Carver is a serial murderer," Lani says.

At that moment, her blazer pocket erupts with the heart-stopping ringtone she has yet to change. She whips out her cell phone and answers. "Yep, yep, you got it. And thank you again."

When she hangs up, French and Brian stare at her expectantly.

"Well, boys, hopefully I'll be holding that proof soon, because I just got us a search warrant on Carver's place."

"The dog was enough?" Brian sounds a little incredulous.

"That, the former colleague's death, the ex-girlfriend's suicide, the question of a problem with the research. String it all together and the judge saw my point. Well, didn't hurt that years ago, when he was still a public defender, I made soups and casseroles for him when his wife was sick with breast cancer. See?" Lani says to Chief Toddler. "I can be nice."

He doesn't take the bait. Simply works his tongue back and forth inside his lower lip.

"So, are you taking me off this case or not?" Lani raises her palms. "If you are, I doubt I need to tell you that if you're wrong and Carver is guilty, you'll look awfully bad for steering me away from investigating him."

The chief's jaw turns to stone. Lani is surprised he hasn't bitten off his own tongue.

After a string of curse words, he says, "Whitaker, you better be right about this."

CHAPTER TWENTY

C ATHERINE

In my despondency over failing to make the lady constable notice the murder weapon hidden inside my bark yesterday, I might as well die today. What reason is there left to live?

My emotions heave and crash, and like Lake Erie during a storm, they drown me with their intensity. I was so close, so close to making her see. Those fallen acorns, which I have strained for months (years?) to release, were not enough to make her understand. Why should they be? It was madness to think otherwise. At least the squirrels, who were grateful for the mid-April feast and have since snatched the acorns away, got something out of the deal.

Something out of the deal. That is an idiom I've heard characters utter in those movies that flash like magic on Mr. Carver's outdoor screen.

But Tony? Tony got nothing out of the deal.

Still, in between my waves of self-pity, determination finds me. Did I admit defeat as a woman navigating a man's world? Did I wilt under the cruelty of Curtis Mayfield, or the lecherous Dr. Frederick Morrison, or my own critical brother? I did not, and I can't here either.

Even the most unlearned child can see my tree is not long for this world though. Despite the recent cold spell, nature springs to life around me, but my branches remain barren and brown like a dendritic corpse. Oh, a few leaf buds here, a tiny drop of sap there, but I'm no more than a crippled woman in the final breaths of life.

Every mysterious and wondrous sensation I've experienced in these many years has dulled: the fluttering of my leaves by a breeze, the tickles of scurrying critters over my branches, the earthy moisture of the creek that bathes my roots in a downpour. My keen perceptions are a mere fraction of what they once were, and I no longer sense that communal energy from my fellow trees. Even my thoughts are less sharp.

Will I make it to another fall? Whether woman or tree, it's always been my preferred season, with its autumnal hues and crisp air. Or will Mr. Carver's arborist return before then? He mentioned a delay at his initial consultation, but does a delay mean weeks or does it mean months? If I'm not agonizing over my ineptitude to bring Tony justice, I'm agonizing over the arrival of the tree-cutter's saw, both for my own demise and for the permanent removal of the murder weapon it will bring.

And yet, a fickle spirit pokes through my dejection once again and reminds me I can't lose hope. Where there is still life, there is opportunity, and should God see fit and find me worthy, I might still have the chance to help Tony. This is what I must believe.

My thoughts grow tedious, and with no Iggy at my base to talk to, the beagle tucked away in the house while Mr. Carver is at work, I surrender myself to the nature around me. This submission is the healthiest way I've found to hold onto my sanity in this prolonged existence. The songs of sparrows and robins soothe me. The vibrations from the passing cars on the woodland road lull me into a daze. The scent of the sprouting soil satiates my restlessness. Circling me, beauty radiates in all four directions, both God-made and man-made, and despite my bouts of boredom or my frustration at whatever bizarre molecular reaction transformed me, I'm grateful to be part of it.

Sometimes I—

Like a scream that shatters a peaceful dream, squealing tires on the driveway break my trance. If I had a heart, it would leap out of my trunk and into my highest branch, its pulse thumping in surprise. Behind the cumulus clouds, the sun's positioning confirms it's now afternoon, but the hour seems too early for Mr. Carver's return. It's his car and not the arborist's, and that at least quiets some of my alarm.

When the carriage house door lifts completely, Mr. Carver pulls in and jerks the car to a stop. Through the little windows near the outbuilding's roof, I watch him spill out of the vehicle and rush through the side door. When he reappears under the trellis and speeds toward the house, his phone is already in hand. Who he's talking to I don't know.

"How close are you? Good. Hurry." His tone is feverish. "They'll be here soon."

Who? Who will be here soon? Mr. Carver is inside his house before I find out.

Is it the arborist? Would the homeowner return in such haste for that?

My figurative heartbeat soars anew.

Moments later, the sliding door bangs open, and Iggy bounds out. Mr. Carver remains shielded in his kitchen, the door once again closed. I hear nothing of his conversation, and oh, how I want to hear his conversation. He paces back and forth behind his breakfast table and rubs his left temple with his knuckles as if in pain.

Iggy runs about, leaving his mark on several bushes. When he finishes his rounds, he scratches and sniffs at my tree. The poor thing shivers but doesn't race back to the house.

Hello, doggie, I say to him, longing to nuzzle him close. This sweet beagle shouldn't have to suffer a murderous master, no matter how charming Mr. Carver is on the outside. As if aware of my thoughts, the dog shakes and whimpers, his paws gently digging near my roots. Does he sense I'm dying? Does he feel there is more to me than bark and dwindling leaves? I imagine he will never find out.

No sooner has Iggy settled into his comfort spot at my base than Mr. Carver once again whips open the sliding door. "Get away from there, Iggy. Come! Now!"

The dog whimpers again, and his tail droops, but he stays put.

No longer on the phone, Mr. Carver curses at the beagle and hollers, "I can't have you there right now."

Why? What's happening? A whisper of energy awakens inside me.

Mr. Carver charges out of the house toward Iggy. "I *said* get away from there."

The homeowner's snarl and angry stomping prompt Iggy to dart away from the tree. This cruel behavior makes me want to stab Mr. Carver with a branch. No sooner have I had the thought than a small limb from my midsection plummets to the ground.

Iggy scampers into the house. Mr. Carver turns to follow him but then stops. He pivots around again and trots the remaining distance back to me. He stares at my tree for a long, frightening moment, and I half expect him to speak to me, as if he is aware of my presence. Maybe he feels the same malevolent air from me that I feel from him.

He tugs on the thick branch that abuts his murder weapon's hiding place. Although the limb is cracked and a few strokes of the arborist's saw would remove it, it remains secure. Still, panic seems to swallow Mr. Carver's anger toward Iggy. He stares at the creek to my south, then back at me, and then rotates in a full circle as if looking for something.

What is it? I want to ask, almost as much as I want to thump him over the head.

"Would they search a freaking tree?" he mumbles to himself, thereby answering my question while also leaving me confused. *Who's they?*

"What was I thinking?" He scratches roughly at his hair, which is mussed and falling over his forehead.

Is the arborist coming? Is Mr. Carver worried the weapon will be found? Is he searching for a new place to hide it?

Now I am as panicked as him. The distress causes a flutter through my branches, and another brittle twig breaks free and joins my fallen parts on the ground.

A vehicle pulls into the driveway. It's not the arborist's black truck. I heave a shudder of relief, losing yet another one of my tiny branchlets. A second car follows. It's Constable Whitaker's. Then a third car arrives and pulls off to the side of the road. Before it disappears from my sight, I read the word *Police* through the trellis.

A greater burst of energy swells inside me. Mr. Carver stands there, seemingly frozen.

They have come back. They have come to arrest him. That smart lady constable discovered something that proves his guilt, I'm sure of it.

Here I am! I wish to shout. If I could, I would jump up and down like a child. *Look! Look! Peer into my crevices, and you'll find all the proof you need.*

CHAPTER TWENTY-ONE

CATHERINE

Constable Whitaker must have noticed Mr. Carver in the backyard because she strides our way. Her partner joins two uniformed police officers and takes the stone pathway toward the front door. A jumble of voices and slamming car doors suggest other people are present as well, hidden from my view not only by the house but from my inferior vision up high.

A man in a suit and overcoat hurries to catch up with the lady constable. He spews words like "harassment" and "personal vendetta," and I recognize him from his visit yesterday as the lawyer, Quinton Dunn. The lady constable seems to share an unhappy past with him. Given their history, he must be of similar age to her, but his poor posture and deep facial lines make him appear years older.

Mr. Carver has moved far away from my tree, his reason for doing so obvious only to me. All three of them appear uncomfortable in the near-winter temperature. Constable Whitaker clasps the top button on her coat to cover her neck. The lawyer blows into his hands, and Mr. Carver pulls his blazer more closely around him, not having had the foresight to fetch his coat before dragging poor Iggy back into the house. The wind whips their hair into unflattering patterns, especially the thin locks of the lawyer, and all three seemed determined to make something happen. I imagine that each of those somethings is very much at odds with the other.

"This search warrant is unlawful. You have no right." The lawyer's bluster sounds similar to that of the windbags of my past.

The lady constable ignores him. "Dr. Carver, I have a warrant to search your place. I'm sure Mr. Dunn gave you a heads-up. Tough to keep secrets in this scratch-my-back world."

She thrusts out a sheaf of papers that flap in the wind. Her words and actions remind me of the detectives I've seen in Mr. Carver's movies, and I can't help but feel a swell of pride in watching her. Had she lived in my time, we would have been friends.

"Go inside and let my officers in," the lady constable demands.

Mr. Carver shoots a pleading look the lawyer's way and starts to say something, but the lawyer cuts him off. "This is unlawful," Mr. Dunn repeats. "You can't—"

"My guys'll dust for prints, look for evidence, you both know the drill," Constable Whitaker says.

"Of course they'll find Tony Habib's fingerprints in there." Mr. Dunn's tone drips with outrage, as if the notion of a search is ridiculous. "He's been to Dr. Carver's home many times. No doubt you'll find his hair and DNA all over too."

The lady constable shrugs, but a shadow of frustration tightens her face, as if she has surmised the same. She orders Mr. Carver once again to unlock his front door and let the police in.

"Go ahead, Mark." The lawyer smooths his wayward hair, but it immediately lifts back up in the wind. "But you don't have to say anything, nor should you. This is all a farce on Detective Whitaker's part. She blames me for her ruined cop-reputation long ago, and this is all payback." He lifts a corner of his mouth in a smug smile. "I guess what they say about women is true: they can sure hold a grudge."

I want to slap this old fool across his pendulous jowls, but the lady constable remains calm.

"You know what else they say about women?" she asks. "They say we get things done."

If I could clap my branches together, they would create a symphony of applause for that response.

A voice from the side of the house calls out, and I recognize Constable Whitaker's partner.

"Hey, boss, we're freezing our butts off. Tell Carver to get over here and let us in, or we'll break the door down."

Mr. Carver shakes his head in obvious frustration, perhaps fear, too, and storms off. He enters through the sliding door into his kitchen. If only he would have turned back for another glance at me. Maybe the lady constable would wonder about his interest. Go searching about my trunk. Regardless, I summon my newfound ripple of energy and force my full attention on pushing that metaphorical ocean through that hollow reed and breaking that blasted branch. A small crack is my reward. I want to celebrate this achievement but hold back. Although my precision is improving, I have a long way to go before the thick branch falls.

Before I can gather my dwindling strength for another attempt, the two longtime enemies turn away and move toward the house. The lawyer clings to the constable's heels like an annoying handkerchief stuck to the bottom of her shoe. He tells her that just because two people Mr. Carver once knew are dead and one of them had a dog named Iggy doesn't mean the man's privacy should be invaded.

Constable Whitaker enters through the sliding door. "Come on, Dunn. You can do better than that."

Beyond the kitchen and dining room windows, as well as the portion of the parlor I can see past the kitchen, bodies move about inside Mr. Carver's house. I'd like to observe them, but it's important I keep my focus on the branch. Try to crack it a little bit more but not so much that I expend all my energy before Constable Whitaker returns.

If she returns.

I try not to linger on that thought.

How long I nudge at the branch, I'm not sure, but after perhaps two hours' shifting of the sun, Mr. Carver, now dressed in a coat, bursts out of the house. Mr. Dunn follows behind him. A young police officer exits through the sliding door as well. With arms crossed over his bulky jacket, the officer stands on the patio and watches Mr. Carver, maybe to make sure he does nothing suspicious.

"I know this is hard." The lawyer follows the researcher to the fire pit. "But it'll be over soon."

Mr. Carver prepares to start a fire, but he doesn't get far before the police officer calls out, "Please don't do that, sir. Not until we've searched it."

"Oh, for God's sake." Mr. Carver moves closer to the creek but keeps a distance from me.

The lawyer pulls his coat more tightly around his broad belly. "Maybe we should go inside. It's colder than Detective Whitaker's heart out here."

If he's expecting a laugh from Mr. Carver, he doesn't get one. Nor from me.

"Go ahead, but I'm about to explode." Mr. Carver's face is the color of the fire he wishes to build. "They're going to take my computer and phone, aren't they?"

"Yes, but not your work computer at the university. The warrant doesn't cover that. They're not going to…find anything on your personal laptop or phone are they? Incriminating emails? Voice messages? Texts?"

"Of course not," Mr. Carver says with an angry certainty.

"Tony only spoke face-to-face with me about the mice so we wouldn't leave a—"

"No." Mr. Dunn holds up a hand and lowers his voice. "Don't tell me anything else. I don't want to know if you had anything to do with Tony's death. I only want to prove you didn't."

"They won't find anything," Mr. Carver repeats, looking my way.

Several minutes pass in silence. By the time the police team moves outside, the sun has shifted another ten degrees. Soon a handful of men and women, some in uniform, some not, some carrying equipment, some not, are searching Mr. Carver's yard in what appears to be an organized fashion, directed by the lady constable. They perform various tasks I don't understand, using devices I've never seen, including a long metal tool that sweeps over the ground and periodically beeps. When it does, a coin or a piece of scrap is dug from the ground.

Once I understand the tool's purpose, I strain to use mental powers I don't possess to bring one of those metal sweepers my way. One pass up my bark will give the police everything they need to bring justice to Tony.

But the officers don't. They sweep the lawn. They sweep the edges of the creek. They even sweep areas outside the main backyard and into the wooded acreage beyond.

But they don't sweep me.

My sinusoids ache with invisible tears. Mr. Carver has found the perfect hiding spot, after all.

He, too, must sense this because his stance becomes less angry and more confident. His lawyer checks his phone and whispers off and on to Mr. Carver. The lady constable and her partner seem interested in the creek, but other than pieces of trash and an occasional rodent, they'll find nothing there.

All around me is human activity. Human voices and human peculiarities. The wildlife has scattered. I keep willing my branch to crack further, but with each passing minute, I fear it's futile. My energy has dwindled. My spirit is trampled.

Soon Constable Whitaker appears as dejected as me. Her face hangs long, and her shoulders sag beneath her unflattering coat. She rubs her fingers through her gloves as if they ache. Although she glances my way many times, she doesn't offer me her usual affections, too focused on the search around her. It's not her lack of attention that brings me sorrow. It's failing to give her what she needs that does.

She approaches Mr. Carver. Mr. Dunn lowers his phone, his jowls pink from the cold.

"Satisfied, detective?" Mr. Carver asks, a smile on his face, one that shows both his dimples and his arrogance.

"If you know anything about Tony Habib's death, now is the time to tell us," Constable Whitaker says, but her voice no longer carries conviction. "A confession can still help you."

"You need to get over this fixation on me. Why can't you just let me grieve my student's passing? He was a good friend of mine."

"Yeah, you look real torn up about it."

Mr. Dunn starts to admonish the lady constable, but she waves him away. She joins her partner who stands near the fire pit talking on his phone, and together they mope back to the trellis and out to her car, both silent, both hunched, both doubtless feeling disappointment and pain.

I know because I feel it too.

The sun is deep on the horizon now, and were it not for my melancholy over the failed search earlier this afternoon, I'd marvel at the orange glow suspended in shimmering lines of pinks and corals.

Despite the cool weather, Mr. Carver sits outside on the green Adirondack chair, his back to me but his body close to the raging fire that crackles and snaps in the stone pit. Even from here I feel its warmth, and it's easy to understand why he enjoys the outdoors so much. His backyard is nothing short of paradise, secluded from the world but accessible to everything via his car. How much easier life has become since my day.

The fire must do its job because Mr. Carver removes his gloves and loosens his coat. Even Iggy is seduced by the flames, leaving my cold roots for a seat by his master, albeit on the other side of the fire pit. Maybe he thinks it's best to keep an eye on the man.

Normally, Mr. Carver would talk to the dog. Spin yarns of his grandeur or complain about his troubles. Tonight, however, he slouches near the flames, drinks from a bottle, and repeatedly tries to reach someone on the phone he previously called a *burner*. His other phone must be with the police, but how he hid this one, I'm not sure. Left it at his workplace maybe? Or maybe he purchased another.

When he pushes the buttons yet again, it appears he has at last found success. "Harrison. Finally. I've been trying to reach you." A pause, during which I can't hear the speaker. "You're right. Sorry." Another pause. "Well, that's good, because no one wants a lousy lawyer. If you say he's the best, I guess I'll have to take your word for it." A longer pause and then, "Yeah, he says the same thing. Says Whitaker has a grudge against him, and that her police chief will see right through it and shut this whole thing down, especially after today's disaster. Guess she's retiring soon?"

Mr. Price must confirm Mr. Carver's statement because the researcher says, "Good. Not soon enough though." More silence. "No, of course they didn't find anything. I told you, I didn't do it, but she's more persistent than herpes." Mr. Carver looks over his shoulder at me. The blaze creates flickering shadows on his liar's face, and in that light, he resembles Satan himself.

His attention returns to the fire. "They left my house a

182 | DANNIE BOYD

pigsty. Fingerprint powder everywhere, drawers a mess, crap from their shoes on my floors and carpet. Can't handle being in there right now." After a short pause, his next words are accompanied by a wary tone. "What do you mean a contingency plan? You should stay away from her."

The uncertainty in Mr. Carver's voice worries me. How far might Mr. Price go to keep the finding of cancer a secret? To protect the large sums of money he has invested in this miracle drug? A sum that, based on my overheard conversations, exceeds millions of dollars. I find that amount nearly impossible to fathom. I'm convinced he suspects his prized researcher of murder, and I fear a man like that, a man who doesn't report a fatal crime, would go quite far indeed. After all, look what happened to me, all because I dared to venture into men's territory.

Mr. Carver says goodbye to Mr. Price. Then he places the phone on his thigh and pulls out his wallet. After retrieving a small card, he studies it for a few seconds and then picks the burner phone back up and punches in a number. "This is Mark Carver. *Again.* This is the fourth message I've left since you came out here three weeks ago. I know you're busy, and everyone else I've tried is booked too, but please call me back. I want this giant of a tree cut down and removed before it falls on my house and kills someone. It's not like I can do it by myself."

When he finishes his call and slaps the phone back onto his lap, my branches droop with heartache and fatigue. Mr. Carver is not worried I'll fall over and kill someone. He's worried someone will find the bloodstain of his sin buried inside me.

For him, the sooner I disappear from his world, the better.

CHAPTER TWENTY-TWO

Lani

Despite the passing of Northeast Ohio's cold spell and the buckets of warm sunshine the late-April day grants them, Lani feels about as sunny as a turd. She drives the remaining few miles to Brian's house as quiet as one, too, even though he sits next to her in the passenger seat.

Having to walk around with her arthritic tail between her legs for the past eight days after the fruitless search of Mark Carver's home makes her retirement in two weeks look pretty good. No blood or weapon in the house. No unusual vegetation around the place to match up with Habib's body. No transient evidence outside like blood or other body fluids, weather conditions having long since seen to that. Sure, Habib's fingerprints were found inside the house, but Lani already knew they'd be there, Carver ever the socializer.

So nope. It was nothing, nada, zilch. No proof whatsoever that Carver offered his PhD student anything beyond party games and cocktails. The researcher has known for a couple weeks he's been under suspicion, so of course he wouldn't leave incriminating evidence behind. Still, Lani hoped they'd find something an average Joe wouldn't consider, like trace blood or tissue down a sink drain, even in the unlikely chance it would still be there.

Her partner breaks the silence. "Punish yourself much?"

As they near his place, residential streets with small homes and neat lawns replace stores and office buildings, and the six o'clock hour brings home workers for a Thursday night beer and a hot meal.

When Lani doesn't respond, Brian says, "It's not like you killed the guy. You searched his house and yard, and it was a solid call, no matter what French says. He's just worried about optics, not to mention Price's continued flow of money to the department. Plus, he thinks Habib's murder was a random act. Or at the very least, some past lover we'll never find." When Lani still says nothing, Brian adds, "Thanks for picking me up and dropping me off today."

"Told you not to trust a toy car."

"It's getting a tune-up, that's all."

"Whatever."

"At least you've had time to get all your paperwork done. No loose ends when you leave."

"No loose ends? Are you crazy? What do you call Tony Habib, huh? That's a loose end my old bones don't need." She squeezes the steering wheel, trying to force her hostility onto its leather casing instead of onto her partner. He doesn't deserve that. "I'm sorry," she manages. Loosening her death grip, she fists and unfists her left hand, her knuckles aching from the strain.

"Just because you have arthritis doesn't make you old. My thirty-six-year-old cousin has it. Wouldn't dare call her old. You've got a lot of time ahead of you to try new things, no nine-to-five to tie you down. Well, more like twenty-four-seven in our case."

"Thanks, Dr. Chopra."

"And don't think Habib's killer is gonna get away. Not on my watch. My money's on you about Carver, and I guarantee you he'll stay on my radar when you're gone. Promise, boss."

Lani swallows. "Thanks." After blinking a few times —*stupid sun*—she adds, "You're one of the good ones, Einstein. Don't let them hold you back. We need more guys like you rising to the top." She glances at her partner, who, in his pale-blue dress shirt and patterned tie, exudes pure capability. "And not only for your brains if you know what I mean."

"I do, and thanks. There are plenty of great cops out there, but we've still got a long way to go when it comes to reform."

"Agreed. And quit calling me boss, for feck's sake."

Knowing that Brian will keep an eye on Carver and keep working to solve Tony Habib's case is a dab of salve on Lani's wounds. Takes her pain and frustration down to a tolerable six instead of a raging ten. The deceased PhD student has no close ally to see he gets justice. No one to keep pestering the department. No one but a great aunt with Alzheimer's in a nursing home.

Life really sucks sometimes.

Lani turns onto Chestnut Road and nears Brian's two-bedroom house, its sage-colored siding and white shutters newly repainted.

"Oh crap," he mumbles.

"What's wrong?" When Lani sees a blue Accord in his driveway and a woman with long, wavy hair sitting on his front step, she immediately understands. She pulls up to the curb on the opposite side of the street. "That the one stalking you?"

"I told you, she's not really stalking me. Just keeps calling and stopping by."

"That's stalking, Einstein."

After Brian opens the car door and gets out, Lani rolls

down the window and adds, "You're too nice. You need to tell her in no uncertain—" She squints at the woman across the street. "Holy shite on a sheet."

Lani bolts from the Crown Vic. Well, maybe not bolts, but dang if she doesn't move quickly for an almost sixty-five-year-old woman.

In obvious surprise, Brian pivots back to her. "I got this, boss. You don't—"

"Well, feck me sideways and highways, that's Mark Carver's sister!"

"What are you talking about?"

Lani brushes past Brian and strides to the front stoop. Japanese boxwoods flank the steps, and a dogwood tree bursting with white blossoms offers a patchwork quilt of shade. "Melissa Taylor, fancy meeting you here."

Mark Carver's sister jumps up from the top step, her cropped pants bunched around her knees and her blouse riding up her flat stomach. She yanks it down over her hips. "What are *you* doing here? You told me you were a friend of Mark's."

Lani snorts. "Do I look like someone your brother would be interested in? But the more important question you should be asking is: how exactly do you think pestering a police detective is going to end?"

Brian looks like a stunned deer who's just bounced off an electric fence. "You're Mark Carver's sister?"

"How do you even know who Mark is?" Melissa seems equally shocked.

"Your brother's a suspect in Tony Habib's murder," Lani answers bluntly. "That's why I was at his place when I met you."

"Wh…what are you talking about?"

"Hey, Brian, bet Mrs. Taylor here didn't tell you she's married with a couple of middle-schoolers, did she?"

Brian blinks for a few seconds and then morphs from

stunned deer to miffed hound. Melissa's dark locks whip around as she stares back and forth between the two detectives, as if unsure which bombshell to address first: the one about her prized brother being a killer or the one about her being an adulteress.

"You're Brian's partner?" she sputters to Lani, apparently settling on a lesser bombshell that Lani hadn't factored in.

"Yep. The one and only."

Brian closes his eyes. "Great, now I'm a homewrecker."

Giving the once-lovers some space, Lani strolls over to the white dogwood and inspects its blossoms. She pretends not to listen as Melissa twists the hem of her blouse and pleads with Brian to forgive her, to not tell her husband, how horrified she'd be if her kids found out, how she just needed a little attention from a man, yada yada yada. And then, finally getting back to the first bombshell, which, if it were Lani, would've been the first question she addressed, Melissa asks Brian, "What did your partner mean that my brother is a murder suspect? He'd never hurt anyone."

Lani figures that's her cue to return to the party. Something has just occurred to her. "Did you cozy up to Brian on purpose?" she asks Melissa. "Thought maybe it'd be good to have a cop in your back pocket to protect your brother?"

"What? No. I don't even understand what you're saying." Melissa's shirt hem is now so balled up from her nervous kneading that even a power steamer couldn't flatten it back out.

Still, her confusion seems legit. Although Lani hates labeling things a coincidence—in her experience, there's usually something afoot—in this case, the label might fit. Melissa was sleeping with Brian well before Tony Habib was murdered.

"I met Brian last fall at the Farmer's Market," she says.

Brian, hands jingling his keys in his suit pocket, frowns but confirms Melissa's words. "It's true. Carver wasn't even on our minds then."

"My brother would never hurt anyone," Melissa repeats. She snatches her handbag off the top step and marches toward the blue Accord.

"Not so fast, Mrs. Taylor," Lani says.

Melissa turns back around, her forehead still scrunched in disbelief. Lani supposes the odd turn of events is no less bizarre for her.

"What?" she says with a frustrated snap.

"What do you know about your brother's research?"

"His drug research? What's to know? He's developed a weight-loss drug. It'll be in clinical trials soon." Melissa stands taller. "He's smart, detective. Dedicated too. And Tony Habib was a good friend of his."

"So you know Tony?" Lani asks.

"Sure. He was at some of Mark's parties. It's awful what happened to him, and Mark is distraught over it, but he had nothing to do with the guy's death."

"Did your brother encounter any problems with his new drug?"

"I…" Melissa fiddles with her purse strap and stares off across the street. "No, I mean, nothing major. Tony might have said something about a mouse giving him trouble, but he didn't elaborate, and Mark hasn't had any concerns. He—" A sudden awareness shifts the planes of Melissa's face, as if she's just realized saying anything more about her brother, a murder suspect, to two detectives is not a smart move. "I need to go." She hurries the rest of the way to her car. Once in the driver's seat, she rolls down the window. "You'll never hear from me again, Bri. I'm sorry. I really am."

After she drives away, Brian, obviously still shell-shocked by the whole exchange—heck, Lani is too—says, "She's going straight to her brother now. We'll get nothing more from her."

"Maybe, maybe not," Lani replies. "But that tidbit about

there being a problem with one of Tony's mice might be enough to get us a warrant to search Carver's university computer and research notes."

"Are you kidding me? You really want to go there? That thread is thinner than Dunn's hair, and if it turns out to be nothing, you'll end up in deeper muck than you already are."

"Who cares? I started out covered in muck, might as well go out that way too. But yeah, it's thin, I'll give you that. And assuming Melissa is running off to blab to her brother right now, he'll make sure to scrub his office computer cleaner than a surgical suite. Probably already has. But do me a favor."

"Anything." Brian follows Lani to her car across the street.

"Chloe Sampson digs you. Check with her one more time. See if she'll share their study results with you. That kind of thing."

"Sure."

"Meanwhile, I'll phone Harrison Price. Make sure Carver didn't mention anything to him, maybe something so minor that Price didn't even think about it at the time."

As soon as Lani is in her car, she calls the contact number she has for the venture capitalist. An in-person chat would be better, but in the off chance he and Carver are in cahoots about something, the longer she waits to speak to Price, the more time Carver has to tip him off. She settles for FaceTime, but the conversation is short and unhelpful. Price is cordial but firm and says as far as he knows, everything is going great with the research. He has investments in many areas, but he's especially excited about this one because of the promise it holds.

"I don't understand why you're so focused on Dr. Carver, detective." The investor's lips tighten, and through the phone screen, he gives the appearance of a man much too important to be wasting his time on this discussion. "The only reason I got him a lawyer was because you kept harassing him. He's done nothing wrong, and it's cruel to smear a good man's name. Word gets around. People at the university are already giving him suspicious looks. You think that's fair?"

"I'm only looking for the truth, Mr. Price."

"From what I've heard, your truth-seeking days will be over in a couple weeks."

"Working cop or not, I'll never stop trying to get justice."

"Oh, so you're a superhero now?"

What a one-percenter fecker.

They end their call, but for the rest of the evening, as Lani waters her indoor plants and inspects her outdoor ones, as she grills a pink slab of salmon and steams a head of cauliflower, as she frowns at Old Henry's ashes on the mantle and wonders where to put them, her conversation with Harrison Price replays in her mind, filling her with self-doubt.

Am I off base with Mark Carver?

Maybe she went and got the one thing she warned Brian against: tunnel vision. Ruining an innocent man's life is not a box she needs checked off on her exit interview.

By nine p.m., she's in bed, but her sleep is restless and full of disappointment. Will Habib's case never be solved? Will she end up like Old Henry? Nothing but a lonely, dejected pile of ashes in an urn no one knows what to do with?

The following morning, exactly two Fridays away from her mandatory retirement, the same thoughts plague Lani's mind. It's as if her brain is stuck on replay. Bleary-eyed and stiff, she brushes her teeth, splashes her face with cold water, and gets ready for her dawn walk, the sun just making its cotton-candy ascent.

In jeans and a puffer jacket suitable for the early hour, she holsters her Glock. Her neighborhood is safe, but she's not a fool.

Once outside, as the horizon grows brighter, she inhales

the cool air and admires the colorful blooms that decorate the old neighborhood. Her thoughts travel to Doug, and she wonders how her ex-husband is doing. Their time together was so long ago that she hardly ever thinks about him anymore. He wasn't a bad guy. She just couldn't give him what he wanted, and when they gradually grew apart and divorced, he found someone who could. His new wife, a receptionist at his insurance agency, shot out three kids faster than you can say Huey, Dewey, and Louie. And honestly, Lani was happy for them.

She wonders what those kids, all adults now, are doing. Is Doug a grandfather? She imagines him taking his grandkids to the Cleveland Zoo, or to a Cavs game, or to the Rock & Roll Hall of Fame and then Slyman's Deli for a corned-beef sandwich so delicious it'll make you weep in ecstasy.

An ache pinches off her throat, and she has to swallow a few times to loosen it. A pebble shoots out from under her shoe. She kicks it down the sidewalk until it veers off into the grassy berm.

What is she thinking taking a cruise around the world? Brian is right. That isn't her style. And does she really think she might meet someone who'll be better company than her plants? On a cruise ship, no less? The only single people there will be old widows.

Nope. Playing poker with an eighty-year-old former cop in Peninsula is as bright as her future gets.

So lost in self-pity is she that at first she doesn't register the light taps behind her as footsteps. She simply considers the rhythmic sound to be background noise. But then her cop instinct kicks in, and she turns around.

Too late.

A figure springs toward her. Dark hoodie, ski mask, gloves. Tall, white skin around his eyes, no crow's feet. That's all Lani makes out before he stabs her through her coat and into her belly.

The pain is so sudden and unexpected that a blast of air whooshes out of her. Before she can even process what's happened, she fumbles for her gun beneath her jacket, but another stab to her belly keeps her from reaching it. He's too strong, and she's too taken by surprise.

She cries out, but who will hear her? Most of the homes are still dark, full of sleeping families. After a few more quick slashes, which she tries her best to fend off with her arms, he sprints away. The assault is over in seconds. Lani falls to the ground, the attacker's weight no longer there to support her.

Blood pours from her abdomen and saturates her coat. Cries of help whisper from her throat, but even to her ears they are barely audible. She tries to grab her phone from her back pocket, but her body is too contorted from the fall. A bolt of pain sparks through her belly. Lightheadedness blurs her vision. Eventually her fingers graze her phone, but that's as far as she gets.

Footsteps run toward her. A distant voice asks if she's all right. Her eyes close into blackness.

CHAPTER TWENTY-THREE

CATHERINE

It is difficult to keep track of the passing days and nights in my tree-ensconced world. So much of nature is monotonous. One day looks much like the next.

That's not to say changes don't happen in a constant fashion—they do. Some are incremental, like the emerald leaves that have sprouted on the surrounding birches and oaks over the past few weeks. Some seem to happen with a snap of the finger, or in my case a dry branchlet, like the bursts of color from the flowering trees. Same, too, of the warblers and hawks who land on my branches overnight every spring. Even the scents absorbed through my pores change with the seasons: the smoky, crisp scent of autumn, the clean frost of winter, the fecund and floral aromas of spring and summer.

And yet, days blur together. Were it not for Mr. Carver's marks on his calendar, I wouldn't know it's now the thirtieth day of April or that almost a fortnight has passed since the lady constable conducted her search. I've seen nothing of her since, although her partner stormed over here five calendar marks ago. What he discussed with Mr. Carver, I'm not sure. Their conversation happened inside the house, and I'm not privy to that. What goes on inside is left to my imagination, beyond what I can see through the windows.

Sometimes that surveillance is more than I want, like when Mr. Carver parades nude around his home or shoves Iggy rudely with his foot. Fortunately, I've never witnessed him lay a hand on the beagle beyond that. Sometimes he is even kind to his stolen pet, sharing a morsel of steak from his plate or petting the dog in the parlor while he watches a flashing screen on the wall. But sadly, this inconsistent behavior only makes the dog more distrustful.

During all Mr. Carver's actions, from the most mundane to the most heinous, there is no one to see him but Iggy and me. The wooded acreage offers a killer all the privacy he needs. Maybe that was his intention when he bought the home.

Since the police search two weeks ago, Mr. Carver's sister also visited, but they ate their meal inside the house, Melissa not quite as outdoorsy as her brother. They appeared to have a heated discussion at the central bar in his kitchen, where four high-backed stools line the counter. Neither seemed interested in the food in the white boxes in front of them. Melissa pushed her meal about on her plate, and Mr. Carver rubbed her back as if to comfort her. Then they stood and embraced, and he mouthed what must have been soothing words because even through the window I could see his face shift into a smile. She nodded and smiled back, as if relieved by his speech. His demeanor was so reassuring that I myself might have been fooled had I not witnessed his true depths.

Despite his reassurances to his sister on whatever matter they discussed (did she learn about Constable Whitaker's interest in him? Was one of her children ill? Did her boutique business fail?), Mr. Carver seems more nervous of late, his confident carriage more guarded. Ever since the lady constable's partner visited five days ago, the researcher paces his kitchen or performs more exercises than usual outside, sometimes at a frenzied pace.

Unfortunately, his growing agitation has made his discussions with Iggy less frequent, leaving me an outsider to his thoughts. The exception was two evenings ago. He sat out by the fire pit in the green Adirondack chair and muttered something to the beagle that left me anxious.

"I should just get rid of you," he said to the dog. "Believe me, I would if I didn't think it would make me look more suspicious."

Iggy, enjoying the fire instead of the cool dirt by my roots, tilted his head at Mr. Carver and whimpered, as if he too felt the weight of the words.

Many times over the past few days, Mr. Carver has stared in my direction, even approached me and re-examined the deep crevice that hides his crime.

"I don't know, Iggs." His fingers tapped my bark. "Should I throw it out? But what if someone finds it? Or spots me on a camera getting rid of it?" He shook his head and knelt down to the dog, giving him a distracted pet. "No. This seems the best place. They did a thorough search and found nothing. Even when Lockhorn cuts the branches off, he won't see that deep in the trunk." From his crouched position, Mr. Carver glanced up at me. The soft laugh that followed was not at all calming. "We made the right decision, Iggs, I'm sure of it, but I'll feel much better when this old beast comes down."

In an exhausted but often scattered state, I wait every day for the arborist's black truck. The fact it has not yet come no longer fills me with the relief it once did because I fear I'm already dead inside. A block of iron has crushed my spirit. My trunk and boughs are fissured pieces of a listless soul, not because of my imminent death, either natural or by the arborist's saw, but because I failed the lady constable. I failed my Tony. From my bark prison, I am useless.

Bright rays of sunshine warm my branches, and with the sun almost directly above me, it must now be noon. My decaying roots sense a vibration, and I feel as much as see and hear Mr. Carver drive up to the carriage house. Sometimes he returns during the lunch hour, so this isn't a complete surprise, but what is a surprise is the other car that pulls up, a fancy vehicle with a metal figurine on the front. I recognize it as Mr. Harrison Price's car.

His visit arouses my interest, and I hope they'll talk outside, but both disappear into the side of Mr. Carver's home by way of the trellis. To my relief, they reappear a few minutes later through the sliding door of the kitchen and sit at the clear table on the patio. Iggy darts out and performs his ritualistic squirts around the yard before settling at my base. Both men hold checkered mugs, and Mr. Carver has also brought out a bowl of cubed watermelon and two small plates. If I still possessed a tongue with taste buds, my mouth would be watering, because what I wouldn't give for a bite of that succulent fruit. Even after all this time, I remember its sweet juice.

"It's crazy," Mr. Carver says, scooping cubes of watermelon to his investor. "I can't believe someone stabbed her."

Stabbed? Who was stabbed? Alarm breaks my lethargy.

"Two deep wounds to the abdomen." Mr. Price removes his suit jacket, forks a piece of watermelon, and slips it into his mouth as casually as if the stabbing of a woman were no more than a swat to a fly. "Wow, warm out today. Must be near seventy. This roller-coaster weather is insane."

"She still in the hospital?" To Mr. Carver's credit, he doesn't sound as callous as his investor. His tone seems wary, even, and I still wonder who they're talking about.

"Yeah."

"Good thing I couldn't sleep that morning and went into the lab early to check on the mice. Otherwise they'd blame her attack on me. Her partner tried to, you know. Came to my house the Friday it happened, but I told him to check the university's security log."

Oh no, oh no, oh no, please not the lady constable.

"It'll show my badge was logged in during that time, and I'm sure I'm on a security camera too. He must've checked because I've heard nothing from him since." Mr. Carver sips his steaming beverage and shoos an insect away from his fruit.

"How'd you find out about it?" the investor asks. "The news?"

"My sister, of all people."

"How did she know?"

"Turns out she…" Mr. Carver hesitates. "She knows Brian Dupree, Whitaker's partner, and found out from him."

I want to wail in sorrow for the lady constable, to tear at my hair and pound something with my fists, but of course I cannot. The most I manage is a shivering of my branches, which neither man acknowledges.

You might think a tree incapable of grief, I lament to Iggy at my base, *but I assure you, I suffer it.*

Although the people who come and go from these premises know nothing of me, I have considered many of them my friends. Not Mr. Carver, to be sure, but Tony, the lady constable, the intellectual couple who lived here before Mr. Carver, the family before them with their special son who shared the same affliction as one of my preceptor's children, both of whom I adored. (I later learned it was called Down Syndrome.) Decades ago, the sweet boy would hold picnics on a blanket not far from my roots, and his laughter and imaginative talk entertained me for hours.

So in hearing of Constable Whitaker's attack, it feels as though I've lost yet another friend because even though she isn't dead, I doubt I will ever see her again on this soil.

Mr. Carver sets his mug too firmly on the table, and coffee spills over the sides. "That Dupree guy threatened my sister. Said if she knows anything about what happened to Whitaker, he'll personally haul her into a jail cell and make sure she never gets out." The researcher's face flushes with an intensity I haven't seen since he killed Tony, and before that when he smashed the glass against my bark. "My sister is off-limits. She doesn't know anything."

"So she doesn't..." Mr. Price chews his final cube of watermelon. "She doesn't know about the mice finding?"

"Of course not. And even if she did, she wouldn't say anything. She wants no part of this mess. The last thing she needs is her family finding out about... Well, let's just leave her out of it."

"Well, someone said something. Detective Whitaker called me last Thursday to ask if I knew about any problems with your research mice. I got the impression she wouldn't stop looking into you."

Mr. Carver bolts up from his chair. His sudden movement startles Iggy. "Why didn't you tell me? Man, that's not good." He begins pacing the patio. "She was already suspicious about the research. Now she's also convinced I..." His voice trails off, but I imagine he's thinking about the former university student and girlfriend who are both dead, likely from his monstrous hands.

"She's retiring in a week, and she's in the hospital," Mr. Price says. "She won't be back at work, so this is where it ends. Your research is safe."

That this is the wealthy man's main concern while Constable Whitaker lies wounded incenses me.

Mr. Carver rocks back and forth on his leather shoes in front of the sliding glass door, but then, as if having a sudden realization, his forehead furrows. "Wait. Did you... Did you stab her?"

"Of course not."

"But...did you *get* someone to stab her?"

The investor holds Mr. Carver's gaze. "I'm as innocent as you, Mark."

For a moment, they stare at each other. Then Mr. Carver pinches the bridge of his nose and shakes his head. "You've just taken this from bad to worse. Everything will come out now."

Once again I wish I could throttle him. I wish I could throttle both of them. I want to use one of my heavy branches to beat them senseless. Never would I have thought myself capable of such hatred, but never before have I seen the people I love so brutally treated.

Mr. Price rises from the table and approaches Mr. Carver. "We wouldn't even be in this mess if it wasn't for you."

"No, we wouldn't be in this mess if you hadn't pressured me so much."

The two men face off against each other like bulls, one tall, one short.

Mr. Price exhales loudly. "Look. No one else in the police department suspects you."

"Well, they sure will now. Whitaker gets confirmation there might be a problem with my research and then gets stabbed? Everyone will be looking at me."

"No they won't. Chief French gave me his word they won't be bugging you anymore, not without evidence."

"Whitaker's partner will. The guy looked like he was about to strangle me with his bare hands."

"Don't worry about Dupree. He just got assigned that double homicide. I'm sure you heard about it. Rich couple slayed in their home. He'll have his hands full with that, and Tony Habib will soon be an afterthought." When Mr. Carver narrows his eyes at Mr. Price, the investor grunts and makes a face. "No, I didn't kill that couple. Good God, what do you take me for? It's just what we call dumb luck."

If I thought it was impossible to be repulsed by anyone more than Mr. Carver, I was wrong. Whether Mr. Price killed that couple or not—which, from his tone and body language, I don't believe he did—his relief over such "dumb luck" and his casualness over the lady constable's stabbing—which I *do* believe he was behind—is as frightening as Mr. Carver's duplicity.

I may be nothing but a giant oak tree rooted to the soil, but one doesn't live over a century and a half without personal growth. What I have learned, particularly over these past five weeks, is that it's not only the Curtis Mayfields and the Frederick Morrisons of the world who should make us leery.

It's also the people we would never in a million years suspect capable of committing such evil deeds.

CHAPTER TWENTY-FOUR

Lani

Other than Brian, the last of Lani's cop visitors—uniformed officers and detectives alike—file out of her house.

Today was supposed to be her last one on the job, but because she's still recuperating from the attack, her colleagues arrived in small groups throughout the afternoon to wish her well. It's been a steady flow of paper plates covered with pizza, plastic cups overflowing with beer or soda (depending on who was still on the clock), and colorful Happy Retirement napkins, many of which are now scattered throughout her kitchen and living room like a rainbow of vomit.

Anderson, the bulldog of a detective who struggles nobly but imperfectly to jump on board the Me Too movement, brought a pink cake in the shape of a tulip. Although his nod toward her love of flowers and plants was touching, its effect fell short when he followed it with, "Think of all the men you can do now that you're livin' the free and easy life."

She threw him a bone and retorted, "Who needs a man when you can buy any size you like?" That got a round of guffaws from the guys she's worked with over the years, some for as long as three decades.

But now with everyone gone except Brian, the house feels as still as a funeral home, nothing but the occasional passing car outside and the flap of napkins on her coffee table from an overhead ceiling fan.

Lani eases herself down on the recliner and winces at the discomfort in her still-bandaged abdomen. "Dang it if I'm not going to miss those guys."

Brian takes a seat on the overstuffed sofa across from the fireplace and mimes a finger gun at her. "I *knew* you'd wanna see them today. You made such a stink about not wanting a retirement party, but there was no way those guys were going to let you get away without a decent goodbye. They'll be lost without you. Even French showed up."

"Chief Toddler just wanted to check if I was dead yet. Hoping to save money on my pension."

Brian laughs. "He knows what a great detective you are, boss. Don't kid yourself. Just because you didn't solve Habib's case doesn't negate a lifetime of achievement, even if the last few months have thrown a few curveballs."

"'Negate.' Big word, Einstein."

"If the name fits."

He smiles his charming smile, and Lani *pfft*s as she fights back her own.

"But between you and me, how are you really doing?" he asks. "You needing many of those pills they gave you?"

"Well, I took a crap last night without needing a laxative, so that's an achievement."

Her partner doesn't react, and she knows he isn't going to let her off that easy. But what is there to say? Two weeks ago she was stabbed by some lowlife they still haven't found. She spent six miserable days in the hospital, the first one for abdominal surgery after a cat scan showed a "penetrating splenic and bowel injury," and five more to make sure she didn't rebleed, get infected, or fail to fart.

"I'm all right," she says. "Dr. Oprah took good care of me."

"Dr. Oprah?"

"I swear to God that's who my surgeon looked like. In my drugged-up brain, I thought I was being punked. But she was all business. No free-car handouts on her watch, that's for sure. But she did manage to perform a 'spleen-preserving' surgery, so I guess I owe her for letting me keep that nifty little organ."

"You're lucky that scumbag's knife didn't do more damage."

"Doc Oprah said the same thing. Now I just have to keep two giant maxi-pads taped to my belly and a bunch of gauze on my arms." She pretends to lift her sweatshirt. "Wanna see my wounds?"

Brian, who just picked up a paper plate holding another piece of Anderson's tulip cake, drops it back on the coffee table and raises his hands in a *no way* expression that makes Lani chuckle.

"Relax, Einstein. You look like Chief Toddler when he spots me ambushing his office. And don't make me laugh. Hurts my stitches."

They grow serious again, and, as if reading her mind, Brian says, "Don't worry. We'll find the guy."

"You and I both know that's unlikely. Couldn't give you much of a description. He wore a ski mask. Tall white guy with brown eyes and no wrinkles around them isn't much to go on. But here's my question: You think this was a random act like Chief Toddler seems to believe? That the guy was hoping for cash but then gave up and took off? He didn't even steal my phone, for crying out loud."

"I think that's horse crap."

"Thank you. Knew I trained you right. The guy didn't make any demands. Didn't even give me a chance to tell him I had no money on me. Just started stabbing. Could've been worse, I guess. He could've found my gun and shot me." She closes her eyes. A cop for over forty years and she couldn't defend herself?

No wonder they're sending me out to pasture.

Brian, who's now eating the tulip cake, its pink frosting coating his lips, says, "It could've happened to anyone. You know that. You were caught off guard in your own neighborhood where you've felt safe for years."

"Okay, Dr. Freud."

He ignores her. "Like you, I doubt this was random. I think it's got Carver's stench all over it. Wanted to silence you, either permanently or just scare you off. But I don't have any proof of that. He was at the university during your attack, and there's no trail to suggest he hired someone."

"I really, really hate it when the bad guys win." As if her sleep hasn't been rotten enough since her surgery, now it's full of raging anger too.

Brian wipes his mouth. With the amount of butter in the frosting, it takes an entire Happy Retirement napkin to do so. "He's not going to get away with Habib's murder, not if I can help it. I promised you I'd keep at him, and I will. And I'm going to find the guy who stabbed you."

"That's good of you, kid," Lani says, "but you'll have better luck finding a contact lens in a swimming pool. Whoever planned my attack made sure of that. Plus, you've got your hands full with that rich couple's homicide."

"We caught one of the suspects. Only a matter of time before we find the second."

"Yeah, and in fifteen minutes there'll be another murder, and then another, and another, and well, you know how this is going to end. Tony Habib becomes another cold case. Meanwhile, his killer gets to keep on truckin'. Or in this case, keep on throwing outdoor parties and soaking in his hot tub like some sort of hotshot celebrity."

They sit in silence, Lani's feet up on her recliner's footrest and Brian's stretched out beneath her coffee table. His suit jacket is still slung over the couch, where it's been since he arrived several hours ago, only now it's stained with pizza sauce from a sloppy cop who ate too close to it. Probably Anderson himself. She's going to miss that dinosaur. Who does she have around to flip off now?

"Decided what you're going to do with those yet?"

Brian's voice breaks Lani's thoughts. He points to Old Henry's ashes up on the fireplace mantle.

"Nope," she says. "Wish I knew if he had a special place. His journal is too clinical. Not much about his personal side, although it's clear he had a thing for the med student who disappeared. I thought about scattering him in my flower garden, but that seemed creepy."

"What about scattering him around Lake Erie. He lived in Cleveland, right?"

"Yeah, thought about that too. Might be breaking the law though. There are rules about that kind of thing."

"Or you could just keep him here. He looks pretty content snuggled up with your ferns."

"That's even weirder. And what happens when I go? Who's going to keep him then?" She doesn't elaborate, but the implication is clear. With no siblings and no children, she's the last of the Cleveland Whitakers. She swallows a knot of despondency. "Ah, just flush us both down the toilet. No use for either of us anymore."

Brian sits up and rests his elbows on his knees. "Okay, here's how it's going to play out. I'm going to give you two more weeks of wallowing. Okay, maybe four. You've been through a lot, and a six-week, post-op grace period is fair. But then you're going to stop this crap. Despite my teasing of you,

you're not old. You're not washed-up. And some cases just don't get solved."

Lani starts to make a snide comment, but he cuts her off.

"You can do lots of things as a former detective, many of them on our own doorstep. Or you can become a PI. Or you can take the cruise you've reserved, where you'll wonder what possessed you to board a floating petri dish with a bunch of drunk people who'll show you more skin than you ever wanted to see. Or get a dog or five cats or twelve snakes. Or apply for a job in the tropical house at the zoo." Brian waves an arm at her army of plants. "You've got the greenest thumb I've ever seen. But for God's sake, quit feeling sorry for yourself and do something. If I can nail Carver, I'll nail him. Keep you in the loop every step of the way. But you've got at least another couple decades left in you, and you are so much more than just a detective. Got it?" He blows out a blast of exasperated air and sinks back against the couch.

Lani raises an eyebrow. She gives him a thumbs up. "Okay, Dr. Phil." She even puts two fingers in her mouth and whistles, despite the pain it causes her abdomen, to show him what he wants to see.

But on the inside? On the inside she feels like the ashes in Old Henry's urn. Dried up and soon to be forgotten.

CHAPTER TWENTY-FIVE

Catherine

I knew this day was coming, and yet as the black truck with the name Lockhorn Landscaping turns into Mr. Carver's driveway, a thick tar plugs my pores and chokes off my air.

While the man exits his truck and lifts his tools from the vehicle's back compartment, I fret with terrified unpreparedness. My memories flood back to one of my preceptor's dying patients in City Infirmary. Old and frail, the man had lived a good life, but as I wiped his brow in the stifling room, he cried hoarsely, "No, please, I'm not ready. I can't bear to never again feel the touch of another's hand, or hear the melodies of an orchestra, or taste the sweetness of a peach. I tell you I'm not ready."

At the time, my tears joined his, and I sat with him until he departed this world. I worried such a weepy display would make me look weak, would prove to all my naysayers that a woman was unfit to carry the title of doctor, but Dr. Clifton assured me otherwise. "My dearest Catherine," he said. "That is the very quality that will *make* you a fine doctor."

But there is nothing fine about this moment. There is only a fearful tremor working its way from the base of my roots to the tips of my branchlets. If I were still a living woman, my heart would bruise my ribs with its pounding and my throat would twist itself closed.

Mr. Carver must have been watching for the arborist from his parlor window because he exits the side of the house and enters my line of sight through the trellis before the arborist can make his way to the front door. Although Mr. Carver is dressed casually, my killer wears leather boots, orange-colored pants, and a long-sleeved shirt stitched with his company's name. A sturdy hat with ear protectors and a clear frontal flap sits on his head.

"Took you long enough." Mr. Carver's tone carries none of the usual charm he reserves for visitors.

"It's been barely seven weeks since I gave you my estimate. That's quick for this time of year."

"I just don't want it to hurt anyone." Mr. Carver stands in the driveway, arms crossed, feet wide. "Those branches are dry, and the smaller ones are falling off."

This is the excuse he offers, but both Iggy and I know otherwise. The researcher's eagerness to have me removed has nothing to do with preventing harm. It has everything to do with preventing discovery.

The arborist nods. "Yup, that's a concern with any dying tree." He pulls on a thick pair of gloves. "Let's get started. My son will be here soon to help me haul it away."

My alarm heightens, and the shake in my branches is worse than what today's wind can blow, but neither man notices. Like my preceptor's patient who died in my arms, I want to scream, *No, please, I'm not ready. I tell you I'm not ready!*

The two men stroll toward me. Iggy peers out from the sliding door window, and as soon as he sees them, he starts barking and jumping in the kitchen. Maybe it's nonsense, but I believe he understands my plight. I long to tell him goodbye.

Long to feel his fur against my bark one last time or witness his joy as he darts around the yard to make his rounds. *I'll miss you*, I call out to him in my thoughts. I pray that some part of him knows how much I've loved his companionship over the past ten months since he and Mr. Carver moved here. He's saved me from loneliness many times.

Mr. Carver and my killer reach my side.

"I'll first make a seventy-degree cut facing the direction we want it to fall." The arborist with the weathered face points toward my northwest, where my thudding impact will spare the carriage house by landing behind it near a copse of trees. It will also avoid the creek to my south. "Then I'll cut out a wedge."

Mother, I cry in a speechless voice, my thoughts skittish. *Will I see you again soon? Is heaven still open to me after all these years? Or will I disappear into nothingness? I'm so frightened. How I wish to feel your arms around me.*

"Then I'll make the felling cut on the other side here." My killer thumps the southeast patch of my bark. "That way it'll be sure to fall in the direction we want."

My brothers and sisters, I hope to see you again. To play marbles and Annie Over like we did as children. Even you, Charles, who used to take me to the orchard to pick apples long before you disapproved of my calling.

"Once the tree is down, I'll cut off the branches," the arborist says, the saw resting against his leg.

Despite my rattled state, I sense Mr. Carver's unease at these words. His gaze darts to the deep crevice that hides his secret, and I imagine him calculating whether the arborist will notice the letter opener. Given how deep it's wedged, it seems unlikely, but if the arborist does find the weapon, Mr. Carver will doubtless find a way to explain it. "So that's where my mischievous niece and nephew put it," he might say, praying the blood was wiped clean by my insides. "I've been looking for it forever."

"Then I'll cut it into manageable pieces and haul it away."

My killer rubs his gloved hand once again down my bark, and my few remaining leaves shudder in response. Inside the house, Iggy scratches at the glass door. "That's where my son —who's my partner in crime—comes in."

Though the arborist clearly means this as a joke, he has no idea how accurate he is. Ending my tree life does indeed feel like a crime.

"Good," Mr. Carver says. "This decaying beast has outstayed its welcome."

With these words of his, so callous and disrespectful to me, to Tony, to anyone else whose life he has ruined, an anger billows inside me and quiets some of my immediate distress. Who are men like Mr. Carver and my first killer to decide who shall live and who shall die depending on how it serves them? Who are they to take us away from everything we love for their own personal gain? To keep us from what we might have been?

In angry frustration, I ponder these questions as my killer (the second killer in my lifetime!) clears the area around me of debris and advises Mr. Carver to step back to the patio.

Because of my killer in 1853, I never practiced medicine other than as a student. I never worked alongside Dr. Fitzgerald and helped those less fortunate. I never again dined with him and his wife Ruth, who, with her remarkable skill with a needle and thread, might have one day sewn and delivered a dress to me. I never again laughed alongside Mr. and Mrs. Clifton—a finer preceptor and second mother a student could never know—or enjoyed the company of their special son. I never again walked with Mr. Mansour Younis, my arm entwined in his as we marveled at the beautiful Euclid Street homes.

And now, because of my modern-day killer, I'll never again see Constable Whitaker and her partner. Or Melissa, or Mr. Carver's friends, or my fellow trees who, although harboring none of my humanness, still forged a connection with me. Or my dear sweet Iggy who stares and whimpers at me from behind the glass door.

No, because of men like Mr. Carver and Curtis Mayfield (or Dr. Frederick Morrison or Dr. Jedediah Cartwright or whoever it was who killed me), I will never again do any of these things.

My fury boils like a kettle of water on an iron stove. With this growing rage swells a wave of energy I feared I'd long since spent. Without thought or intention, it floods my entire corpus and crashes into my branches, sending them into a violent shudder. I will expose Mr. Carver's deadly deeds, I will. I will avenge Tony and make that weapon fall from my insides.

With my whole being now a convulsing mass of dry and brittle branches, the arborist looks up at me in surprise, his saw still silent. From the patio, Mr. Carver stares at me in wonder and shock. "What the—"

I hear it before I feel it. One of my high boughs cracks free, and with the arborist peering up at my trunk, his protective face shield not yet lowered, the severed branch plummets down and skewers him in the eye.

He drops the saw and cries out in what must be a mixture of shock and pain. Mr. Carver runs toward him. Iggy's barking grows frantic inside the kitchen.

The branch has fallen to the ground, but blood pours from the arborist's eye and through his fingers as he presses his thick glove against his face. "Oh God, oh God, oh God," he cries.

Oh God indeed—what have I done? I never meant for that to happen. I let my rage flame bright without trying to control it, a control I've worked so diligently to develop over the years. Using it to release trapped acorns is one thing. Blinding an innocent man is very much another.

Mr. Carver rips off his shirt and presses it to the man's bleeding wound, just as my mother once had me do with a linen towel during a childbirth gone bad. With the other hand, Mr. Carver flounders for the phone recently returned to him by the police and calls someone to say he needs an ambulance. It's a word I've heard only in his outdoor movies but one I instinctively understand. At the same moment, the arborist's son comes running back to join the mayhem. In my panic, I didn't notice the young man arrive.

When the ambulance comes and hauls the arborist away, his blood staining my bark and the soil around my roots, I remain tortured by what I've done. I never meant to hurt him. I only wanted Mr. Carver to know my fury. To know how much he wronged Tony and others.

But in my haste to expose the weapon used to kill Tony—and my violent shudder did indeed loosen the branch that hides the crevice—have I not become Mr. Carver? Or Curtis Mayfield, who I'm convinced to this day poisoned me? Have I not used my potential danger to others to achieve my own goal?

No, I tell myself. Injuring this man was never my intention. I harmed him, yes, maybe even blinded him, and for that I feel great remorse, but I am not Mr. Carver. I can't let my shame and grief cripple me because look at what I just managed to achieve. Maybe I can make it happen again. Not to hurt someone else, of course, but to free the bloodied letter opener.

I must seize this opportunity and pray the chance comes again for me to expose Mr. Carver and get justice for Tony.

I will live another day.

I must not lose hope.

CHAPTER TWENTY-SIX

LANI

Nearly three weeks after her stabbing, Lani feels like a bear caged inside a breadbox. Bad dreams over her attack and daily restlessness leave her cranky and frustrated. To make matters worse, her birthday was two days ago. She is now officially a sixty-five-year-old retired woman.

How in the world did that happen?

Turning thirty didn't bother her. She was too busy angling to become a detective. Forty twinged a little, mostly because she had to accept she was never going to have any kids, at least not by her own body, and fifty got her pondering life's dismal meaning. But sixty? Sixty smacked her in the face like a hockey puck. The realization she'd lived seventy-five percent of her life—give or take a few years—sent her into a deep funk, one from which she still hasn't surfaced. If anything, she's only sunk deeper.

To celebrate her miserable birthday milestone, she made her infamous chili and reread Old Henry's journal, hoping to glean something about the missing medical student she hadn't before and maybe solve his case. She failed at that, but she did succeed in proving that three weeks post-abdominal surgery was not long enough to wait before chowing down on spicy chili. Her gut hasn't quit hollering for two days.

She also dug out an old jigsaw puzzle her parents had stashed in the hallway closet next to some frayed beach towels and a tattered game of Risk. The puzzle's image is of downtown Cleveland in the 1920s. In the center of the city's radiating streets and growing skyline sits Public Square, with its village greens and Soldiers' and Sailors' Monument. She set the puzzle up in the screened-in porch on top of the mosaic table she and Doug bought in a consignment shop decades ago. With its terra-cotta surface, it's one of her favorite holdovers from their marriage.

Now, grunting in irritated boredom, Lani grabs her cell phone and heads out to the back porch to work on Downtown Cleveland.

Easing onto one of the wrought-iron chairs, her movements still cautious, she squints against the late-afternoon sun and stares through the screen's mesh at her vegetable garden. Now that it's mid-May and the frosty nights have passed, she'd like to transfer her indoor tomato seedlings and do some weeding, but she doubts she's up to the task. Walking around is fine, and she even drove to the grocery store to restock the fridge, but the up-and-down motion of gardening might still be too much. Dr. Oprah would no doubt agree.

Lani flutters her lips and returns to the puzzle. After she selects a piece that might be part of Euclid Avenue, her peripheral vision catches sight of a squirrel foraging the exposed roots of a white oak near the fence.

"So is this my future?" she asks him. "A fecking puzzle?" Pretty soon she'll become her old cop friend in Peninsula, just waiting for the younger Brian Dupree to stop by for a few rounds of poker, his good deed for the day.

In one of those bizarre coincidences Lani hates to acknowledge, her phone rings and the caller is Brian.

"Just checking in," he says. "Making sure you're not sitting there wallowing in self-pity again."

"Jeez Louise, I was just thinking about you. You're a regular soothsayer."

"Did you know Nancy Reagan consulted a psychic to make sure the stars were aligned for her husband's dealings?"

"Gee, thanks. I'll sleep better tonight." Lani finds where the Euclid Avenue puzzle piece fits, snaps it in place, and grumbles at the satisfaction it gives her. "Heard you guys caught the second suspect in that couple's homicide."

"We did."

"I never doubted it for a second. You've got topnotch skills and instincts. You know that, right?"

"Don't go getting all soft on me."

"I wouldn't say it if it wasn't true."

Brian clicks his tongue. "Don't I know it. You and platitudes go together about as well as snakes and mice. But seriously, you doing okay?"

"As well as I was yesterday when you called. But I don't recommend you come over. I made chili the other night."

"Thanks for the heads-up. Hey, got something you might be interested in hearing."

"About the Habib case?" In her excitement, Lani's hand sends five puzzle pieces to the porch floor.

"Whoa, slow your roll," Brian says. "Kind of, but nothing that'll help find his killer. Just an interesting side bit."

With her foot, Lani slides the fallen pieces closer to the table. "So, what is it? Don't keep me in suspense."

"I was just about to leave the station earlier when Benson, who was going through the morning's 911 calls, yells over to me: 'Hey, Dupree, isn't this the guy Whitaker thought killed that PhD student?'"

Lani sits higher in her chair, sore abdominal wounds and dropped puzzle pieces forgotten. "And?"

"Turns out Carver had a guy come over this morning to cut down that old tree. You know that big one the dog was always sitting by?"

"I do. A beauty on its last legs."

"So the guy is getting ready to cut down the tree, clearing away the area or whatever, when he looks up and a branch breaks off and hits him right in the eye. Didn't even get a chance to lower his face shield."

"Are you kidding me?"

"Carver's voice is on the 911 call."

"Is the landscaper all right?"

"Actually, he's called an arborist because he cuts down—"

"Oh man, Einstein, I'd slap you if you were here."

"Yeah, he's all right. Got a deep gash in his cheek they had to sew up, and at first they thought he might lose the eye, but they were able to save it. Hopefully, he'll retain some sight, but it won't be great."

"Wait, how do you know all this?"

"Because I stopped by the ER to see him this afternoon. They were watching him after the eye doctor took care of him. I thought it might be worth asking him a few questions."

"Okay, *now* if you were here, I'd high-five you. God forbid, I might even hug you."

"Hey, I learned from the best. Anyway, I asked the guy what happened, and he said it was the weirdest thing. Said that out of nowhere, the tree started shaking and the branch fell. Claims there wasn't even a blast of wind, although of course there had to be."

"Of course." Lani peers through the porch screen at the motionless trees in the backyard. Was it windy this morning? She doesn't recall any big gusts when she fetched her mail. "Did he say anything about Carver?"

"Said Carver was helpful and concerned. That he felt really bad about the injury."

"Not exactly what I want to hear."

"Maybe you'll like this better then," Brian says. "Apparently, Carver had been 'a real pain' up until then. Kept calling about getting the tree cut down, left some angry voice messages. The arborist said he got to it within seven weeks, which was a decent turn-around time in his opinion, and that he'd never seen anyone want a tree removed so badly."

"Carver's a narcissist, no surprise there."

"Well, now that the arborist nearly lost an eye, he says he has to admit Carver was right in wanting it down. As soon as he's recovered enough, he'll remove it. Or at least he'll talk to the city about it. Guess his son, who's his business partner, found out the tree actually falls on city property. Carver must not have realized that. He could've saved himself the liability. It's lucky the arborist didn't get impaled."

"God, even Carver's trees are dangerous," Lani says.

Brian moves on to a story about Chief Toddler, but Lani is no longer listening. Instead, her mind remains on Mark Carver and his tree. She replays their interactions in his backyard oasis, how he always seemed so agitated when she went near the tree. She assumed it was because he didn't want her petting Iggy, afraid she'd connect the dog to his dead girlfriend—which she did. But what if it was something else? What if there was something else he didn't want her to see? Like something buried around the tree or in the creek behind it that they missed in their search?

"Boss? You still there?"

"Yeah, yeah, I'm here." Prickles of excitement race down Lani's spine. She shares her thoughts with Brian. "I think we need to go to Carver's place one more time. We need to check around that tree, see what he's hiding in the dirt and—"

"Whoa, stop right there. We—and especially you, Ms. stab victim—aren't going anywhere. Carver's lawyer has finally quit threatening to sue the department for harassment over your 'personal vendetta' against him and his client, and Price has stopped hinting to Carver's lawyer that he might pull his funding to the PD. So going over to the research professor's house is the last thing you're going to do. I only told you about this to keep you updated, just like I said I would. Believe me, I'm watching him, and when something new comes up that I can *legitimately* use, you'll be the first to know." When Lani doesn't respond, Brian says, "Is that understood?"

"Sheesh, all right already. Man, who's being bossy now?"

"Besides," Brian adds, "you'd be trespassing, and he could press charges."

"Not if I ring his doorbell first and ask permission."

"I mean it, Lani. Don't go over there."

The tone in Brian's voice and the use of her first name show his concern, and that gives her pause. But her hesitancy doesn't last long, because at the same time she's telling him not to worry, that she won't do anything stupid, she's pushing herself to a stand.

By the time they end their call, she has her car keys in hand, her personal handgun in the back waistband of her jeans, and her cardigan halfway on her arm.

CHAPTER TWENTY-SEVEN

CATHERINE

All day my worry over the arborist grows. The warm sunshine and vibrant spring life around me do nothing to lessen it. My shame at harming the man, maybe even blinding him, leaves me despondent, and yet if his saw *had* made its cuts, I would no longer be here.

He will come again, to be sure. Or if not him, then another. Mr. Carver will see to it. Or maybe an arborist won't be needed at all because my natural death is not far away. My growing fatigue and drifts of consciousness prove that.

But then what? Will I simply cease to exist? Will I become a new tree or a new blade of grass or a new tulip come this spring or the next? Will my molecules fuse with the bullfrogs that speak to me at night from the creek? Or maybe I'll be reunited with my loved ones in heaven.

That's the outcome I hope for most. My future partner, Dr. Fitzgerald, and his wife didn't believe in such things, although they wouldn't admit that in public. They spoke to me in confidence over supper one night, and now I pray they were wrong because the thought of my soul disappearing to nothing fills me with despair. Fear too. Even though I'm old and tired, and my branches crack at the slightest breeze, I'm not ready to *not be*, to not exist either in one form or another.

A car approaches the house, and when it slows down, I'm startled out of my morbid rumination. I hear and feel the car but don't yet see it. Mr. Carver's vehicle is in the carriage house, so it can't be his. Plus, he left for a run a while ago, dressed in loose shorts and a shirt as snug as a corset.

Lately, his confidence has returned fourfold, and despite this morning's accident with the arborist, he once again carries the air of a man who thinks nothing can stop him. His students and friends have visited over the past week, and from what I've heard of their conversations, his research is going well. If any more cases of liver cancer have developed in his study mice, he's either missed them or ignored them.

When the vehicle comes into view and pulls into the driveway, I recognize the dark, boxy shape of the lady constable's car.

At first, I wonder if I'm hallucinating, like those disturbed patients at the asylum, but then my scattered energy coalesces, and both relief and confusion course through me. While I'm grateful for this temporary surge of aliveness, I don't understand her visit. According to Mr. Carver's calendar, it's been four weeks since I last saw her. A short time after that, Mr. Price and Mr. Carver discussed her attack, an attack in which I'm convinced the investor played a role. Has she recovered enough from her injuries to be here?

With a wince on her handsome features, she exits her car. Her obvious discomfort answers my question—no, she's *not* well enough to be here. And yet there she goes, walking the stone pathway toward Mr. Carver's front door, at which time I lose sight of her. Moments later, the bell rings from inside the house. Loud knocking and Iggy's barking follow. Soon she'll realize Mr. Carver is away. Will she leave? I want to shake my branches to stop her, shudder them like I did before I injured the arborist, but my life force is nearly depleted, and I can't risk wasting what little I have left for an act she won't witness.

When she gives up her ringing and knocking, she rounds the home and makes her way toward the backyard with tentative steps. Whether from pain or from uncertainty as to Mr. Carver's whereabouts, I'm not sure. Maybe both.

An optimism I haven't felt in weeks fills my venules. I have one last chance to help her solve her case and get justice for Tony. I've already felled one branch. Can I not break another? Can I not rip apart the most critical branch of all and draw her eyes to the deep crevice hidden within my bark? It loosened during my unplanned attack on the arborist. One more shudder of energy might be all that's needed.

When Constable Whitaker sees that Mr. Carver is not on his patio, nor near his fire pit, nor up on his deck, her body seems to relax. Still, her steps are still slow and controlled, and she guards her abdomen as if worried something might spring out of her. She wears a plain shirt, a long sweater open in the front, and jeans. When she turns and the breeze lifts her sweater, I notice a gun in her waistband.

Iggy watches through the sliding glass door and scratches at the pane, his barking reduced to a few yips. Constable Whitaker waves to him and begins to crisscross over Mr. Carver's lawn, her gaze traveling everywhere, as if making sure she missed nothing from her previous search.

Here! I am here! I want to cry out. *Hurry, before he returns. Who knows what he'll do?*

Her sweater lifts again, and this time I notice metal loops poking out of her front pocket. From Mr. Carver's outdoor movies, I recognize these as handcuffs, and that can only mean one thing: she came to arrest him. She must have found something new.

I remind myself I have had this same assumption before and was wrong.

She walks toward me, her gaze searching every spot from my gnarled roots poking from the ground to my tallest branches. My imaginary heart soars with elation because the determined expression on her face suggests I'm the target of her return. When she starts kicking at the dirt along my exposed roots, circling my wide circumference, and rubbing my bark with her aged but capable hands, I realize she recognizes my importance, especially when she says, "What's so special about you, huh? Why is he so eager to have you cut down?"

How she knows, I'm not sure. Maybe she received word from someone. Maybe she noticed Mr. Carver's nervousness whenever she approached me. Whatever the reason, I use all the conscious energy I can muster to transfer my thoughts, to shake my branches in unison, to funnel a force strong enough to break off the branch that marks the weapon. She must find it before Mr. Carver returns.

At my shuddering, she looks up in surprise. Her gaze travels toward the defining branch, cracked and gaping away from my bark. A few inches to the right, and she'll notice the deep crevice that hides what she seeks. I'm so near victory that only a miracle could be responsible.

She knows something is there. She knows!

Completely immersed in my arboreal thundering and shuddering, which I can't sustain much longer, I failed until now to notice Mr. Carver returned from his run. He hovers mere feet behind the lady constable, sweat dripping down his forehead, dark hair matted against his scalp.

My shuddering stops so abruptly that if not for my roots, I'd topple over. *Watch out!* I scream unheard to Constable Whitaker. *He's behind you.*

She keeps staring at my bark, as if trying to work out the possibilities of what could make Mr. Carver so interested in me. In the same moment, Mr. Carver, aware of where the constable's focus is directed, shows a flash of fear and indecision. For a second, I think he'll surrender. That he would rather give up than hurt her.

Foolish me.

When she pats my bark, not too far below where the weapon hides, a steeled jaw replaces Mr. Carver's brief uncertainty. He lunges forward and grabs the lady constable around her chest.

In his hardened and soulless eyes, I see what he's thinking.

He plans to kill her.

CHAPTER TWENTY-EIGHT

CATHERINE

Mr. Carver's arms clasp together around the lady constable's torso, her own arms pinned to her side. In her shocked expression, the natural world seems to come to a stop around me. Birds no longer sing. The creek no longer rushes. Insects no longer buzz. My only focus is on Constable Whitaker, who is outpowered by a man at least eight inches taller and many pounds of muscle heavier.

Mr. Carver speaks in an eerie tone. "Trespassing now, are we? You shouldn't have done that."

"Hurting a cop—retired or otherwise—isn't going to end well for you, Carver." The lady constable's speech is a hoarse croak, the grip on her chest maybe too tight for anything else. "Every cop in the city will be looking for me."

Indecision finds its way back to the researcher's face. If he plans on killing her, I imagine he's searching for the most logical way to proceed. A way that will not trace back to him.

Constable Whitaker attempts to wriggle free, but his hold of her tightens, and she cries out in pain. Although I don't know what abdominal wounds she suffered, I'm certain they're not healed enough for this.

I'm desperate to help her. I want to whip Mr. Carver with my branches and force him to the ground. Stab him like I did the arborist. But I'm useless. I've expended myself, my remaining energy tapped away like syrup.

Mr. Carver's gaze darts around his yard and stops at the deck. He mutters something, but between Iggy's feverish barking inside the kitchen and my own terror for the lady constable, I don't hear it. When he starts dragging her back toward the wooden deck, she struggles and kicks out at him, but he's too strong for her to overcome.

Scattered and panicked, I will my remaining consciousness to think clearly. Dear God, is he meaning to drown her in his bubbling tub?

The lady constable does not make the backward travel easy for him. Halfway there, as they near the fire pit, she drops her head forward and whips it back like a cannon ball against his lower jaw.

He grunts in pain, and although her attack is not enough for him to release her, his hold must loosen because she twists out of his arms, spins around, and kicks him in the genitals.

With that, he buckles over but doesn't fall. Almost immediately, he stands back up and lurches toward her.

She reaches behind her back.

The gun. In my rattled thoughts I forgot about it. *She has a gun.*

It appears Mr. Carver, too, underestimated the older woman in a sweater and ill-fitting jeans, because when she points the weapon at his chest, he stutters to a stop. His eyes widen in surprise, maybe at the gun itself or maybe at his own stupidity for not considering she might have had one hidden beneath her grandmother clothing.

Her back is to me, but the heaving of her torso and her

rapid breaths tell me she's winded and likely in significant pain.

"It's over, Carver," she says, slowing approaching him.

He starts walking backward, as if he might run away.

"Seriously?" she pants. "You know I'm in no condition to chase you. I'll just shoot you instead. That what you want? Believe me, these swollen knuckles can still pull a trigger and shoot straight."

He pauses, as if trying to decide whether she would really shoot him or not. He must decide *yes, she would*—the same decision I've happily come to—because his stance slackens. From inside the kitchen, Iggy whimpers and scratches the glass.

"Now, head to the deck," Constable Whitaker orders. When Mr. Carver complies, she follows him. "Go up the stairs. Come on. Up. Up."

Despite her hunched and halting gate, her free arm holding her abdomen, she manages to climb the stairs after him, her gun aimed at his back the whole time.

Once at the top, she retrieves the handcuffs from her pocket and hands them to him. "Here, put one end around your wrist and the other around one of these." She taps the deck's wooden slats. "Good thing I had them in my car, don't you think?" Her speech is still breathless. "And if you try to get cute and throw them, I'll shoot you. Don't think I won't. I'm angrier than a bear, and my stomach feels like a grenade exploded inside of it, thanks to you."

At this point, I think both Mr. Carver and I are convinced of her sincerity.

After he complies, she strains to drag a heavy chair over from the table and delivers it to him. "Sit." When he does, she scowls and says, "Now, let's see what's got you creaming your jeans over that tree." With cautious steps, she descends the stairs and approaches me, gun in one hand, phone in the other, as if she is about to call someone.

I know it's now or never. This will be my final chance. It might kill me, drain the very last of my withering vitality, but I'll do it for Tony. My beautiful, beautiful Tony who deserved so much more than what he got.

I close my metaphorical eyes. I concentrate on my gnarled roots, most of which carry nothing but dead matter and rot. I conjure the remaining life force inside them and carry it up the sinusoids and fibers of my trunk. I flood it into my branches, biggest to medium to the very tips of the smallest. I visualize the veins in my few remaining leaves. Then I make the branch that hides the murder weapon the center of all this arboreal energy and let blow the concentrated rage that's built up inside me, where it explodes into every part of my being. I shudder and rattle and splinter like never before. A reverberating wave rumbles through the soil like an earthquake.

For you, Tony.

From their different positions in the yard, the lady constable just past the fire pit and Mr. Carver handcuffed to the deck, they stare at me in shock, eyes wide, postures frozen. Even Iggy behind the glass falls silent.

A thunderous crack splits the air, and that low, thick branch that abuts the murder weapon thuds like a cannon ball to the ground.

And then just as suddenly the world falls still, as silent and as empty as a crypt.

I did it. Oh, dearest mother and father, I did it. I have finally accomplished what I believe I was meant to do as a tree.

But it has cost me. It has cost me dearly.

My consciousness floats away.

CHAPTER TWENTY-NINE

Lani

Lani looks from the seizing tree back to Carver, who is hand-cuffed to the deck. He seems as startled by the oak's inexplicable shaking as she is. The branches were rattling before Carver attacked her, sure, but nothing like this.

What. The feck. Is happening?

The ground rumbles beneath her feet. Is it an earthquake? Is that it? It's rare, but Ohio *has* seen them. But nothing else seems to be moving. Just that big oak.

Craaaaack.

A branch thicker than a bodybuilder's thigh breaks away from the tree and hammers to the ground. If Lani had been a foot or two closer, she would've suffered a fate worse than the arborist's.

And then, just as abruptly, the tree and ground stop shuddering, the sudden silence noise itself.

Lani blinks. "What in the world?"

From inside the house, the dog resumes his scratching and whimpering.

Lani turns back to Carver on the deck. Spots the anxiety on his face. It sure as heck isn't out of concern for her welfare. She knows in her stabbed little guts that something is buried in that tree. Knows it like she knows Carver killed Tony Habib. Knows it like she knew her and Doug's inability to have kids was because of her, even before that stone-faced doctor showed her the ultrasound of her mutant uterus. Split-second instinct is a real thing, and anyone who doesn't heed it is a fool.

Avoiding the fallen branch, caution in her steps, phone and gun still clutched in opposite hands, Lani approaches the massive oak. At the same time, a car pulls into the driveway, and in a few seconds, Brian appears. He takes one look at her through the trellis, shakes his head, and trots toward her.

"I knew I'd find you here," he says. "I knew you wouldn't listen to—" His words cut off when he spots the fallen branch. "Are you okay?" He hurries the rest of the way to her.

Lani waves him off. "I'm fine."

"You don't look fine."

She supposes she doesn't, hunched over, still breathing heavily, her belly screaming. And yet she smiles at him. "I'm doing better than Carver." She points to the deck.

When Brian sees Mark Carver handcuffed up there, he shakes his head again. "Oh man, you're killing me here, boss."

"Hold your judgment. I know what I'm doing. There's something in this tree. Ain't that right, professor?" Lani calls out to Carver.

Dr. Carver jerks his arm tethered by the handcuff. "You don't have a right to search anything," he yells. "You're trespassing. Leave now, or my lawyer is going to have a field day with you."

Lani hesitates a moment. The last thing she wants is to find evidence she can't use. She runs through any legal tenets that might be on her side, but then something Brian said earlier pops into her mind. The landscaper's son learned the tree was on city property.

Like the Grinch on Christmas Eve, a wicked smile lights up Lani's face. "Well, seeing as how this tree occupies city land, I think we're good."

Carver jerks upright from his confined position on the deck. "No, that's not…" Uncertainty clouds his face. "It can't…"

Covering more bases, Lani adds, "Plus, you assaulted me, so I could argue a post-assault search, and if we leave, you'll destroy any evidence we might find, so I'd call that exigent circumstances. Not to mention a branch from this *city* tree injured a landscaper, and another one almost killed me, so I think that gives me the right to inspect it. Don't you agree, Einstein?"

Instead of waiting for Brian's answer, Lani returns her focus to the oak. She examined the exposed roots earlier, before Carver jumped her, thinking maybe he buried some-thing near them, but now she wonders about something inside the tree itself. Her guys never found anything with their metal detectors, but who would think to run it up a tree?

It seems insane, and no doubt Brian, who is silent behind her, thinks she's one M&M short of a cookie, but there *is* something about this tree that bothers Carver, Lani is sure of it.

She touches the bark in various places and then focuses on the splintered area where the heavy branch fell. Feeling around above her head, she continues to palpate its surface, much like Dr. Oprah palpated her injured belly. She pats higher.

"Careful, boss. Another branch could fall and hurt you. Already been two so far today."

She stands on her tiptoes. Her fingertips feel an opening. "Oh my God."

"What?" Brian is now at her side. "What'd you find?"

"There. Where my fingers are. Reach inside there."

To his credit, he doesn't question her. Just pulls a pair of disposable gloves from his pocket and, using the advantage of his height, reaches inside the fracture she found in the bark. She glances over her shoulder to the deck where Carver is handcuffed. He's slumped over at an awkward angle, as if in defeat.

Oh yeah, something's in there.

Brian pulls out clumps of slimy leaves, rotted acorns, and damp sticks, filling the air between them with a cloying, earthy scent. "There's nothing here." His hand digs deeper. "It's just a—oh, man."

"What?" Lani asks, scared he might have cut himself.

Her partner, her incredibly smart and competent partner who she'll miss not seeing every day like a mother misses a son, pulls out an object with a metal blade.

"Jeez, boss, you were right." Fumbling in his pocket with one hand, he pulls out another pair of disposable gloves and gives them to her.

"Well, aren't you a prepared little fecker." She grins like a lottery winner and puts on the gloves.

Brian hands her the object. A letter opener. A heavy, fancy, engraved one.

Lani winks at Carver on the deck and calls out, "Hey look, it's even got part of your name on it."

Brian whistles. "Got some dried blood on it too."

"Maybe even some DNA," they say at the same time, and then high-five their synchronicity.

The next few minutes are the most satisfying minutes of Lani's life. She inhales the beautiful May air, absorbs the natural beauty around her, and ignores Carver's sputtering about having no idea how the letter opener got in there—blah blah blah, yada yada yada, balk balk balk. She savors the moment as Brian walks him down the deck and toward her Crown Vic.

"Wait," Carver says. "I can't leave Iggy alone."

"You mean the dog you stole from the woman you murdered?" Brian asks.

"I...I don't know what you're talking about. I just don't want him to get hungry."

"Well, whaddaya know. Look who's suddenly got a heart." Lani trails behind Carver and Brian, her wounds hollering at her to slow down, but her adrenaline too pumped to let her. "Or maybe you're worried about him being another piece of evidence against you." She glances through the kitchen window, but this close to the trellis the angle is off, and she can no longer see the dog. He's back to barking though.

"Give me your keys, and I'll get him," she says. "I'll even keep an eye on him for a while because you're gonna be tied up for the next few days."

She smiles and adds, "Besides, I'm pretty sure he likes me better."

CHAPTER THIRTY

LANI

Eight days after arresting Mark Carver, Lani sits alone in his fancy backyard on one of his fancy Adirondack chairs near his fancy fire pit. Her great grandfather's ashes and a small shovel rest near her feet. Although the day's wind is hefty and the cloud coverage threatens rain, the temperature is near seventy, and she's comfortable in a Browns sweatshirt and jeans.

Brian will arrive soon. She doesn't need him for what she's about to do, but she wants an update on Carver's case, and he didn't want her out here alone, so voilà. Carver's bond hearing was denied the previous week, but things are getting messy between him and Harrison Price, and Lani won't be surprised if Quinton Dunn gets Carver out on bond on appeal.

Iggy, who's been keeping her company at her house and learning to stay away from her plants (the toxic ones have all found higher homes on her shelves), lounges over by his beloved tree. Crime scene tape blocks off its perimeter, not only for the investigation, which was already conducted, but for safety purposes until it can be cut down for good.

Lani tried to keep Iggy away from it by securing his leash to one of the Adirondack chairs, but he whined so much, she didn't have the heart to keep him restrained. Once loose, he bolted straight for the tree. Hopefully, if a branch cracks off, he'll dart away quickly.

A shame to see it go, though, Lani thinks. Despite the oak's splintered bark and paucity of leaves, it remains a majestic sight.

A few minutes later Brian saunters over, decked in his usual nice duds minus the suit coat, which was probably left behind in his car. His gun is holstered at his waist. "He shouldn't be over there." He indicates Iggy with a nod of his head.

"Try telling him that."

Her partner—ugh, *former* partner—plops down in the green chair across the fire pit from her. "Melissa wouldn't take him, huh?"

"Apparently, her husband is allergic to dogs."

"Wonder if he's allergic to being a cuckold too."

"Ha, good one, Einstein. Or maybe she doesn't want the dog of a woman who her brother might have killed."

Brian's expression softens. "Yeah, she's pretty distraught. She and Mark are close. If the guy ever does confess, she might be the reason he does so. When I mentioned her, he got all agitated and said to leave her out of it. He clearly loves his big sister."

"Even sociopaths have their soft spots. And I *am* convinced he's a sociopath."

"He didn't hurt Iggy when—*if*—he overdosed his ex-girl-friend, so that's something, at least."

"Or Iggy was his trophy. He might have trophies from other victims too. We just didn't realize they were trophies during our search. Better look into that." Lani heaves an exaggerated sigh. "Fine. Guess I can keep the beagle a little longer if need be."

"Yeah, right. You love having him, and you know it."

"I would've called Mrs. Walker. She should have first dibs on her daughter's dog. But she told me she couldn't keep pets, and since we can't yet prove Carver was behind Cindy's overdose, I didn't want to worry her unnecessarily."

"Makes sense." Brian jerks a thumb toward the dying oak. "Still think that thing has magical powers?"

"Oh for feck's sake, I never said such a thing. It was just a tiny earthquake."

"You claimed, and I quote, 'the tree did what it had to do.'"

"Plants are living things, you know."

"Yeah, and so is Iggy. One that eats and craps and needs the outdoors. How're you going to take him on that cruise?"

Lani uncrosses her legs, her movements still cautious, and places her feet on the fire pit's stone ledge with its decorative maroon tiles. It's been four weeks since her attack, and although most of her pain is gone and her nightmares have tapered off, the memory of the event hasn't. A knife to the gut isn't easy to forget. At least she's started her daily walks again, but only during the hours when her neighbors are out and about. For that, more than the wounds he inflicted, she hates her attacker. He deprived her of her sunrise walks, one of the things she loves most in this cesspool of a world.

"Hello? The cruise?" Brian prompts her.

She waves him off. "Not taking it. Got my deposit back."

"Good. You'd never have survived. Or maybe I should say your poor shipmates wouldn't have survived *you*."

"Thinking of buying an RV instead. Just me and Iggy wandering the U.S. a bit." She throws Brian a self-conscious glance. "Think that'd be dumb?"

He grins. "Now that suits you. Good for you." He cups both hands around his mouth, as if speaking through a megaphone. "Watch out, America. Here comes Lani Whitaker. If her surliness doesn't kill you, the aftermath of her chili will."

That gets a laugh out of her. Not far from the truth either.

"So no teaching then?" he asks. "No new job? Thought you couldn't stand the thought of retirement."

Lani shrugs. "I dunno. Retirement might be growing on me, at least from the police department. None of Chief Toddler's grief, no more slimeballs, plenty of time to garden. I'll see how I feel after Iggy and I storm America. Then maybe I'll find something that fits."

Brian puts a hand over his heart. "You're filling me with joy, boss. You're filling me with joy."

"Shut the feck up."

"So, you really gonna bury that here? Technically, we're trespassing. Again."

"So arrest me." She glances down at Old Henry's urn. "Can you think of a better place to put him? He couldn't solve the case that plagued him, but maybe he'll be at peace in the place I solved mine." She rolls her eyes at the *aww that's so sweet* smile Brian flashes her and pivots to Tony Habib's case. "Carver still claiming innocence?"

"Yep. He and his lawyer confirmed the letter opener was his, given to him by his investor, but he claims it disappeared. He had no idea where it went. Us finding it in the tree was as much of a surprise to him."

"My sweet butt it was."

"Says he was horrified to learn Habib's blood was on it and that the ME concluded it was the murder weapon, based on the analysis of Tony's vertebra." Brian rubs at a chip in the Adirondack chair's green paint. "Why would he leave it in the tree? Wouldn't you toss it?"

"Where? Always a risk it's found if he tosses it in his own trash."

"Could've dumped it somewhere else."

"Sure. Probably what I would've done," Lani says. "But hiding it in the tree is smart too. That was an awfully good spot."

"How so? It's still near his house."

"We all missed it in our initial search, didn't we? Besides, he was getting it removed." Lani stares across the yard at the oak tree, Iggy nestled between two of its exposed roots. "Once it's cut down, it'll be turned into mulch and anything in it will get mangled in the machine. Could it come back to him? Especially with the one-of-a-kind design and engraving? Sure. But it also might not be recognizable. Just a chunk of metal caught up in the blades that gets tossed."

"They might cut the tree up for lumber instead of mulching it."

"True, there's a risk, but there's also a risk to him dumping it somewhere else. Everybody's got an outdoor camera these days. At least this way he knew where it was at all times."

"Bet he's kicking himself for not paying closer attention to his property line," Brian says. "If he was smart, he would've tossed the letter opener in the middle of Lake Erie."

"This isn't a movie. His renting a boat all of a sudden would've looked suspicious."

"True, but he's a good actor," Brian says. "Claimed he *might* have mentioned to his investor there was a snag in their research. Let that kind of linger in the air."

"So he threw Price under the bus?"

"So fast it left skid marks. He also claims Price hired someone to silence you."

Lani winces. "And what's Mr. Richy Pants got to say about being implicated in the murder?"

"He claims any research snags are news to him. Says all he knows is that Carver was worried Tony found something that might hurt their drug advancement, and when Price asked what it was, Carver told him not to worry about it. Said he'd 'take care of Tony,' and Price claims he didn't know anything else about it."

"And what do *you* think?" she asks.

"I think they're both telling the truth and they're both

lying. It's trying to figure out who did what that could be tricky."

Lani shrugs. "You told me Fry concluded the killer was taller than Tony, based on the angle of the neck wound. Price may have big pockets, but he's a physically small man. Still, I'm with you. Carver was the one to kill Tony, but both men played a role."

"I've got something else you'll find verrrry interesting." Brian wiggles his eyebrows like a kid with a secret.

"Spit it out. I don't have all day." Lani tilts her head. "Oh wait, I do."

"You remember the suicide we investigated last month? The woman with the Crocs and the unmade bed?"

Lani drops her feet from the fire pit ledge. "Of course I do. Why?"

"It kept eating at me. How you didn't think she committed suicide. And then we learned Carver had an ex-girlfriend who killed herself."

"Wow, you think Carver killed that woman too?" Lani's tone is so spirited Iggy's head shoots up. When she calls out to reassure him, he lowers his snout back down.

"I don't know yet. I'm working on it. But I did some digging around. The woman didn't have a door camera, but a gas station down the street has a security camera. Catches a portion of the road in front of it." Brian pulls out his phone, swipes his finger a few times, and crosses around the fire pit to Lani. He plays the video. "See here? That black Subaru Forester driving past?"

Lani is fully upright now, stabbed abdomen forgotten. "That's the same SUV Carver drives," she says. "A hybrid model. Please, please, please tell me the license plate number matches."

"The license plate number matches."

"Please, please, please tell me that footage is from the day she died."

"It's from the day she died."

"Ha! I knew something was up with that suicide."

"Slow down, granny pants, I still need to prove it. The camera doesn't show far enough down the road to see if he stopped at her house. He could just be driving by."

"Bull."

"Agreed," Brian says. "But like I said, I need to prove it. Learn more about the woman. Find out if Carver knew her. You know the drill."

"I have no doubt you'll figure it out. And I have no doubt you'll bring Tony's case to a complete close too. Make sure the right man is charged with the right crime and get the recognition you deserve."

"Okay, now you're freaking me out with all the kindness. Besides, you should get the glory. You're the one who cracked Habib's case."

"Nah. I just want to see Tony get justice so he can be buried in peace. Get out of the medical examiner's freezer, for God's sake. That's all that matters to me." Lani glances at Old Henry's urn and is relieved to feel that's the truth. "I'm in a good place now, Einstein."

"I'm really glad to hear that, boss."

They enjoy a bit of shared silence, and then Lani eases herself out of the orange chair and picks up the shovel. When she reaches for the urn, Brian rushes to grab it.

"Too heavy for you," he says. "You're not even six weeks out yet."

"I carried him here, didn't I?"

They approach the tree. Iggy jumps up and taps his paws on Lani's lower legs. She gives him a pet.

"You could sprinkle the ashes in the creek instead," Brian says.

"What, and have Old Henry float away into the murky abyss? God would slam heaven's gate in my face if I did that, and Old Henry would be right behind him. I want to bury the whole thing, urn and all." Lani pokes the shovel in a few places near the tree's back roots, thinking a spot between the creek and the tree might be best, but when Iggy plops back down in his usual place in front of it and whimpers, she glances at Brian. "Maybe Iggy's spot should now be Old Henry's spot."

Brian flashes a patient smile. "Do what you gotta do." He takes the shovel from her. "But here, let me do the digging."

"You don't have to go too deep, and be careful. Don't want any more surprise branch attacks." Lani glances warily at the thick branches above their heads.

After nudging Iggy away from his coveted spot between two roots, Brian starts digging, gauging the appropriate depth to bury the urn completely. The more he digs, the more Iggy prances around and paws the ground. Then he starts barking.

"What's the matter, Iggy?" Lani holds him back so Brian can work.

And then she sees something.

"Brian, stop," she orders.

Brian does, and when Lani carefully drops to her knees, he crouches to join her and says, "Is that a…"

"I think it is." Lani sweeps with her hands, slowly at first and then more rapidly, her knobby joints barely up to the task.

There, buried hardly eighteen inches beneath the surface, is a human skull. Or what remains of it anyway.

"Oh my God," Brian says. "Who's he got buried here?"

Lani shakes her head. "No, the flesh is gone, and parts of the bone have deteriorated. Carver's only lived here eleven months or so. Whoever this is has been here much longer."

She sweeps away more dirt, careful not to damage anything but desperate to uncover more before they get a team out there. Brian is already on his feet, calling it in.

Maybe I trained him too well, she thinks.

But at the same time, his good instincts and proper techniques fill Lani with a warm satisfaction. Maybe she left her mark on the Winston PD, after all.

Soon she scoops away enough dirt to find fabric covering a torso of decayed bones. The material looks like velvet but is too degraded to be certain. Lani knows she should stop digging, but her human instinct refuses to listen to her cop brain. Brian recites the address to someone, but his voice sounds a thousand miles away.

After several more gentle sweeps, pushing the dirt to the side, Lani's breath catches in her throat.

Something is buried with the body. Something hard.

She pulls it away from the torso. It's a wooden plaque with six metal plates, each engraved with words too encrusted with dirt to make out.

Not wanting to ruin anything, Lani gently lays it aside and finds a second surprise in the shallow grave. A scroll of some type, thick and covered in dirt. Delicately, she places it next to the wooden plaque. Although she'd love to unroll it, she fears it would fall to pieces in her hands if she tried.

She sinks back on her haunches, forgetting all about her residual pain. Who in the world is buried here?

"They're on their way, boss."

She nods without looking at Brian. Instead, her gaze catches one last thing, wedged in the dirt next to the decaying clothes. She reaches for it.

"You probably shouldn't touch anything else before—"

She pulls it out.

A piece of plaid fabric. In the shape of a flower. A flower she's read about.

Lani stares up at Brian. Her mouth opens and closes, but for the first time in her life, she's incapable of speech.

"You okay?" He frowns in concern.

Something incomprehensible squeaks from her mouth. She clears her throat and tries again. Nothing.

Trying to process what her eyes are seeing, imagining the

incalculable odds, she finally recovers her voice. "I think we found Catherine Miller," she sputters incredulously. "How she ended up near Hudson, I don't know, I really don't know, but…" She lifts the plaid flower and stares at Brian in disbelief. "I think I just solved Old Henry's case."

CHAPTER THIRTY-ONE

CATHERINE

I drift in and out of a foggy lassitude, my remaining life force so small not even my malformed leaf buds will move voluntarily, but when I see what the lady constable has dug from my soil, a stunned awareness revives me. It can't be. How can it be? And yet, as marked by the evidence within her hands, it is.

Constable Whitaker has found me.

She found the woman I once was, no longer of flesh and personality, but of decaying old bones too wasted to fill out the rotting cloak and gown that holds them. Near Hudson, no less. How did I get here? All these years I haven't known with certainty whose soil grew my roots. I assumed Cleveland because that's where my life was stolen, but my environs are not those of a city. Even in Hudson I must be at the outer limits.

But if there were any doubts the remains are my own, my diploma, which the lady constable lifts from the dirt and places alongside my engraved class tickets, offers indisputable proof. I was clutching both when I ran down St. Clair Street and into the woods.

My temporary buoyancy fades, and I have to force whatever soul remains inside me to concentrate on the scene at my base, to focus on my corporeal body buried between the roots of my arboreal one. The voices of the lady constable and her partner are distant now. Even Iggy, who prances in and out of my awareness, seems to no longer share our connection.

But wait, Catherine, I tell myself, *wait.* Don't fade yet because what did Constable Whitaker just find? What did she pluck from the dirt like a dandelion?

A scrap of plaid cloth.

A plaid flower.

Oh my Lord, I recognize that flower. I saw it only once, during an evening meal as an invited guest, but it's hard to forget such a distinct object.

It's a flower from Ruth Fitzgerald's trunk, the trunk Dr. Fitzgerald added wheels to so his wife could deliver her gowns to the women of Cleveland and beyond.

How can it be? Oh no oh no oh no, how is this possible?

It wasn't a man who killed me. It wasn't a man who smashed me over the head and stole my human life. It was a woman. The wife of my future partner. A woman who seemed nothing but cordial and welcoming to me.

The shock of learning the identity of my killer taints the joy of finding my remains. Why? Why would Ruth commit such a heinous act?

I fight to stay conscious, fight to replay our interactions. She seemed pleased her husband would have help in his clinic. "Oh yes, he's very busy," she said. "What a pretty addition you'll be."

But now, as I stand here dying, soon to enter another world or simply not exist at all, other things about Ruth Fitzgerald come to light. How she always doted on Dr. Fitzgerald, often touching him in my presence. How she laughed, almost nervously, when he smiled and delighted at my jokes. How she asked if I worried my work as a doctor might keep me from finding a husband.

Was she jealous? The thought is ludicrous to me because I had no interest in Dr. Fitzgerald beyond his medical practice and mentorship. Was she worried I might somehow lure him away from her arms and embrace him in my own? At the time, they had no children yet to tether him. Maybe she worried that would be reason enough for him to leave. If that's the case, it pains me to think she imagined me capable of such improper acts.

But how did she do it? She was a tall woman, to be sure, but how did she manage?

She must have followed me down St. Clair Street. In my haste to escape the excitement, I didn't notice. She had informed her husband she would leave the commencement celebration early to take a train to Hudson to deliver a dress and tend to her mother, but was that a lie? Did she remain behind, hiding in a store or cafe until I passed by? How could she be sure I would be alone?

Or was it simply an impulsive act on her part? Maybe she was waiting for a coach to take her to the train station when I came flying out of the medical college and set off down the street. What if she only meant to speak with me, not hurt me?

No. She wouldn't have snuck up on me if that were the case. She would have made her presence known before she clobbered me over the head. The thick clusters of trees offered the perfect seclusion, and I must have been so distracted with my whirling thoughts that I didn't hear her or her trunk approach. The blowing wind and squawking seagulls near Lake Erie are all I remember.

After she struck me—with what, I don't know—she must have stuffed me into her trunk, which she'd brought with her that day. What she hadn't planned on, however, was one of the plaid flowers catching on my cape and remaining with me as proof of her crime.

I imagine her dragging me in her trunk over the bumpy terrain of the woods, grunting and jerking in exertion. Or maybe the wheels made it no exertion at all. Wasn't that the point? I hardly weighed more than a hundred pounds.

When she reached the walkway and returned to the city limits, her passage would have been smoother. From there, she could have hailed a coach to deliver her to the station, boarded the train, and stepped off in Hudson, just as she'd done many times before. Or maybe a coach waited for her not far from where she struck me.

Given my remote location in Hudson, she must have dragged me some distance to bury me, along with my identifying possessions. Did she have a shovel in her bloodthirsty trunk as well?

Still, it seems a difficult feat for a woman, even one as tall as Ruth Fitzgerald. Did Curtis Mayfield help? I'm convinced it was his hand that poisoned me. Or maybe one of the other doctors had been her accomplice, ready with a coach in Hudson to deliver me to a far-off burial place. Perhaps the spurned Dr. Frederick Morrison or the outraged Dr. Jedediah Cartwright who thought no woman belonged in medicine.

Then again, maybe I only wish this because I could never commit such a heinous crime myself. I thought those types of evil doings were the acts of the Mark Carvers, Harrison Prices, and Curtis Mayfields of the world, not the Ruth Fitzgeralds. Ruth appears to have joined the most exclusive of all male clubs.

And yet, with the right motivation and determination, hadn't I, Catherine Miller, shown that a woman can do anything a man can do? Shouldn't that extend to murder as well?

A chill runs through my trunk. Maybe it's more disturbing than that. What if her blow didn't kill me? What if I was unconscious and didn't die until I was buried in the ground? If that's the case, thank heavens I have no memory of it. Yet maybe that awful, tragic, slow death is what made my molecules blend with the surrounding earth. Made them circle and swirl and fuse until a sprouting sapling was their reward, one that grew into the mighty oak that has housed my thoughts and sensations for one hundred and seventy years.

I...I...

...I must have drifted off. Maybe for quite a spell because two men and a woman who weren't in Mr. Carver's yard before are here now. More shadowy forms crowd in the distance. My vision is fading, the images blurring together. Only the closest perimeter to me is visible now.

The team tends to my decayed remains, carefully uncovering the rest of me with a small raking tool that passes like a comb through the soil. When did these people arrive? The lady constable is still here. Her partner too. He must have brought one of Mr. Carver's colorful chairs over for her to sit on while she watches my unveiling. Iggy—oh my sweet Iggy—rests on her lap, and I feel a peace in knowing he has said his goodbyes to me. He's aware I'm on my way to heaven's gate. At least I pray I am.

I'm so desperately fatigued. My determined attempts at breaking that thick branch likely hastened my demise, but for Tony I would do it a thousand times over. Still, even though my entire world—my thoughts, my sight, my sensations—grows dusky, I perceive awe on the lady constable's face. Or maybe it's satisfaction. Perhaps it's both.

I don't know why I am so important to her.

I don't know who the "Old Henry" is that she's mentioned many times to her partner.

I don't know why she wanted to bury his urn near my roots.

I am only happy she did.

As they begin to remove my human remains and gently

place them into a vessel I can't make out, my life force depletes at an alarming rate. Fatigue is an understatement. It's more like a shrinking. A fading. It's as if I am disappearing from the giant oak and sinking into my bones, as if my spirit longs to be home.

But as I experience my arboreal death, I feel no distress. I feel none of my earlier fear or restlessness or hopelessness because I exit this world with so many beautiful completions.

Tony has seen justice. I have been found. My killer has been identified. Although Ruth is long gone and can never be tried, the knowing is enough for me.

A peaceful calm washes over me. I am no longer connected to the beautiful tree that graciously extended my life, but that is as it should be, for I—we—are dying. My fear of disappearing is gone. Indeed, I welcome it.

Like a whisper of an angel, a silky curtain envelops my soul...

...and caresses me into eternal sleep.

CHAPTER THIRTY-TWO

LANI

Without a trace of abdominal pain, Lani exits her loyal Crown Vic and steps onto Mark Carver's driveway. A city truck, bearing the logo of the Urban Forestry Department, is parked near the curb.

She leans back into the car and calls Iggy over to the driver's seat. He obeys but looks affronted when she attaches the leash. "Sorry, big guy. Can't risk you getting hurt."

Once the beagle is by her side, she closes the car door and heads toward the backyard oasis. Chief Toddler told her to consider the Crown Vic a retirement gift, but she knows the truth. The thing is too old to make a trade-in worth the department's time. Nonetheless, she gratefully accepted the metal heap, leaving the chief open-mouthed at her lack of sarcastic reply. She didn't even ask how his wife was doing or if he'd been to Peninsula lately, that was how charitable she felt. She's seven weeks out from her surgery; her pain and nightmares are gone, and June is proving to be one fine summer month, so she boxed up her belongings from her station desk with nothing but good cheer, fist bumps, and a few finger flip-offs with Anderson the bulldog.

Inhaling the fragrant blossoms lining the trellis, Lani holds onto Iggy's leash. "Let's watch from the patio. Safer there."

The beagle trots along obediently. His eagerness to spend time with her amazes her. Equally amazing is that, aside from Brian, she managed to find a living being who she can stand to spend more than an hour with.

Two men dressed in protective gear stand near the old oak, arms gesturing as they debate the best approach to cutting the tree down. One of them waves to her, and she waves back, glad she's not too late. She put a word in to the city that she wanted a heads-up when the big moment happened, and they kindly obliged. She feels she somehow owes it to Catherine Miller to be there. Stupid, she supposes, but here she is. She takes a seat at Carver's patio table, and Iggy plops down by her feet.

Given the tree injured an arborist and dropped a mega branch that could've squashed Lani like Silly Putty had she been a few feet closer, the city agreed to chop it down before it caused any more damage.

Its imminent death leaves Lani with a throat-pinching sadness. Death of any kind deflates her, but as she admires the lush growth in Carver's backyard, from the oval leaves of the butternut trees near the creek to the blue buds of the mophead hydrangeas lining the house, it's plenty clear life goes on.

Still, the Northern Red Oak is a beauty, boasting one of the widest trunks Lani has ever seen in that variety of oak, and after putting up with Ohio's deranged weather for what— a hundred years? a hundred and fifty?—it's a shame it has to come down.

"Ain't that right," she says to Iggy, who glances up at her with a rapt interest she doesn't deserve.

Although the tree removal comes at the city's expense,

Melissa is stuck with selling her brother's house since he'll otherwise be indisposed. For quite a while too.

Lani tries to suppress a smug smile, but it surfaces anyway. In what was a surprise to both her and Brian, Carver agreed to make a deal with the prosecuting attorney. It was a smart move, and he is, after all, a smart man. A mountain of evidence now points to him, and he knew when to cry uncle: the weapon with both his and Tony Habib's DNA (and Tony's blood) on it buried in Carver's yard; the lack of Harrison Price's DNA on the letter opener since it had been mailed directly to Carver from the manufacturer; Carver's height consistent with the stab mark on Habib's cervical vertebra; and the fact that one of Carver's other PhD students, who took over the mouse duties when Carver got locked up, was surprised to find one with liver cancer.

Assuming other cases existed and the mouse cancer was the snag in Carver's research, this last morsel provides a nice chunk of motive. A highly coveted new drug with billions of dollars at stake?

"Oh yeah, baby," Lani murmurs to Iggy. He licks her toes through her sandals.

Unfortunately, nothing connects Harrison Price to Tony's murder, or even Lani's attack, but her gut instinct says something rotten is going on behind his protective wall of money. They just can't prove it. At least his drug investment will be put on hold while the research team sorts out the cancer issue, assuming they can continue without Carver.

A saw buzzes to life. One of the men starts on the first cut. Lani winces as the blade screeches and splits its way into the outer bark.

Because of the evidence, and also because—as much as Lani hates to admit it—Dunn is a great defense attorney who portrayed Carver as an upstanding citizen with an impeccable record, Carver pleaded out to voluntary manslaughter. He made up some story about Tony blackmailing him and threatening him in his backyard. Claimed Tony took a swing at him, and when he did, Carver acted in a "moment of rage" and killed the student with the letter opener in his hand. He swore he was "devastated and horrified" by his actions and that it had been a tragic, panicked mistake.

The overworked prosecutor accepted his absurd confession, and the judge approved the plea bargain of a ten-year sentence. Lani figures a more compelling reason for Carver's sudden remorse and resultant guilty plea is because Brian lied to Carver that the prosecutor might go after Melissa for using her affair with Brian as a means to help her brother stay one step ahead of the investigation. Maybe Carver also figured that by being charged with the crime, Brian would lay off investigating anything else, or at least he'd be sentenced before Brian could find any new evidence that might make the prosecutor rethink her decision.

Whatever the reason for Carver's guilty plea and sudden contrition, Lani is livid he didn't at least get second-degree murder. Now he'll see freedom far sooner than he deserves. Everything points to Tony Habib being a studious young man with a bright future, and Carver snubbed him out like he was nothing. According to Harrison Price, Carver took advantage of Tony's crush on him and used it to coerce Tony into hiding damaging research. Carver took advantage of Tony's loneliness, too, because the introverted PhD student had few people in his life. Maybe he hadn't even come to terms with his sexuality yet. Lani doubts very much that Tony blackmailed and threatened his superior.

Then again, Carver's perfect academic life is now destroyed and his career may be as well, so she supposes that's a form of justice too. Beyond Iggy, who isn't yet strong enough proof in the hands of a great lawyer until Brian has more evidence, nothing implicates Carver in his ex-girlfriend's suicide in Cleveland or the PhD student's car accident in California. But in time, maybe, because Brian is trying to track down Iggy's former vet, who moved out of state, to see if they can match Cindy Walker's Iggy to Carver's Iggy.

Even if they do prove Carver stole the dog, it doesn't prove he overdosed Cindy. Brian says he'll keep digging though, and he already put a call into the California authorities who investigated the PhD student's car crash. Furthermore, he's working on getting approval to check the house of the woman who hanged herself. Although the place has been rented to someone new, Brian wants to look for Carver's fingerprints to prove he knew the woman. Having video of him driving down the same street as her house isn't enough.

Lani supposes Chief Toddler is giving Brian a lot of leeway now that she and Brian proved Carver killed Tony Habib. French is probably trying to lick his doubting wounds in the most dignified and camera-ready way.

Einstein delivered on Carver, that's for sure. He told her he wouldn't give up, and he didn't. If she had an ice-cold IPA in her hand, she'd hold up the bottle and give a big cheers to Detective Brian Dupree. Brains, looks, and decency.

"If I'd have been thirty years younger..." she says with a sigh. Iggy's tilted expression seems to reply, *Yeah, right. Wishful thinking, lady.*

After removing a wedge of bark from the first cut, the arborist moves on to the second one. Lani's throat tightness doubles down. No matter how much Einstein teases her, she's convinced that tree helped her find the weapon, not to mention the remains of the nineteenth-century medical student. Most would argue the finds were pure coincidence, but to Lani, that seems equally implausible. About as likely as her becoming a six-foot-tall super model.

Whatever the reason for the discoveries, Lani is happy the deceased woman's remains have finally received a proper burial, back in a small Pennsylvania town at the request of her family's descendants, who, thanks to the internet, were easy to track down. As one of only a handful of female doctors in

1853, the missing woman has been a conversation starter for years in that town.

And as if all that isn't enough to lower Lani's cynicism by a good five degrees, she also solved Old Henry's case. She looks up at the sky. She's not much of a heaven believer, but she hopes somehow he knows.

When the old oak thuds to the ground, Lani's feet vibrate and the table rattles. Iggy jumps into her lap, his body trembling. After barking at the tree a few times, he lowers his head on her jeans and stares at the fallen trunk. As she strokes the saddle-shaped fur on his back and watches the arborists saw off the branches, she hopes Old Henry is at rest too.

A few days after Catherine Miller's remains were removed, Lani returned to the burial site in Carver's backyard. Deciding her great grandfather might not want to spend eternity in an urn, she unsealed his marble tomb and spread his ashes around the area where the med student's bones were discovered. Probably wasn't lawful to do so—states have rules about where ashes can be scattered—but there's a nice symmetry in his fusing with the earth that housed the woman he spent his life trying to find. Although Lani will never be able to ask her father how Henry's ashes got left in the attic, she's grateful they were, because that serendipitous soil around the now sawed-off tree stump seems like the best final resting place for him.

Or maybe it's all hogwash. What does she know? She's just a retired detective with a new dog, a new RV, and a whole lot of new time on her knobby hands to explore North America. She even found a young cop in Cleveland who wants to rent her house for a year, a woman who transferred to the first precinct. Not only can Lani trust her not to trash the place, the soon-to-be tenant loves gardening and will keep Lani's flowers, vegetables, and indoor plants tended.

Lani scoops Iggy out of her lap and returns him to the stone patio. After a final glance at the majestic tree, which is now in pieces, she stands and waves goodbye to the arborists. She makes her way to the trellis.

"Come on, big guy," she says to Iggy. "We've got places to go, people to see."

As an afterthought, she adds, "But hopefully not too many people. There are only so many I can fecking handle."

The End

AUTHOR'S NOTE

Catherine Miller is a fictional character. In 1849, Elizabeth Blackwell became the first woman to graduate from a reputable and recognized U.S. medical school, the Geneva Medical College, in Geneva, New York. In 1852, Nancy Talbot Clark became the second woman to do so, graduating from the Medical Department of Western Reserve College (also known as Cleveland Medical College), which is now Case Western Reserve University in Cleveland.

Five more women would graduate in Cleveland before 1856, at which time a new, less progressive dean considered it "inexpedient" to continue admitting women. It would be decades before another woman would do so.

Since no women graduated in the class of 1853, I chose to make that Catherine's year, and as such, in the book I tout her as the third woman to graduate medical school in the U.S. In truth, that honor goes to Emily Blackwell (sister of Elizabeth Blackwell), who graduated from the Medical Department of Western Reserve College in 1854.

The suburb of Winston and the Winston Police Department are fictional, but the town's location would be south of Cleveland. Similarly, Cardon University is made up. Although

I briefly mention real universities in California and Illinois, the characters I created in them are fictional.

From the historical records I researched, I tried to replicate the actual medical training in Cleveland in the mid-1800s, but the teachers I created are fictional. Also, I could find minimal description of Cleveland Medical College's interior, so I used my imagination there. The actual building, which sat on the corner of St. Clair Avenue and E. 9th Street, was razed in 1885.

ACKNOWLEDGMENTS

Thank you to story coach Kate Johnston for her invaluable beta read. She has such a keen eye for detail. Another heartfelt thanks goes to Diane Donovan for giving *Fractured Oak* an early read, as well as to Jack for his insights. My gratitude also goes out to Officer Johnsen for helping me get the police details right. Any mistakes in that world are my own. Thank you as well to Tea Jagodic for her beautiful cover art. She brought Catherine's tree to life while also conveying the tone of the novel. And, of course, where would I be without my wonderful husband for his endless support, my sons for continuing to make me laugh, and you, the reader, for giving this book with an unusual premise a chance. If we could live on in the physical world, I wouldn't mind spending an extra century or two as a tree.

ABOUT THE AUTHOR

Dannie Boyd is a pen name for Carrie Rubin, a writer with a background in medicine who has several medical thrillers published under her own name. She currently lives in Northeast Ohio ... where there are lots of trees.

If you enjoyed *Fractured Oak*, you might like other titles published by Indigo Dot Press.

Indigo Dot Press specializes in thrillers, mysteries, and suspense—some rooted in realism, others with a supernatural bent, and most with a medical theme. Visit the website below to learn more.

indigodotpress.com
indigodotpress@gmail.com

Printed in Great Britain
by Amazon

21682831R00155